ALIVE AND KICKING

John Milne

ALIVE AND KICKING

FOUR WALLS EIGHT WINDOWS   NO EXIT PRESS

Published in the United States by
Four Walls Eight Windows/No Exit Press
39 West 14th Street, Room 503
New York, N.Y. 10011

http://www.fourwallseightwindows.com
http://www.noexit.co.uk

First Printing September 1999

ISBN 1-56858-145-9

1 3 5 7 9 10 8 6 4 2

Composed in Palatino by Koinonia, Manchester
and printed and bound in Great Britain.

Jeffrey Kime nagged me to write this novel when I couldn't. He died in Paris in October 1992. Jeffrey, *salut*, this kick is for you

Part one

Love and fear

THIS IS CONJECTURE.

On one side of London a woman makes a phone call. It's her second call to her correspondent and she doesn't like speaking to him. It makes her nervous. As she puts down the handset her hand trembles. She lights a cigarette with an out-of-practice hand. The flame shakes and she snaps the old, gold lighter shut.

Later, in a building in the old, eastern centre of the city, a lock clicks and turns. A long-closed hammered-glass door opens. It leads into a dusty room crowded with filing cabinets. The floor is covered with ancient paper debris. A man enters and pockets a key. The man is serious looking, middle-aged. He wears a made-to-measure hand-cut blue suit, has perfectly groomed sandy hair. His shoes are glossy, parade ground black-polished. The man treads deliberately across the rubbish on the floor. Distaste shows on his freckled face. He opens a long-closed filing cabinet, glances at the contents and moves on. The man repeats this procedure with each drawer of each cabinet. One cabinet screams as he pulls the drawer open. His carefully manicured finger moves back along the crystal files. There. Slaughter, nineteen-sixty-eight. There. The man takes out the file, satisfied, and begins to read. The file contains reports, witness statements, black and white photographs, even press cuttings.

The man steps back across the paper debris, still with the file open, still reading, and leaves the room. The deadlock clicks over and the room is quiet again.

One

THIS ISN'T CONJECTURE. It happened to me.

I came out of a pub in the Mile End; L'Etoile, sometimes known as 'Club Etoile', formerly The Star. Foreign name, beer the temperature of a nun's thigh and a prophylactic lemon in the neck of the bottle. It's horrible. I wouldn't go there at all but I like the man who owns it, Terry. I've known him all my adult life.

I stepped over the granite threshold of the Club Etoile and waved Terry good-bye.

Warm yellow light poured from the Star's doorway, then the door swung closed behind me and the light and the fug and the warm and the noise was cut. I shivered. It was the end of October, cold and windy enough for a coat and scarf. I had neither. I moved out of the wind, into a shop doorway, a deep, dark, glassed-in showcase doorway, the sort of window a 'modern' tailor's would have had in the nineteen-fifties. The windows were empty, the glass smeared with a chalky emulsion. Leaves, abandoned papers, cigarette packets and God knows what fragments of London night life blew past me. I was snug for now in my doorway. Across the four-lane Mile End Road a young man sat on a big red Japanese motorbike. It was unfaired, what the Japanese call a 'naked'. The young man wore brown boots, a black bomber, jeans and a full face helmet, but no gloves. He was a big, strapping lad and he sat easily on the motorcycle; relaxed, facing the traffic. He kept his engine ticking over.

I started as a white Ford Granada drew up outside the pub, then relaxed. Not mine. My Ford should have rust stains around the side, like a bath with tide marks, only red and on the outside. Also mine should have lace handkerchief door-skins and be driven by a black garage mechanic, Leon. This was someone else's white Ford Granada. The driver cut his engine and wound up his window. The motorcyclist started

across the road, stopped in front of the Ford and turned on the
Ford's driver. The motorcyclist was holding a pistol. I was
surprised but not as surprised as the man in the Ford. The
motorcyclist raised his arm, aimed through the Ford's
windscreen, then fired his pistol, once, twice. That's why he
wasn't wearing gloves. He didn't want to fumble, he didn't
want to have to shove a gloved finger through the trigger
guard (what was it, a Glock? A Browning? Something like that.
But when someone's waving a gun near you it just looks big,
black and dangerous. You don't peel back his fingers to see
which brand he has chosen). The gun fired fast and the noise
was flat-sounding and very loud. No silencer, no one seemed
to notice the shots except me and the white car's driver. It
jammed on the third shot and the motorcyclist worked the
mechanism a couple of times. No go. The motorcyclist tucked
the shooter inside his black bomber, set his bike into gear and
drove away, quickly. I saw him do something to the gun before
he tucked it inside his coat. What? Probably put the safety on.
It's no good being a cool, calm gunman if you shoot your nuts
off driving away. The motorcyclist was some distance up the
road before he turned on his lights. Mile End traffic passed,
calm, oblivious. I went over to the Ford. The driver, a large
black-haired man of about forty, sat frozen behind the wheel. I
opened his door. Cars rushed past my back.

'Are you all right?'

He took his time, then unclenched his hands from the wheel.

'Did you see that? Did you see that?'

'I saw.'

He stared ahead, muttering, 'bastard' over and over.

'So what's he got against you?' I asked.

'How do I know? Did you see that?'

Now Leon drew up behind us in my Ford. The Ford's door
creaked and Leon joined us. I told him about the motorcyclist
and showed him the bullet holes in the front of the man's
Jenner replica. Leon misunderstood and thought the man was
a friend or with me somehow. Maybe bullet holes are all part of
a day's trade in Brixton, where Leon has his garage.

'You're going to need a new radiator,' said Leon, and handed over a business card.

'And windscreen,' I said. 'I don't know if you're going to be able to pass this off as a stone chipping.'

'Why not?'

'You don't get many stone chips go through the front window and out the back as well.'

'Bastard.' The man said.

'What did you do to this motorcyclist?' Leon asked. 'Cut in front of him?'

You wag, Leon.

'I've never seen him before,' said the man. 'Did you get the number?'

Leon frowned; number? Are we on a crossed line?

I shook my head. 'It wouldn't be any use. The bike'll be nicked.'

'We should call the police,' said the man. Leon looked at me, 'oh-oh' written all over him.

'They'll come, don't worry,' I said. Now Leon's expression was shouting 'let's go'. Leon looked closely at my face, waiting for me to agree. When I didn't he turned angrily on the man and snatched the business card from his hand.

'What do you do for a job?' Leon asked.

'I'm a milkman.'

'And you don't know why would someone want to take pot shots at you in the Mile End Road?'

'No.'

'Well you want to have a look at your dance card, mate, make sure you ain't spending more time than you ought to delivering pints of gold top to some gangster's home address.'

'What?'

'This is jealous-man shootin',' said Leon, 'Stop messin' with other man's wife, milko.'

Leon goes very West Indian when he gets frustrated.

'I don't do any of that, it's against the commandments,' the pot-shotted milko told Leon.

'So is shooting people,' I said, helpfully.

Leon looked at me, then at the milkman. He turned to me again and smiled. 'Commandments? This is a gag, innit? You two are having me on.'

'No, Leon.'

After a pause the milkman said again, 'Bastard.' He wanted to wait for the police and we didn't, so we left him in his car saying 'bastard' while I drove Leon back to the tube.

'Where do you want?'

'The Victoria Line. Anywhere.'

'Tottenham Hale? Blackhorse Lane?'

'Very funny.'

Leon is the London equivalent of a square earther. The northern limit of his world is Essex Road. All right, Holloway Road at a push. The southern end of Holloway Road. Leon lit a herbal cigarette and blew smoke out of the open window. He examined the end of his herbal cigarette, making sure it was well alight before asking, 'Do you think the man with the gun was aiming or frightening?'

'Well, you'd need to be a good shot to get a bullet to pass someone's ear in the dark. I mean an inch is an inch. Ask any girl.'

'Answer, Jenner.'

'I think he was trying to kill him.'

'Why?'

'Shall we go back and ask him, Leon? You can let the coppers have a drag on your funny fag while we're there.'

'Okay, okay. I was only asking.' We queued for roadworks. 'That car, Jimmy...'

'Yes?'

'It could have been you. Same motor, dark-haired spa about your age.'

I didn't answer.

'How about *your* dance card?' He asked.

'Too boring for words.'

'Work?'

'Nothing. My cupboard is bare.'

He looked at me.

'You're a cool one, Jenner.'

'I'm serious. I'm not working.' His gaze was steady. Then he smiled. I caved in. 'Divorce. Okay? I'm doing a divorce.'

'I thought you didn't do divorce.'

'So did I.'

'You're skint.'

'Is that a crime?'

'No.' He paused. I waited. He had a very superior looking face on him, Leon. 'But there must be something special about it.'

'Not a thing. It's pathetically ordinary. I'm gathering evidence so someone's wife can hijack his pension.'

'What sort of someone?'

'A local government officer.'

'Well, he must be very pissed off with you, Jenner, this local government officer. Local government officers don't have much reputation for shooting at people.'

'I don't suppose he knows I exist.' I stopped the car at the kerbside. 'This is you.'

But Leon wasn't finished yet. He didn't move. I waited.

'I know a boy who'd like to learn your trade.'

'I'm sorry?'

'I know a boy....'

'I heard what you said. You've no need to repeat it. How long have you been running an employment agency?'

'He's a good fellow. Big strong fellow. Very tough. Very intelligent.'

Now he waited.

'No.'

'Just a few months.'

'I can't.'

'Vaughan, he's called. He would be reliable.'

'Good for him.'

'You're worried about money...'

'I'm not.'

'You are. He doesn't need paying. I'm sure we could make some arrangement about that.'

'That's not the problem.'

'Just meet him.'

'No.'

'Why not?'

'I can't be responsible for other people, Leon.'

'What does that mean?'

'You saw what happened outside the Etoile.'

'You said that was nothing to do with you.'

'It wasn't.'

'I thought your cupboard was bare, apart from the divorcing civil servant?'

I didn't reply. He got out of the car, made a pistol of his first two fingers and pointed at me. 'Watch your back, Jimmy. You owe me for fixing the car.' He fumbled in his pocket, then fished out a crumpled piece of paper. A bill. 'One hundred and fifty-one pounds seventeen pee.'

'Why seventeen pee?'

'Why? I'm outraged. It's one-five-one-seventeen because that's what it came to.'

'Are you VAT registered?'

He sighed. 'There's no trust in the world any more.' He pointed to the bill. 'Don't die before you sign the cheque. You want a shooter?'

'I thought you were a mechanic?'

'I own a garage. I hope you're not going round telling people I'm a mechanic. Do you want a gun, yes or no?'

'No. It's illegal.'

'Well, at least you need someone with you.'

'No I don't.'

'Protection.'

'No one has any reason to shoot at me, Leon.'

'Have a think. Ring me when the penny drops.'

'Yeah yeah.' I waved him away. I put the car in drive and it stuttered into the flow of traffic. Kangaroo petrol in an automatic car. I owe money for this? Still, Bethnal Green's not on the Victoria Line. I looked at him in my rear view mirror, Leon with his wonky grin and herbal cigarette, standing under a yellow London street lamp. Thin rain fell and he went into the station. A motorcyclist overtook me, zoom, and I flinched. I can't spend my life like this. I made a mental note. Don't flinch every time a Honda passes. All I have to do now is find a way to slip the note under my unconscious self's door. Zoom. There goes another.

When I got home I put the mortice lock on, turned the lights out and peered out of the window after myself. No crash helmeted assassins lurking in the shadows of Defoe Mansions. No motorbikes ticking over in the car park. Chicken Jenner, it's okay. Stoke Newington is neither calmer nor more dangerous than before. The natives have not gone native in Stokey.

I spent the first two weeks in November this way, looking over my shoulder, so that I developed both a flinch in my face and a crick in my neck. It was all for nothing. No one took any more pot shots at me or people who looked like me and drove old white Fords. No motorcyclists armed with automatic pistols hung around outside boozers I frequented. None that I saw, anyway. And though I examined what Leon had called my 'dance card' very closely indeed, I could find nothing that made me a target. No unsettled scores, no psychos newly-released from prison with my name carved on their heart, no debts which would need to be paid off with a bullet. I began to believe that someone really was upset with the religious milko, and he'd been telling me fibs.

Until the penny dropped.

Two

THE PENNY TOOK two weeks to drop and a little Maltese sweetheart called Mickey DeWitt died before it did. The sound of the falling coin was a loud metallic 'clang'. It rang back twenty-five years.

*

I was walking along an East End street when the penny clanged flat. I was in the rain on the same street, the Mile End Road outside Terry's pub, L'Etoile, only it was two weeks after the milko was pot-shotted. The roadworks had slid closer to the Etoile, fetching their temporary traffic lights with them. Now we've all got something to watch while we sit in the traffic jam. Red, red and orange, green; raspberry, marmalade and goosegog, but still you just sit there, jammed.

I was walking in the road because trenches cut the pavement and the flags were up, leaning against each other like tipsy granite brothers. I was plastered, drunk as a skunk with my dead brother's friend, Terry, who owns the Etoile. I've known Terry all my life, or so it feels. We were skittering through puddles, him doing Gene Kelly, me limping with my false leg chafing, singing, 'We are some of the Bermondsey boys'. Terry wasn't drunk, of course. He doesn't drink. And I don't know where that song comes from, have never seen it written, never heard a recording of it, only ever heard it sung by drunken men from Bermondsey.

I came to the bit where you go, 'Doors and windows open wi--ide' and I held my arms out wide and fell on my arse in a puddle. My elbow hurt and water seeped through my worsted trousers. I'd lost my walking stick. I leaned back on my elbows and laughed. Terry laughed. I laughed so much I couldn't finish the verse. Now cold water crept up my back. I didn't care. A Rover car stopped nearby and my ex-wife got out, as if it was the most natural thing in the world. Her new boyfriend sat at the wheel, staring through the windscreen in front of himself, drumming his fingers on the steering wheel.

'Here comes trouble,' said Terry. I tried to get up and fell into a shallow trench, part of the roadworks. It was a bit muddy and so was I, now. Judy stood over me with her hands on her hips, the way women do. I've been watching women do that since the first time I dropped my dummy over the side of my high chair. Spring nineteen fifty-three.

'What are you doing?' She asked.

'I dropped a tanner in here and I was looking for it. Lend us your matches.'

'You know I don't smoke.'

'So you don't.'

'Anyway, it's a gas trench. Look.'

She pointed to a small hoarding propped against a stack of big yellow pipes. NO NAKED LIGHTS. Beyond the hoarding and the pipes her new boyfriend Tom leaned on his Rover and watched. Judy and Tel helped me out of the shallow trench. I held out a muddy hand for Judy to pull. Tom gave me the evil eye from afar, 'what an irresponsible wretch you are, Jenner'. I waved him a muddy little wave. Terry looked at me, then at the trench, then at Tom, then at me again.

'Where's your walking stick?' Judy asked.

'Lost,' I said. 'Like my tanner.'

Terry handed me the stick.

I pulled myself up to full height and began, 'His eyes were glazed, his breath smelt of intoxicating liquor, he was unsteady on his feet...' a refrain I knew she'd remember from both our days as foot-slogging constables. Judy interrupted.

'...what were you doing here?'

'Everybody's got to be somewhere.'

'Ha ha. You're pissed, Jenner.'

'You Metropolitan women are rough, do you know that?'

I knew I was swaying a bit. Judy brushed at my raincoat, as if she were straightening-up a dusty schoolboy. My mother used to do it. Self-confident, un-jealous new boyfriend Tom fetched a bit of old carpet out of the boot of his car and spread it carefully over the back seat. Hoy Baldy! I called in my head. He looked at me as if he'd heard. Judy's face floated before mine.

'What are *you* doing here?' I asked.

'I live here, remember?'

She does. She has a flat on the Mile End. I couldn't resist it, though. 'I thought you lived with the Scottish ponce.'

And Judy hit me with the flat of her hand so hard I staggered back a pace. My face hurt and my good ear rang. She stood in front of me while I gathered my balance again. She pulled her hand back again. I winced. Tom Mack stood by his Rover with the door open, watching; neither in nor out of it, either not knowing or not deciding what to do. Terry stood near the trench ready to field me if I staggered that way again. I met Judy's eyes. Her voice was very soft and shook a little.

'I'm sorry. I'm sorry.'

'So am I.'

'Come on, we'll drive you home.'

'I'm not getting in his car, drunk or sober...'

'Is it worth it?' She interrupted me, her voice raised and angry again.

I looked in the trench while I thought about it. 'A tanner's a tanner. Anyone will tell you that.'

'Always the philosopher. But cheap.'

'It's my line of work. Leaves you with a lot of time for thinking.'

'When you're sober enough.'

Ouch.

'Good-bye,' she swept back to the Rover, making up Tom's mind for him. Terry and I stood watching in silence as they drove away.

'Bleeding trench,' I said. I leaned on the stick, sober now, staring at the shallow trench. Terry stood close by my side.

'You all right?' He asked.

'I'm all right.'

'Dangerous things, trenches.'

'The trench was fine. It was the woman that hurt.'

He shrugged for a reply. I stared into the trench a little longer.

'Trenches are dangerous. Even shallow ones.'

I watched the rain fall into the trench. My clothes clung to me the way women don't. I wiped mud off my trousers.

'Yes,' Terry said at last, with a dry sounding voice.

'Even shallow trenches, Tel. You don't need to get much bigger than that to swallow up a man.'

'Thinking about Joe Boy?'

Joe Boy was my brother. 'Had been', I should say, since he's been dead for all of my adult life.

'I was thinking about the trench, too,' I answered.

'I knew you were.'

And we were silent for a long time, staring at the trench.

'She's right,' said Terry, 'Too much thinking can muck up your head.'

He meant it, too. Just to make sure I got the point he added, 'You want to try and relax a bit, Jimmy.'

Good advice if you can follow it. Terry touched my arm and I followed him away from the gas trenches. Rain fell but didn't wash us clean and I didn't sing or drink any more. If I had been drunk I wasn't now.

Three

BUT LET'S NOT rush ahead. Before I fell in the trench the motorcyclist shot at the milko, and before the motorcyclist shot at the milko I'd been trailing this fellow, Ralph Purnell, for a couple of weeks.

It felt like a couple of years.

Eventually I followed him to Bermondsey. I usually avoid Bermondsey. It turns me maudlin. Sometimes I feel as if everything in my life started and ended in Bermondsey. I know it started there.

*

If you cross Tower Bridge to the southern shore of the Thames, then turn directly east, things deteriorate fast. I know. I was born there. Past the nick, past the docks, past the Catholic church, and that was me, in the council flats. Our balcony was the third from the left on the second floor. In my day Bermondsey Borough Council painted the balcony rails council sky blue. But things have changed, and not just in the rusting of the handrails and lack of naval jelly. Nowadays, cross Tower Bridge, turn left and you're immediately among converted wharves and ponced-up former factories, security lighting and wine bars. Tooley Street's river side has gone up-market, and is looking up. Ignore all that. It doesn't take long to get among the heaving masses of Bermondsey proper. The people in the converted wharves spend more on parking their cars than the old ladies in Jamaica Road spend on living. Wring your hands if your conscience bothers you, but it's the way of the world. Apparently. Press on the accelerator. Keep going, past the entrance to the Thames tunnel and head instead for Brunel's tunnel. A million bricks can't all be wrong. Head for the bleakest, most wind and rain-lashed quarter of all of Thames-side London. You'll find yourself in Downtown. Just as I did a few days before the moody motorcyclist extended the hand of extreme road rage towards the milko in the doppelganger Jennermobile.

*

I was sitting alone in my old Ford Granada, nearside wheels hugging the gutter mud in a line of parked cars. I was outside a building site in Downtown. All around me homes were being built at an heroic rate. Nearby was a promised tube station, so far only a hoarding. Downtown is big on hoardings. The street was screened from the building site with Sterling boards. So was I. That was the idea. I was playing Injuns with Ralph Purnell again.

The fence carried two yellow-and-black signs facing the street, one threatening site workers with instant dismissal for urinating except in the comfort zones, the other warning they would be sacked for failing to wear appropriate headwear. The workmen were all inside, sporting hard hats and zipped trousers. The notices were moonshine, designed to convince would-be Downtown residents – real heroes – that this muddy patch piled with cinder blocks and facing bricks was a quality operation. If the would-be residents would only brave Jamaica Road, Brunel Road and all points east, something special awaited them here. Downtown was on the way up. Nearby, older, nineteen-fifties blocks of flats had been capped with verdigris decorative pyramids, as if that would improve matters. Early morning mums emerged from the flats, passed under the green pyramids, dragging their kids to school through the rain, heads down as they passed the yellow signs and pushed their prams. I sat listening to a phone-in in the Ford, a recently acquired habit. That's false; I wasn't so much listening as sitting with the radio switched on. 'Wayne... Wayne? We seem to have lost Wayne. Now to Tony in Tooting.'

What about Jimmy in Downtown? Jimmy was supposed to be keeping tabs on Ralph Purnell, Esq., local government officer. Ralph was a surveyor in his sixties, a long-time employee of Downtown Borough Council. I'd been following him for weeks. I was getting considerably over my daily rate to watch

Ralph, and I should have been awake and alert, but the surveyor had tired me out.

Ralph had a relationship with a girl working in an architectural practice in Dewsbury, outside Leeds. Looking at Dewsbury, you'd think they recruited their architects from the RNIB. Or maybe it was the same chap who'd thought it a good idea to put green hats on flats in Downtown. The architects had a twenty-five-year-old blonde bombshell called Louise who worked as typist and receptionist and had exploded over Ralph. Every architect should have a blonde bombshell in his or her office, if only to blind local government officers on compliance checks. Or maybe Ralph and Louise's relationship was romantic love. The real thing. It could have been.

Ralph and Louise maintained their sweet little attachment by car. A couple of times a week each motored a hundred miles or so to a motorway service station hotel in Birmingham. Not many people would associate Birmingham with love, fewer the M40. Ralph was one, coming from London in his official car on official petrol (of course), and preferring to travel west up the M40. I don't know why. Louise came from Dewsbury in a second-hand, slightly lived-in looking metallic green Porsche Ralph had bought her. I know Ralph paid for the Porsche because I had a man, Boycey, find the garage who'd sold it. Even a second-hand slightly lived-in looking Porsche costs a lot of money. Boycey also camped outside Louise's place for a couple of the nights we were watching them. Just to check. She was a dreamboat. A nun. In Dewsbury Louise went to bed early and alone. She saved herself for Birmingham and Ralph.

When they reached the motorway services hotel Ralph and Louise would go directly to a room and spend the night locked inside, presumably making whoopee. I say 'presumably' because I don't know. I didn't spy on them making whoopee; I wasn't hired for that and anyway, you have to have some standards. I suppose they hadn't hired the room because it offered Sky Sports big match satellite TV and a first rate minibar.

Once booked in, the happy couple never went out, sending for sandwiches if they were hungry. It was like a twice-weekly

honeymoon, an arrangement to envy. When I managed to bribe
the buffet service waiter he said they didn't seem to be doing
much, just sitting around in pyjamas waiting for a sandwich. I
don't know if he was very simple or just the broadest-minded
buffet waiter in Birmingham.

Last night was just such a honeymoon night, the second I'd
attended. Though Louise had put a spring into Ralph's step
she'd played havoc with my sleeping arrangements. You have
to move your car every now and then in a motorway services
car park otherwise some jobsworth will accuse you of being a
camped-out diddicoi and serve you with a ten quid overnight
parking bill. I never dozed for thirty consecutive minutes. At
five-oh-three Ralph left the motorway services hotel and
headed back to London. I expect he left Louise asleep. She
wasn't rushed. Architects don't open early. They're not
newsagents, and at this stage milkmen still held only the usual
significance in my life. At five-oh five I began to follow Ralph
back to London, hips and neck aching, sleepless and feeling
dismal. We ploughed the M40, through a rain front which
hovered nervously on the edge of the Chilterns, then followed
us and the other early-bird commuters down into the Thames
valley and on into West London. I trailed Ralph through the
city to Downtown. We stopped as the sun rose. I parked
opposite a cream-paint and tea-stain coloured mobile tea bar.
Building contractors had done their best to turn the wholly
urban road into a muddy track. Ralph parked his car, pulled on
a hard hat and went through Sterling board security gates to
collect bribes or anoint plans or whatever it is borough surveyor persons do. I watched the security gates through heavy-
lidded eyes for a few minutes, looking in an amused way at
those comfort zone signs, trying to read a Midland newspaper.
'ALBION IN CRISIS.' Sometimes headlines are bigger than the
writer intends. I was bored and cosy. I folded the paper and
settled in my seat. Then I just blinked, or so it felt.

I was woken by wheezing air brakes. A white, box-type
delivery lorry double-parked next to me. *Right* next to me. I
couldn't have got out of my car if I'd wanted. I'd have shouted

if I'd thought the lorry driver would have heard, but there was no point. The Ford's off-side window-winder came off in my hand. Again. The lorry driver climbed down and crossed to the mobile tea bar. I didn't see him at first, but I heard the driver's door slam. Then I saw his legs quickly crossing the road under the lorry. I was baulked by a parked car in front and a parked car behind. Someone with two legs would have wriggled across and out of the nearside door, but I haven't got two. I've got one-and-a-half legs plus a prosthesis and a walking stick. I was stuck, unable to leave the car by the nearside door except head-first. I could see the lorry driver's legs under the lorry, standing at the mobile tea bar. Polished brown boots, new blue jeans. Very smart for a lorry driver. A thin veil of road dirt had been thrown over the cream coloured paint of the tea bar by passing lorries. The man in blue jeans and polished brown boots stood in relief before the veil. Another pair of legs stood next to him. A man in formal trousers with sensible cleated brown country shoes. The two pairs of feet turned towards each other and relaxed, as if they'd ordered their teas and were now having a chat. I did my best to relax, too. Why worry? After a while the lorry driver climbed back in his cab and started the engine. I'd managed to force the handle back onto the winder and open the window, so I got a nice lung-full of unburnt diesel fuel as the lorry drove off. When I stopped coughing I looked towards the mobile tea bar. The man wearing the sensible shoes and formal trousers was Ralph Purnell. He stood at the tea bar with his yellow hat on his head, a sheepskin coat on his back and his tea in his hand. He was looking straight at me. We made eye contact. I lifted the Midland newspaper and feigned interest in the Baggies. Ralph put down his tea and walked back into the well-regulated building site. His steps were confident. He looked calm. He didn't seem rushed or as if he was embarrassed. There was nothing urgent Ralph had to do.

Had he seen me?

Of course he had.

Damn.

Four

O N TO MICKEY DeWitt. Did I say he had been involved in Tommy Slaughter's gang in the nineteen sixties? They never mentioned that on the news when he died. It was all public munificence, private magnanimity and 'what a lovely family man'. No one mentioned the knives in the back, the slashed faces, the girls' lives ruined. Mickey, depicted in the press as an endlessly caring if literally incredibly swarthy father of two blonde daughters, had spent the sixties turning other people's daughters into prostitutes. Presumably he'd never ruined a news editor's daughter; or grandmother, bearing in mind their relative ages.

No one mentioned – either – the specially adapted mole wrench pipe-clamp he was reputed to use to crush his rivals' knackers. Not for Mickey the sophistication of the Richardson hand-generator. The sixties are a long time ago and Mickey DeWitt had spent the intervening years cleaning up his reputation. Journalists nowadays all look younger than policemen, who look like sixth-formers to me. Mickey DeWitt's past was far enough past to have slipped beyond the grasp of any but the most persistent investigative journalist. All the crime beat wallahs who would have remembered Mickey had long since succumbed to cirrhosis. And the new generation? He'd committed his best crimes while they were still hanging off their mothers' tits.

But I remembered.

*

The radio man gave the weather for the London region. Rain. Cold spells. More rain. Rain predicted. Low pressure out in the Atlantic, heading this way. Cold front descending from Norway. You get the picture. It makes you want to ask why this stuff is described as 'changeable'? Then the man on radio news said, 'And in Sydenham last night Michael Conrad DeWitt, a businessman aged sixty four, was shot dead by a gunman as he left the Glass Balloonist public house. The victim was known for his philanthropic work throughout London. Police are seeking a slim grey-haired man who was seen in the area at the time.' And then actualities, a woman witness speaking in one of those classic, nasal cockney voices you associate with the spirit of the Blitz.

'Well, love, I was carrying my shopping across and then this little bloke came out of a pub and walked across the car park.'

'Did you see him?' Asked the reporter.

'I just said,' said the woman. 'It was dark but he was a little bloke in a suit. Swor-vy.'

'Sworvy?'

'Hairy. Like a g'rilla. And he walked across the car park and another bloke came up behind him and shot him.'

'Was the gunman alone?'

'It was a pub car park.'

'What was he like?'

'Little.'

'The gunman?'

'Old. You think you'd be safe from being shot by pensioners.'

'Was it a gang killing?'

'I didn't stop to ask him, ducky. Bang bang and I was off,' she pronounced it 'orf' and the news editor, tired of non sequiturs, had cut the report right there.

But I was there. The old lady's story was spot on. Sometimes pictures on the radio are more real than being there. Bang bang and she was orf. She ran right past me.

I had heard the bangs. I was drawn towards the source of the sound as if someone was reeling me in. But I was in a dream as the old lady ran past me. I didn't know what had happened or who (if anyone) had been shot. I could only think, to be on the scene of a shooting in London is bad luck, unless you run with a certain crowd down the over-excitable Old Kent Road (which I don't). Two shootings in a few days is very bad luck indeed.

Five

TOMMY SLAUGHTER HAS been dead since nineteen-sixty-eight.

In the sixties Mickey DeWitt was in Slaughter's gang.

I met Tommy Slaughter once.

My brother was in a car with him and a man I can't put a face to – I never saw him clearly. I think it must have been Slaughter's driver, Freddie Phillips. I can't say for sure.

Be fair. It was more than twenty-five years ago, and I was a schoolboy on an errand for my father. I remember the car, I remember the dusty street it was on, I remember walking along the street. I remember an american-cloth bag full of spuds hanging from my fingers. Spuds and brussels. No one ate broccoli then, just stuffed themselves with roast spuds and brussels and beer and relied on open windows and forgiving friends. I crossed the road. The Jag pulled up beside me. Slaughter was on the passenger side, the man I can't put a face to – but was probably Freddie Phillips – was at the wheel. Joe Boy was on the back seat with Janice. I couldn't see Janice all that clearly in the shade. I remember or do I invent her great big neon lips? The car stopped at the kerb right next to me and I didn't stoop. Joe rolled down his window. I could see Janice's long white legs shining on the seat beside Joe, not so much marble as Twyford porcelain.

'Jimmy... Jimmy. Come here,' called Joe. And then to Slaughter. 'This is my brother, James. He's sixteen.'

Slaughter was wearing super-dark sunglasses, shiny jobs. They were rare in England then. Slaughter took the sunglasses off and stared at me. I'll never forget those eyes. Blue grey, flat, no fun. Psychopath's eyes, though I didn't know the word then. He wore a black suit. Joe got out of the car and put his arm around me. There was a gun in his waistband. I could feel it. I said nothing.

'Big for his age, isn't he?'

'Yes,' said Slaughter. He had the glasses on again. His face was set, as if it never smiled.

'Good muscles. A big strong lad.'

'He's just like you, Joe. Two peas in a Jenner pod. One younger than the other.'

'One for you in a few years, Tommy,' said my brother. I just wanted to get away.

Slaughter didn't speak again. I broke free of Joe and began to walk away. I looked over my shoulder once or twice. They were still there, sitting in the Jag. The door was still open and Joe stood next to the car still. A motorbike passed; an old man on a big bike wearing a cork-lined helmet, a Cromwell. I remember the helmet strap was loosely buckled and he had a fag hanging out of the corner of his mouth. A paradox, being safe but taking risks. Joe got in the car but it didn't drive away. I went straight home. The american-cloth bag cut into my fingers. I didn't tell my father. It would only have caused a row. Later that week they had a row anyway, when my old man found Joe showing me the .38 Smith-and-Wesson I'd felt in his waistband. I'd forced Joe to do it by threatening to tell Dad. But Dad found the gun in Joe's pocket for himself. I mean, it was a bit big for a Mars bar.

'What are you, a Lilliput Lancer? Or have we joined the Officer Training Corps?' Said the old man and confiscated it. I don't think real gangsters have their guns confiscated by their Dads. I told Joe so. He was nearly in tears.

'I'll get it back,' he said. 'I know where he puts things. I've just let him *think* he's taken it. It's important to let the old fellow have his pride. He hasn't got much, Jimmy, apart from you and that pride. I can't take that away from him. I have to play along.'

Oh *sure*, Joe. Even across the twenty-five years and more; oh *sure* Joe.

'Why have you got a gun?' I said.

'It's a frightener.'

'Why do you need a frightener? You work for the Gas Board.'

'I'm biding my time, Jim.' He winked. 'Digging holes is a cover. I'm on Slaughter's payroll now.'

Six

I REMEMBER MEETING Tommy Slaughter. Bully for me. It's hardly tea with the Queen. Later he was murdered and rumoured to be propping up the M40. So I should remember him. The meeting of him should have been memorable. And memorable events are popularly believed to be high tide markers of our lives.

Aren't they?

It's supposed – for example – that we know where we were when John Kennedy died, as if he'd been President of England as well as the other place. If that's true, if we're so bound up in a sort of communal diary kept in Bush House, how did we manage before TV and radio news actualities existed? Perhaps we were slower, or simply didn't care. I don't believe either is the case. The news of Waterloo took a couple of days to reach London. The first day of the Somme made the next day's newspapers. The news of Kennedy's assassination was played on the radio minutes after it happened. In Bosnia they saved their ammo and refused to fight until the news crew turned up as promised. What's the good of fighting if you don't get on the news?

I quite agree. I wouldn't want to bleed for nothing. I just can't make myself believe any of this represents an improvement, which is why – according to my ex-wife Judy – I'm always letting the battery on my mobile phone go flat. She thinks it's a sub-conscious rejection of the late twentieth century. Very female, that is. Whichever way you turn they've got you.

Memorable events are supposed to be high tide markers of our lives, exceptional high water springs. Higher water than you'd ever expect. Not the sort of thing you'd expect a boy brought up on the side of the Thames to forget. I played on that Thames-side mud as a child. Every spot of flotsam is etched on my memory. I can replay the tape of each sucking slurp my feet made as they moved along the strand below Bermondsey Wall.

So why did it take so long for the penny to drop?

*

I was brought up on a council estate in Bermondsey, by the river. I was brought up by my father. My mother died when I was a kid. The years have dulled my memory of her, and even though I don't see what I could have done about it, this fact makes me ashamed. I remember my Dad and my brother well, though. Just as I know where I was when John Fitzgerald Kennedy died.

I was helping my father and my brother Joe paint the kitchen, an activity for which none of us was particularly suited. I expect the old chap was out of dosh – why else use a dreamy twelve year old and a sullen late-teenager for something as unlikely as dabbing duck-egg blue all over your kitchen pipes? You could never know whether my father was well off or skint; as my step-Aunt Kate said, 'You could never tell whether your old man had a tanner or twenty quid in his pocket.'

We covered our white-spotted red Formica-top tables and chairs with well-worn copies of the *Daily Herald*, then Joe and I sploshed away on one side of the room while our father glued wood-effect damp-resist wallpaper on the other. My father's glue was fungicidal. As I remember it Joe and my old man had a row about whether they ought to match up the knots in the wallpaper, then the Roberts radio said Kennedy had been shot. We paused amongst the fake cladding and the perfectly matched printed brown knots, paint brushes in our hands. Stinking blue paint trickled down my wrist. It was then that my father spotted the tattoos.

'Why have you got "Love" written on your knuckles?' He asked Joe.

Joe didn't have an explanation, except to say 'It's a tattoo, isn't it?'

My father grabbed the other hand. 'Fear.'

'"Fear"... fear, you pillock. What am I going to do with you?' It was rhetorical. Joe turned on me.

'Why have you got blue paint all over my best screwdriver?'

'I had to open the tin somehow.'

That was more Joe's level. I made tea.

Later that year Joe had 'Made in England' tattooed on his arse, which he thought was hysterically funny. He had no sense of humour to speak of, my brother Joe, though he thought he did.

My brother was much older. Joe. Joe Jenner, Jimmy Jenner. Brothers. Our flat ('my father's flat' as I always thought of it, though it was my home as much and as long as it was his) was on the first floor of our council buildings, near the Drill Hall, and from our balcony you could watch the world go by. Sometimes we did just that.

My father was a contrary man, quick to grow tired of others' failings.

'There you go. Eyeball that one,' said my brother Joe. It was a hot evening in the summer of nineteen-sixty-eight. Joe was pointing to a glossy red Mark II Jag rolling slowly towards us from the Abbey Street arch. Though the steam trains had long since finished the brickwork of the arch was still smoke-blackened, so that the red Jag came from the most unutterable blackness into the greasy heat of a London late summer evening.

'Look at that.'

'Don't tell me what to do,' said my father, and huffed and puffed and rubbed his elbows on the ragged concrete of his balcony.

No one induced bad temper in my father more readily than Joe did. God bless him, Joe Jenner, for now he is gone (and my unbelieving father too except he'd probably curse me for the benediction). What a pair! Each time Joe would come up with some extraordinary 'fact', my old chap would call his bluff, and Joe would be hurt, and unable to answer. He would gag, the words would catch in his throat as if he'd been swallowing hard bread, or rags soaked in diesel oil. Or Bermondsey mud. Poor Joe. How could he have all the answers to all the traps my old chap laid for him? My father had an infinity of traps and

the better part of forty years start on his elder son. Joe didn't
stand a chance. Being younger, I understood I didn't stand a
chance, and at fifteen only wanted to stand in my old man's
shadow. Joe's trouble was he wanted both to be like my old
man and unlike him all at the same time. To no one's surprise
but his own, Joe couldn't pull it off.

There were other things Joe wanted to grasp which stayed
puzzlingly (for him) out of his reach. Joe wanted to be rich.
Since he had no idea how to become rich, Joe restricted himself
to owning two expensive pieces of clothing (a bottle green
mohair suit and a mauve and soft pullover he often wore under
it – was the pullover cashmere?), and hanging round with a lot
of hoods in Soho when he wasn't working. Now I think of it,
he also had a pair of Italian shoes; black, made of smooth-
surfaced leather, with the most delicate welts imaginable. I
envied him those shoes.

Even Joe knew that lolling around side streets in Soho in a
cashmere pullover wasn't much of a get rich plan... but he
wasn't clever enough to think up anything better.

My father wanted little or nothing in the way of material
goods, and certainly wouldn't visit what he called 'Up West'.
As the years went by my father appeared to live more and
more like a monk – even if the monk was one who drank Guinness, smoked rollies and was in the big league of bar-room
raconteurs. Joe recognised that my father's story-telling and
fluently expressed opinions were the source of much popu-
larity in Bermondsey, and so wanted to be like him in these
things. But Joe was little league, with brains to match. And the
only people Joe managed to impress that he was a good egg
were the kind of pin-brains who thought Tommy Slaughter
was a good egg too, and so were the Krays and the Richard-
sons and all the other dross who financed their nights in
Mayfair casinos and Soho night-clubs by organising gangs of
numbskulls to knock over sub-post offices, or by scaring Jewish
or Asian shopkeepers so they'd pay twenty pounds a week to
be allowed to keep their shops along the Old Kent Road open,
or by breaking bookmakers' legs, or chucking Molotov

cocktails into minicab offices. Or by getting desperate girls to go on the game for them. My father despised the people who liked Joe, detested Joe for wanting to be liked by them, disdained any interest in his elder son. Joe might have managed detestation, but disdain was out of his range. Joe couldn't cope.

That warm night late in nineteen-sixty-eight we stood on the soft tarred balcony of my old man's flat and we looked down on the Jamaica Road, watching the asphalt gleam through the glistening oily air. You could almost taste the petrol off that road.

The red Jag, polished bright and with a couple of mohair-suited spivs inside, swept down to the junction of Abbey Street and Jamaica Road. My brother Joe said, 'That's Freddie Phillips' motor. He's in Slaughter's gang, he is.'

The Jag paused at the lights and a girl got in, giggling. She had long blonde hair and wore a white nylon-type blouse and a short, black semi-matt skirt; maybe it was leather. I don't remember her face but I do remember that giggle. Who was she? Just some blonde daisy, getting into the Jag. She was local and she'd been waiting for the spivs, talking to a kid on a motor scooter while she waited. I think, but I'm not sure, that she must have lived in Arnold Estate. I knew everyone around there in that invisible way kids do. Why didn't I know her?

You didn't need to be a genius to work out where Freddie Phillips and the other man were taking her; I mean, I didn't and I was only sixteen then.

My father peered at the Jag, then at Joe, eyes screwing tighter together. I watched as he wiped his left hand back across his widow's peak. My father's hair hardly went grey, just got thinner and thinner. He puffed his cigarette from his right hand before saying, 'So what?'

'So... it's as good as saying, he's worth a hundred and fifty a week,' said Joe. 'Minimum.'

'It's as good as saying, he's a pratt,' said my father.

'That's your view,' said Joe. 'Not everyone's as stick-in-the-mud as you.'

'Pratt,' said my father. 'As thick as a docker's sandwich. I know who that is, swanning round in the Jaguar and buying rounds of gins down the Greg for floozies every Friday and Saturday.'

'There are no floozies in the Greg.'

'Not when you and your pals jump back in your Jaguars there aren't.'

'I haven't got a Jaguar.'

My Dad, Alf, looked at him long and hard.

'So you haven't. How long do you think that pratt can go wandering around London, acting like he's Baron bleeding Rothschilds, without no one noticing he hasn't got any visible means of support?'

'He's got a wife,' said Joe.

'*Wives*,' said my father, tipping papery cigarette ash off his roll-up, 'are not a means of support. Wives get pregnant and load men down with bloody mill-stones like you.'

Which was not fair. Joe was independent, not a kid like I was then. Joe had a job digging holes for the gas people, and it was well-paid, a good job. Secure. Holes always needed to be dug. Joe would let anyone who would listen know it was his plan to get out, but for the moment he had a job. He had too a flat down Southwark Park Road and a girl living in it with him. Janice Conkey. She was as common as brass curtain rings, with a mouth like a coal hole. She didn't need a phone, all Janice had to do was swing open their kitchen window, fill her lungs with air and she could let the whole world know about whatever she wanted to let them know about. She often did it. Joe didn't care. They weren't married, either, which was important in the sixties in Catholic Bermondsey. It was a statement. I sometimes think Joe only really shacked up with Janice so he could flaunt her and her slattern sisters (because Janice came from a large family of mouthy sisters, too many to count or know by their faces, but all recognisable by their short skirts, long legs and willingness to assume the horizontal mode) in front of my old man. There's an example of Joe's misjudgement of our father. What was there about some birdbrained bint shacked up with Joe in the Southwark Park Road that would

rattle Alfy Jenner's cage? Nothing. My old man just thought (or
gave out that he thought) Joe was a biscuit short of a packet. If
he wanted to squander his life digging holes, hanging around
with mentally deficient Mediterranean types in Soho and
impregnating sluts down the Blue... well whose fault was that?

'You're a big boy, Joe. *You* choose,' my father had said. The
irony was lost on Joe, of course. Joe was going to choose, even
though my father clearly meant 'Don't choose; obey'. Joe never
got it. By the time Joe moved in with Janice he'd already
chosen the method of his escape. The visits to Soho were part
of it. He told me often, enigmatic little hints. 'I won't be doing
this long. I won't have to put up with this long. I've got plans.'
He had plans. He had a method. I was too young then to
understand what was implied in his method, I was too young
to read the hints the way my father did. I spent my early
twenties figuring Joe out, and when I did I only got it wrong:
Joe did very little – the method chose him.

I can picture them now, over twenty-five years later. Joe Boy
in his Stay Prest trousers and his polished black Italian casuals,
his short black hair smoothed close to his head, trying to look
relaxed and composed. Joe had pushed his sleeves back up his
thick forearms, revealing his tattoos. It was some years since
'Love' and 'Fear' and Joe had moved on to frozen doves and
twirling girls. An anchor concealed the Sharon Janice had
replaced, though Joe had never been nearer the sea than Margate
beach. He rested one tanned forearm against the chipped blue-
paint rail of my father's balcony and smiled, as if he had a
secret and my old man was going to have to prise it from him.
Not yet.

'You wouldn't understand these things,' said Joe, waving his
hand at the Jaguar.

Now the blonde had settled in her seat and the Jag accelerated
away towards Tooley Street. I never saw the man at the wheel
of it; Freddie Phillips, as Joe claimed. I never saw him in the
flesh, not to recognise. Joe turned away from my old man and
followed the Jag with his eyes. 'It's more complicated than that.'

'What's more complicated? You mean he's got a couple of

Rozzers in his pocket? Big deal. So old mouth and trousers gets dressed up like a Jamaican pimp and goes floating round Bermondsey like he owned the place on *what*? On the strength of buying coppers' drinks? What's he got, a different coloured one of them Jaguars for every day of the week?'

My father pronounced the three syllables 'Jag-you-ares' like some vile insult. Conspicuous consumption revolted him.

'Slaughter has.'

'Slaughter has. Bully for him. Another over-rated big-mouth.'

'Shows you what you know,' said Joe, smiling and playing his 'secret' card again. My father didn't answer, just 'tutted'.

'And, for your information the floozies, as you call them, don't drink gins,' Joe went on.

'Except days with y's in them.'

'And,' said Joe Boy, with a look of triumph on his face, 'you couldn't be more wrong about who buys drinks for which coppers. But what would you know?'

My father shook his head slowly, as if he was dealing with an imbecile.

'It's not Freddie Phillips, I can tell you,' said Joe.

'Of course not,' said my old man, stubbing his cigarette carefully in an Old Holborn tin he kept on the balcony specially for the purpose. 'It's his pratty mate. Slaughter.' And he mimicked my brother's voice, *'That's Freddie Phillips' motor. He's in Slaughter's gang, he is.'* My father paused, then tugged at the waistband of his charcoal grey worsted trousers so that they came where he liked them, half-way up his chest. He looked keenly at Joe, who turned half away. 'You're easily led, Joe, and you're easily led into admiring the wrong people. You will end up with your honesty tested, son. How will you fare?'

Joe didn't answer. It wasn't a tack he'd expected my father to take. We all went indoors and I made tea. Joe wouldn't drink it, preferring to walk back to Southwark Park Road and Janice. My father spent the evening in a sulk. I watched *Beat the Clock* on my own. That Bruce Forsyth spun a career out of nothing. Perhaps that's the trick.

*

Joe didn't get a chance to find out if he was honest or not. First
Slaughter copped it in Crooms Hill, Greenwich. One night the
Jaguar was found red both inside and out, doors swinging, seats
covered in blood, panels pierced by bullet holes. Slaughter was
gone, rumoured to be propping up part of the elevated section
of the M40. Phillips was simply gone, as if he'd never existed.
A power struggle developed amongst London gangsters.
Brother Joe's tenuous connection with Slaughter's gang was
cut. He never had a chance to make other connections. A few
months after our conversation on my old man's balcony a spoil
truck collapsed the wall of a gas trench he was digging. In
January nineteen-sixty-nine Joe drowned in the Bermondsey
dirt we were all struggling to stay above. Twenty-four years
old with arms as hard as larch posts. No use at all for
swimming up towards the tarmac street through Bermondsey
marsh clay. Joe's hands stood out of the dirt, Love and Fear, but
they couldn't drag him clear. They dug him out of the Neckinger-
soaked soil as quickly as they could but he was blue, and his
chest was all caved in. His mouth was full of Bermondsey
mud. I remember going round to Albins, the undertaker by St
James's Church. Old Albin had put kid gloves on him, to cover
the torn fingers and missing nails. Albin's assistant had made
up his face too, ghastly-looking orange ending at the neck, so
that Joe looked like he had had a couple of good weeks in
Jersey, but had kept his suit on all the time. Joe had a nice
white rim under his collar. I couldn't bring myself to kiss him,
as my Auntie suggested I should. My father didn't force me,
either. We both saw that look on Joe Boy's face. Utter horror.
My old man cried a little, and was angry with someone. I
didn't push too hard to find out, in case it was me. When I was
a kid I always felt as if I had just done something wrong. The
feeling persisted in me until I was quite grown up.

My father followed Joe two years later, via the more usual
methods – Old Holborn, Guinness, Teacher's whisky, general
self-abuse until his heart caved in. Or out, depending which way
round an infarction goes. They said he shouldn't have lasted so
long. He'd had something wrong with his heart for years. I

interred him at Hither Green in a parking space he'd booked seven years before, a reserved seat next to my mother. My mother had been there since I was ten, and no doubt had a good deal to discuss with the old fellow by the time we stuck him under the turf next to her. She was that kind of woman... built things up inside herself.

I grew up and became a copper, which is about as far as you could have got from sixties cockney gangsterism; the kind of copper I was, anyway, seeing old ladies across Forest Road, Romford and ear-wigging kids a couple of years younger than myself for riding their bikes down the pavement. I'm sure I once saw Bobby Moore pass in a Roller. Or was it Ian Dury? Anyway, someone with sideburns. That was the highlight. When I was twenty-eight I transferred to a central London nick, expecting to broaden my horizons and become a detective, also to impress a bird I was after who worked in central London. I married her later but never managed to broaden my horizons as a flatfoot. Instead I got blown up by an Arab suicide squad in Regent's Street, for only crossing the road and asking to see their driving licences. I'm glad I never asked for their passports or they'd have really got the hump.

Today I'm not a copper any more and the right leg below the knee isn't me any more, being a nylon, stainless-steel and Terylene prosthesis. Let's be fair – who wants to be a one-footed flatfoot? Now there's only two arms and one leg of Clan Jenner left to go, all the others, my mother, my father, my brother Joe and my right leg, having snuffed it long since. My Uncles Tony and Red are dead too. I've got a persistent Auntie (Kate) but she's an acquired one, being the second wife of my Dad's brother, Red. I don't remember my Uncle Red who is dead and I barely remember my mother. My memories are composed of a few mental snapshots of my own and things my Auntie Kate said about her. Not so much a selective memory as a selected memory. At sixteen going on seventeen you do remember everything, of course, and so I do have the memory of my brother Joe. It's only a memory though, just pictures and words, nothing approaching comprehension. My memory of

him is like reading about a man in a history book. Words,
sometimes pictures, a bit of sound if you're lucky. Nothing you
could put your hand on. Movement and sound is a bit jerky
and very demanding of memory space, like a clip on a CD rom.
I'm bang up to date, me.

As for my old man... well, I'm not like him at all, despite
what my non-Auntie Kate (who retired once, but has now
come back to haunt the licensed victualling trade, and runs a
boozer down by the Elephant) says, 'You're the dead spit of
your Dad, Jimmy. Except you're taller of course. The boys in
your family always did look alike,' she was the second lady
publican called Kate that Red married, which must prove
something. He'd seen off the first Kate but the second had seen
off Red. My mother was a Kate too, a Jenner predilection, but I
made an alliterative marriage with a girl called Judy. A nice
blonde girl, with a sharp brain, lovely figure, blue eyes and a
right like Henry Cooper.

*

I was in the Mile End when the penny dropped.

I was walking in the rain with my long dead brother's
friend Terry. I've said that. And Judy Jenner was there. I've said
that too. And that she hit me.

The night the penny dropped I stared into the trench at the
side of the Mile End Road for an age, unable to answer Terry.
Internalising. Philosophising. A dollop of mud slipped into the
shallow ditch. Plop. Thus I dispute my own past. I was
thinking about the past. I was thinking about my brother Joe
Boy, who is dead and has been for more than twenty-five years.
With all our faults, yours and mine, you are mine, Joe. I would
not ditch you in a ditch, of whatever depth. I would not dump
you under a truck of any sort nor allow a truck to dump on
you. The penny has dropped.

You always wanted to know how things would be after, Joe
Boy. Well, this is 'after' and all the years since the last time I
saw you are 'after'.

Now the future has come to pass, and I am the last living

Jenner, as much as there is of me. Alive and kicking. Now the past is peopled with ghosts. Jenner family business is my business alone, however ghastly. The buck stops here.

Seven

Tommy Slaughter is dead. You know. We've been through all that. He died in nineteen-sixty eight. Mickey DeWitt was reputed to be responsible. Maybe he was, I don't know. I wasn't there. I think I know who shot Mickey DeWitt in his turn, more than twenty-five years later.

In the nineteen-sixties Mickey DeWitt had been a big-time Maltese gangster based around Soho. Then, every copper, every hood in London knew DeWitt. He was a star criminal, or at least he had been. Of course his name then wasn't Mickey DeWitt. His real name was a mixture of English, Italian and unpronounceable Arabic. Spit while you're saying Mickey Bellini. Mickey thought DeWitt gave him an air of grandeur, as if he was old money. How can a man five feet four inches tall who has to shave three times a day be 'old money'?

In the sixties the Metropolitan Police had created gaps in the organised crime market by putting capital figures behind bars. Mickey DeWitt filled the gaps, personally or with a relative. Mickey was not only in girls, porn clubs and slot machines... he was in everything, owned it all, ran it all. Nobody did anything in Wardour Street and Old Compton Street, all the way to the Charing Cross Road, without Mickey's say-so. Both the trade and the location were a tradition amongst his countrymen.

Mickey was the big fish the cops never reeled in. By the time they were ready to have a go – at the end of the seventies – Mickey was spending more on information than they were. The word was he got word and went for an extended holiday to Malta, leaving various brothers and cousins in charge of the family business. By nineteen-eighty-one he was discovered to be both a born-again Christian and a born-again property developer. Investment portfolio, church membership, nice clean English wife, two blonde teenage English daughters. Big house in Egham, Surrey. Convenient for the river. He didn't know nothing about crime and he didn't want to be seen around no criminal characters. If you've got the dosh people will believe anything. Mickey DeWitt had never done a day's bird in his life and pitched himself at his new non-criminal peer group as if he was the regular, legitimate businessman who'd just got out of the Mercedes.

Of course, no matter how many times he changed his name, his face or his address, Mickey was going to be famous among a certain class of person. Me, for example.

*

Tommy Slaughter is dead. You know. We've said it all before. He died in nineteen-sixty eight. Mickey DeWitt was reputed to be responsible. Maybe he was, I don't know. I wasn't there and can stand witness to nothing. I think I know who shot Mickey DeWitt in his turn, more than twenty-five years later. I was there. I was sitting in a Ford in Sydenham, watching the rain fall on shoppers. I was not exactly waiting for Mickey to die but it was going to happen next.

Mickey DeWitt must have thought his criminal days were years past him. He must have believed himself safe, or he'd never have gone to that pub.

I sat in the Ford watching the pub, the Glass Balloonist. I was bored. I'd spent too many hours doing this. On the pavement near me a bored child threw a tantrum, flinging himself at his mother's feet and bawling. Rain fell onto his open mouth and his breath came in sobs. Throw one for me, kid. I can't remember screaming so. I must have done once. A few minutes later the woman passed with the child again, the screaming mouth stopped full of chocolate. Sympathetic as ever, I was suddenly reminded I was hungry. My guts ached from hunger, but I couldn't get out of the car. A dog approached the child, who gave it a piece of chewed chocolate. St. Francis of Sydenham. The mother shooed the dog away. And all this happened before Maltese Mickey, once Mickey the killer, lately Mickey the philanthropist, got it. Mickey the Martyr.

I know. I was there.

Here's how it happened. We sat in the Ford in the half-light, me and a man called Boyce. The rain fell on shoppers. It wasn't dark but it would be soon. The lights were on in the shops. We sat without speaking for a long time. Across the road a couple of navvies packed up their pneumatic drill, closed down their compressor, adjusted their signs in the falling rain, 'Beware, Works.' It could be paraphrased as '*hole, don't fall down here*'. If you're so stupid or pissed you're going to fall down a great big hole in the street, what use is a sign to you? I know. I mean of all people *I* know.

Water dripped off the navvies as they bent to put sacks full of sand over the feet of the signs. They got in their Transit van and rubbed their hands while the exhaust blew condensation.

We talked. The man sitting next to me did the speaking. I listened mostly. I tried not to reply. The man sitting next to me in the Ford was Malcolm Boyce. I wish I hadn't been with Malcolm Boyce when Mickey DeWitt died.

We were sitting outside a pub car park. Ralph Purnell was in the pub. He's not the sort of man you'd associate with having a few bevvies, but he had adjourned to the pub and so we'd adjourned to the street outside. Boycey and I were watching, waiting for something to happen. Nothing ever happened on this job. It was good money for nothing; a cakewalk if it hadn't been for the problem of sitting in the car with Boycey all day. That was hard work. He either listed to radio phone-ins, tried to ring them or told smutty and exaggerated stories about himself. If he listened I listened involuntarily, if he rang on my mobile phone I paid. Anyway, the phone battery was flat and I'd left the curly lead for the cigarette lighter socket I knew not where (and more importantly cared not). If I neither paid for Boycey's phone calls nor wanted to listen to Harry in Havering or Bert in Balham's attempts at economic forecasts over the radio I had to suffer Boycey's stories.

'I knew a woman round here once... '

Boycey began a sort of demented 'once upon a time'. I tuned out as he launched into an entirely imaginary anecdote about an entirely imaginary woman. The tumbler in the Ford's electric clock fell back, clunk. If I was richer I'd have a car with a digital clock.

Time had never passed so slowly since I'd left school. I stared through the blue-tinted glass screen and wished the time away. Another hour at the most and I'd be able to leave. My wandering mind tuned in to Boycey for long enough to realise he was on another sexual fantasy. A girl was walking past us; eighteen-going-on-fifty, with already a brassy look to her, badly-dyed blonde hair, a tight skirt, a wiggle-wiggle walk. Few young women are improved by make-up.

'Eyar...eyar,' he called after her, laughing. He sounded like a donkey braying. His tone turned confidential, 'I've done it with her sister.'

'Boycey, this is the first time you've been in Sydenham....'

'How do you know?' he interrupted. 'I went to school in South London. I know lots of people here. It's in my blood.'

'You haven't got any blood.'

'Ha *ha*. You think you're so smart. You think you know everything Jenner, that's your trouble. But you don't.'

'Really?'

'Why am I here?'

'Because you think you are. From my point of view, because of all the noise you make.'

The girl walked past us again. Wiggle wiggle. Boycey photographed the girl, one for his collection, then put the camera down. He stared at me. I could almost hear him ticking. Bing! Got there.

'*Why do you need me here*?' I mean.'

'I often wonder.'

A white, box-type delivery lorry parked in front of our target pub, the Glass Balloonist, blocking the view. Fifty men could have gone in and out and we'd never have seen. Boycey started the Ford's engine.

'I'll move,' he said.

But there was nowhere to move to. The street was full of parked cars and old ladies de-bussing.

'Wait,' I said.

The lorry-driver lifted out a very small parcel and went into a shop, a ship's chandlers. He'd left his engine running. Why is there a ship's chandler's in Sydenham? It's so far from the sea. Who was the driver? I felt I knew him. Not his face, not his lorry, not even his clothes or just the way he walked, but something. I knew him from somewhere.

Who are you?

A fit-looking white-haired man in a blue wind-cheater stood next to the lorry. He was near the cab, as if he was eyeing it up as a prelude to nicking it. It looked comical. The white-haired man was nearer seventy than sixty.

'One day that driver's going to come out and find someone's legged-it with his lorry,' said Boycey.

I didn't answer.

'Still, he's a bit old for a hijacker. Maybe the goods aren't valuable.'

'What are you now, Boycey, a loss-adjuster?'

He turned away as a reply.

The driver came back, still carrying his tiny parcel. Brown boots. He was wearing polished brown boots. I hadn't seen his face before but I'd seen his boots, under the lorry in Downtown. The driver ignored the white-haired man standing next to his lorry and walked round to the back doors. He still hadn't taken the keys out of the cab. The lorry driver opened the back doors and put the tiny parcel back in. He didn't close the back doors immediately. He leaned inside and took something out. I couldn't see what. It was wrapped in a yellow duster cloth. The white-haired man took the yellow duster package from the lorry driver and tucked it inside his blue wind-cheater. It takes a long time to describe but it happened in an instant.

Boycey spoke with his eyes closed.

'I did like her. Oh I did.'

'Who?'

'The sister.'

'So you did.' I tried to sound resigned. Un-encouraging.

'She had a fat, rosy-looking face. Trusting, like a cow. And she was as happy as they come when she was....'

'All right, all right Romeo. Spare me the details.'

The delivery driver jumped back in his lorry and Boycey cut the Ford's engine. Now we could see the pub again.

'So where did she keep her stick?'

'What stick?'

'Oh. She had a guide dog then.'

'Ha ha. You may take the rise if you want. You wouldn't understand, Jimbo. No.' He paused to let this sink in. 'You're like most men, a bit slow in these matters.' Boycey leaned back in his seat with an expansive gesture, farted and smacked his lips appreciatively. 'You see, I *know* women. Your female of the species goes for something a bit out of the ordinary. Something a bit different. I know what that is and I can provide her with it. Even when I was a kid that was true.'

I stared into his pallid, pock-marked face. His shirt collar was spotted with blood from shaving. His clothes looked like he'd slept in them for more than one night. He was different, okay. Everything about Boycey was cheap, for a start. He wore cheap perfume and he wore cheap clothes. He seemed to choose clothes with as little natural material in them as possible. Boycey was happiest in a nylon shirt, extra-long paisley-pattern green Terylene tie and a Courtelle jacket. He always wore the tie, as big as Harry Carpenter's, tucked in his trouser-waistband. That wasn't the only way Boycey was different. When Boycey shaved he must have used a blunt cheese-grater, then slapped on some highly perfumed aviation spirit he'd bought from a stall down the Petticoat Lane. He got the razors and the alcohol cheap, dirt cheap, otherwise he wouldn't have bought them. Boycey bought himself new shoes once every six months, always brown jobs with brothel-creeper soles which are the cheapest shoes the cheapest shoe-shops in London do. Boycey wore the shoes, never polishing them, until their crepe soles were worn through. Then, a few weeks too late, he went and bought another pair. The result is he was almost always down-at-heel.

Poor Boycey. Boycey didn't see himself as poor Boycey, he didn't see he was unattractive. Who does? Boycey thought all those shivers he gave girls were thrills of anticipation. I know. He'd told me so over the last couple of weeks. Over and over.

'Probably you'd find you're a bit more of a prospect now,' Boycey went on, 'with only the one leg. You could find a lot of girls who'd be turned on by that. It could be a great asset.' He looked carefully at my face. 'Maybe your only asset. You've just been a bit slow in realising it.' He grinned.

The character in the blue wind-cheater was crossing the road behind Boycey's head. Closer to, he had a thin, drawn-looking face and turned-over shoulders, as if he were permanently doing a moody.

'Thanks Boycey. Where's the camera? Cop the bloke in the blue wind-cheater. Come on! Snap to it!'

Boycey duly photographed the man in the blue wind-cheater. Click. Blue windcheater, blue grey eyes. Boycey put down the camera quickly as the man turned and looked at us. He stared a flat stare at us, almost through us and I returned it, resisting the temptation to wink.

The man in the windcheater was on our side of the road now. He went into a newsagent's shop. 'Well done, Malcolm.'

'Who was he?'

'I dunno. He seemed to like you taking his photograph, though.'

'Bollocks. He never clocked me.'

Did he? I thought he may have, but Boycey was so certain. Sometimes I can't be bothered to argue.

'There's our girlfriend.' Boycey said a few minutes later, pointing through the windscreen at a woman. The woman was in her mid-twenties, tall and dark-haired, smartly dressed in a business suit and carrying a briefcase. She was very elegant, with a thin face, full lips and sharply cut features. If she wasn't clever she looked it. She walked briskly towards the pub. She'd had appointments with Ralph before. Strictly business. We hadn't been able to figure out who she was. We hadn't really tried. Women Ralph wasn't screwing were outside of the brief.

'Everywhere we go she goes. She's driving me mad, Jimbo.'

'Try some of your sexual attractiveness on her.'

The woman paused and looked towards our old Granada for a few moments. Now I dropped the camera to my lap, but she didn't seem to see us. Smart-dressed smart-brain girls don't even notice two scruffs sitting in a beaten-up car.

'I'll have a print of her when they come back from 'Boots'. I could give that one. I really could..,' Boycey said.

She looked away and I raised the camera and snapped again. The camera's motor whined.

'... bosh, just like that, across the kitchen table.' He laughed. 'Or perhaps I could give her the word about you. Maybe this could be your lucky day, Jimbo... *"Hello, darling. My mate wears a leather harness on his knee. How would you like to sit on his face?".'*

'Terylene.'

'Terylene?'

'Harness. Like your tie, only plain grey not green paisley. Pink plastic leg, grey Terylene harness.'

'I'll tell her you're cool, Jimbo. *"Don't rush him, babe. He's too cool for that. Treat him right. Your patience will be rewarded."'* Boycey laughed, opened the latch on the car door. 'I'll go into the pub. I could do with a closer look at our target, anyway.'

'Sit still and keep your mouth shut, Boycey.'

'No harm in looking.'

'I'm running this. You sit back, cakehead.' I put my hand on his shoulder.

'Let-go-a-me.' Boycey said in the most menacing manner he could muster. He thought he looked tough. I let go.

He shrugged. 'That's better.'

'Don't be so tough,' I said. 'You'll come to harm one day.'

He grinned. 'But not from you, Jenner.' He looked down at my false leg. He let go of the door handle, was quiet for a second, and then laughed and cried, 'Bosh! She'd love it.'

Boycey held his crotch with both hands and leaned back in his seat again and grinned again.

The elegant woman went into the pub. I closed my eyes for a moment, wishing him gone. Thinking about the cast of characters assembling. Some thread held them all together. It was like the actors in a play assembling on stage. Brown boots,

the white haired man with the flat stare. The elegant woman.
Ralph Purnell waiting in the pub is now joined by the elegant
woman. All we're waiting for is the action. DeWitt would be
the action, but of course I didn't know he was coming.

'Out of film, Jimbo.'

I checked the camera, then the glovebox. I had two extra
rolls of high speed film, but where?

'Last one,' Boycey said helpfully.

'There's some in the back.'

'I'm the driver.' He wasn't moving.

I got out of the car, then got in again, only this time in the
back seat. During the past couple of weeks the rear seat of the
Ford had deteriorated into a squalid pile of crumpled papers
and half-filled plastic bags; some of the papers were notes,
some important. All of the bags except one contained plain
debris. But which contained the spare films? I found it.

'Eyeball,' Boycey said.

I twisted forward and looked between the head-rests.

'Mickey DeWitt. I don't know the geezers with 'im. Do you?'

'No,' I said, struggling with the camera, 'but I want their
pictures.'

Why do mechanical devices refuse to co-operate when it
matters? I couldn't feed the film into the slot. The rain began to
fall again, making blobs of water form on our dirty windscreen. The more I rushed the more the film refused to go in. I
glanced up as DeWitt was getting out of his regular, legit businessman's Mercedes, powder-blue, a new model. There was a
tough-looking young man behind the wheel. DeWitt shook
hands with a couple of regular straight-looking businessman
characters who'd got out with him, then turned away and
walked alone towards the pub. The men got back in the Merc.

'Come on!' Said Boycey, laughing. He had pulled a little
instant camera from his pocket and was snapping away.
'You're useless Jimmy!'

I got the camera-back closed and began snapping too. The
men with DeWitt had begun to get back in the Merc. Snap snap
snap. 'Get DeWitt,' Boycey said.

'I know what DeWitt looks like.'

'Get DeWitt! This camera won't do it.'

I took a couple more of the Merc until it drew away, then turned the lens on where DeWitt should be. He'd gone.

'He's inside,' Boycey said. 'You should have got him while you could.'

'He's got to come out again, Malcolm. Even you could figure that out.'

Boycey didn't answer. He slipped his instant camera back into his pocket. I handed him my camera and searched among the papers on the back seat until I found my notes. I stayed where I was and started writing DeWitt up.

And then it happened.

'Was that a car backfiring?' Boycey asked.

'No.'

Bang bang. There it went again. Bang bang. We looked at each other, stupidly.

I climbed out of the Ford, and set off to have a look. I crossed the road and walked towards the pub. God knows why I was going this way rather than the other. It's not genetic, I know. As I strode towards the boozer Ralph Purnell, our target, walked towards me. He was walking quickly, looked shocked, carried a pistol dangling from his fingers, his arm hanging unmoving at his side, as if the pistol was a mason's plumb and Ralph's arm the string. Ralph walked right past me. He had steel grey hair, cut short, and wore a fine, expensively cut blue suit. With the arm held still by his side and the expensive conservative clothes he wore he went past people as if he was invisible. No one paid him a second glance. They certainly didn't stare. I did. He was like a man in a trance. Ralph swept past me, then on up the road. I carried on to the pub. I've never seen a boozer empty so quickly in my life. An old lady nearly ran me down. Mickey DeWitt lay on the tarred parking ground outside the pub, dead as his ancestors but nothing like the veneration. He lay on his back and his chest was covered with blood. His face was covered with blood too. His eyes were shot out. What's that? Superstition? They wouldn't get a picture of the killers from Mickey's eyes. Or maybe a warning. Given Mickey's background I'd have bet on the latter. A barmaid in a cheap black skirt and almost transparent white nylon blouse stood over him, shaking. She had blood on her ruff, was wearing no shoes and she was screaming fit to break the windows. The smartly-dressed woman and the man in the windcheater were nowhere to be seen. I went back to Boycey.

'Someone's shot him.'

'Who?'

'Kennedy, you dipstick, who do you think?'

'DeWitt? Someone's shot DeWitt?'

'Someone's shooting Christians.'

'What?'

'First the guy in Mile End, now DeWitt.'

'Why did they do it?'

'Shall we go?'

'What?'

'Malcom, start the engine or move over and let me do it.'

I walked around the car. Boycey moved into the passenger seat.

'What Christians? What bloke in Mile End?' He asked. I didn't reply. We drove away before the cops arrived. We had plenty of time. It's not just a question of lifting the phone and then they're round sirens screaming, like on the telly. Ambulances are normally quicker and firemen quicker yet, but neither of those would do any good for Michael Conrad DeWitt, aged sixty four, who was past the aid of paramedics and was not on fire.

Eight

T HOUGH I WAS born in Bermondsey and brought up there too I can never relax in transpontine London, and presume people live there to be close to their work, or because it's better than living in Kent or something. Driving back from Sydenham I looked in that rear-view mirror a lot; guilty. Why? I was a witness. I'm not one of nature's narks but... but, but we're all *citizens*. Everyone else had it away on their toes when Maltese Mickey died. Why not us? Why should *I* be the one feeling guilty? I'd shot no one. The Blackwall tunnel sucked us in, then spat us out again in the East. At Old Ford, the Roman Road, we stopped outside a pie shop. We were near my girlfriend's studio. Less than a hundred yards. I would have gone to her place only I had Prince Charming with me, complete with nylon shirt and itchy crotch. I climbed in the back of my old Ford and wrote up notes. I can't pretend my hand wasn't shaking a little.

'Still the copper, Jenner?'

I ignored him.

'What are we going to do?'

'I don't know.'

'We should have reported it to the police,' he said, and held up the mobile phone, as if to help me or offer a clue.

'I think you'll find someone will have already done that.'

'We should go and see Menke.'

Menke was the lawyer who'd hired us to follow Ralph Purnell. Presumably he hadn't been planning on us witnessing Ralph involved in a murder.

'It's too late for his office, Malcolm.'

'At home then.'

'He lives in Stoke Newington, for God's sake. Once it gets dark they lock their doors and don't open them round his way.'

'Why?'

'They're frightened the electric light will escape. Why the hell do you think?'

'Do you know,' Boycey accused, 'Do you know, you've a very sarcastic mouth on you, Jenner?'

'Piss off.'

Boycey got out of the car and crossed to the pie shop. I wiped my face with my hands and thought, unhappily. Say someone had copped our number? I stared at the clipboard and tried to get my thoughts together. When Malcolm came back he was munching a pie and carrying a styrene cup full of eel liquor. He got back in the car and quaffed eel liquor like it was the elixir of life.

'Do you want some?'

'I did... but I've gone right off it,' I said. A woman passed under a sodium light before us. Boycey 'cooed' through a gobfull of cheap steak. Pale green eel liquor dribbled down his chin.

'Look at this.'

I scribbled. I didn't look.

'Five-ten, nicely-sized medium-to-large bristols, hips crying out to have your hands round them, an immaculate pair of legs going all the way up to where it matters and a ginger-top at that, Jimbo. Even you must fancy that, Jenner.'

I kept writing and still didn't look up.

Boycey stuffed pie in his mouth, bit off a piece and talked through it. 'I've had everything. I've had Chinese birds, I've had black birds, I've had blondes and brunettes, Jimbo. I've had girls all over the world. I've had tight ones and loose ones. I've even had girls I couldn't understand a bleedin' word they was saying. But I don't mind admitting, Jimmy Jenner, I've never had a ginger bird. And I think this one is just about gorgeous enough to make me break my duck.' He 'cooed' again and I heard the creak as he began to wind the window down. 'Just get a load of it. I want a plateful of this ginger pussy, oh yes.'

I put the clipboard down, tucked my pen away in my top pocket and leaned between the head-rests. I took hold of Boycey's long paisley tie in my left hand and leaned my right around the seat so that I had hold of his shirt front. As if I was embracing both Boycey and the seat. I did this very quickly. I pulled his head back with the paisley tie and turned the tie once round the base of the head-rest. I heaved on Boycey's tie as hard as I could one way and on his shirt front as hard as I could the other. He choked, made a strangling sound. I could see his features in the mirror. His eyes were popping and his face went red, the first time I ever saw colour in it. I could smell his greasy scalp near my face. I let the tie loose for half a second, then pulled again as hard as I could. The auburn woman was crossing the road towards us.

Boycey had taken half a breath.

'Jim...' he gasped, 'please....'

I kept pulling. He went purple and his arms started flapping, then his legs too, slamming up and down against the bottom of the steering wheel. Boycey's mouth opened and closed silently, like a newly-landed fish. The camera fell to the floor between his legs.

The auburn woman came right towards us, staring at us. She opened the car door beside me.

'Jimmy?' she said. 'I saw your car,' she pronounced my name 'Chee-mee'.

I pulled a second longer.

'Jimmy! What are you doing?'

I let go of Boycey's tie. He flopped forward and hit his head on the steering wheel. I grabbed my walking stick from the front passenger seat and used it to lift his head.

'I've had enough of you!' I yelled at him. Tension, see? Usually I'm very reasonable. I let the stick fall and his head dropped back on the steering wheel.

'Jimmy?' The woman asked. Chee-mee?

I said, 'We were arguing who was the best. Harry Cripps or Barry Kitchener.'

She just looked at me. What do French women know about Millwall in the sixties? *Rien.*

'There's no comparison, really,' I went on, 'they played on different parts of the park.'

Boycey's breath was screaming in and out of his chest, in and out. His whole body was trembling.

The auburn woman helped me out of the car, then looked at

me reproachfully.

'Don't start all that "*I can't stand violence*" bollocks,' I said.

'I wouldn't dream of it.'

'Good.'

We looked at each other for a moment, then I ducked back into the car. 'Boyce,' I said, 'can you hear me?'

He nodded, forehead against the steering wheel still. His breath was even now coming in wheezes.

'When you work with me, you do your job, you keep your trap shut and then you push off. No mouth and trousers, no ribald commentary, no puerile stories and no eating beans and drinking beer. Okay?'

Again he nodded.

'Also, my name is not "Jimbo", all right?'

Another nod against the wheel.

'Now you get you home, Boycey, because you are going to need to be at Ralph Purnell's bright and early tomorrow morning to see where he goes and what he does in response to the demise of Maltese Mickey.'

He could barely speak but he did anyway.

'You don't know he's dead. You ain't a doctor.'

'You don't need to be a doctor to count the holes in someone's head.'

I began to walk away with the auburn woman. My hand hurt where I'd held the tie and my fingers ached on my right hand. I was holding the walking stick too hard. I slackened my grip. She squeezed my arm.

'How do you feel?' she asked.

'I've got a headache. You?'

'Excited.'

'Excited?' Sometimes her English gets a bit inaccurate.

'Come down here and make love to me.'

No, it wasn't inaccurate.

'Where?'

She pulled me towards a perfectly ordinary sidestreet.

'Here.'

'Here?'

'Now.'

'Now?' I looked about myself. 'Er... why don't we go to your studio?'

'Now.'

'No.'

'*Now.*'

'*No.*'

'Homosexual.'

'Listen, Piaf, never ask a one-legged man for a knee-trembler.'

'What's a knee-trembler?'

She laughed when I told her. We walked arm-in-arm for a hundred yards.

'I'm sorry.' I said.

'Meaning?'

'About him.'

The auburn woman screwed her face up to show distaste.

'He's disgusting.'

'Don't beat about the bush, Amy,' she doesn't. You don't meet very many French women with a light touch.

'Jenner!' screamed a cracked voice from behind us. I turned and looked. Boycey's body was hanging out of the driver's door to the car, as if he were drunk, or a lunatic. His head was almost touching the ground. His green paisley tie flapped before his face, white again now. Soft drizzle fell on the three of us.

'Jenner!' he screamed again. Then, after pausing to get his breath he called, 'You could have killed me!'

He looked so peculiar even my serious auburn friend smiled. I smiled too. Sashes flew up, heads leaned out of windows, each craned towards Boycey, so they looked like coconuts all in a shy. People stopped and stared. An assistant came out of a closing baker's shop so she could see better. She folded her arms across her blue nylon coverall, as if she might be watching a parade or chatting over a garden fence. The whole of Roman Road was staring at Boyce, upside down on the pavement.

'Killed me!' he yelled again, but without as much enthusiasm. Boycey fell onto the pavement, all in a pile. My auburn friend and me, we just turned and walked away.

*

Amy's studio was reached via a lot of stone steps. She had an eyrie in the loft of a warehouse by Old Ford. It was near the canal, convenient for bedstead and supermarket trolley dumpers, fly tippers, rapists, muggers and God knows who else. The warehouse was owned by a load of painters and sculptors who'd got it cheap in the mid-seventies and seemed to think it was convenient for painting as well as being mugged, and rather handsome, too, with its view of the canal. Amy chose the eyrie for the light, and she could afford the rent of the best space. I'd have found it easier for the stairs if she'd been an artist in the dark basement.

We climbed the stairs together, keeping step. Amy lived in her studio, so it had skip sofas and a fashionably battered seventies TV. In one corner was a modern shower cubicle. Of art there was little sign. Amy was conceptual. Her presence was the work. Her studio was full of the possessions of a previous tenant, canvases stacked against a wall, paint-brushes parked permanently in a catering-sized jam tin. Five litres of Seville Orange Marmalade. FOR HUMAN CONSUMPTION screamed huge letters around the lower half of the label. They don't muck around in the catering trade.

I took my coat off and stretched. It was dark outside but I could still see beads of rain on the skylights, tiny spheres reflecting light thrown up from Amy's studio.

'I'm sorry.' I meant the fight with Boycey.

'Don't talk about it.'

'But I'm sorry.'

'It doesn't matter. It was rather charming.'

She took her clothes off and ran a shower. She stepped into the cubicle. I stared at the skylight. Sydenham was like a dream. I was in the only safe place in London. Old Ford *inconnu*.

'It's never going to stop raining,' I shouted over the shower.

She didn't answer.

'From now on. All winter, till next July. Then it'll stop for two weeks and start again in August.'

'What are you complaining about? You were born here.'

'Doesn't make it any better. It's dark and it rains too much. We should live underground, then we'd be dark but dry.'

'Dark, dry and vitamin D deficient.'

I could smell the scent of her soap as she lathered up.

'Your girlfriend rang.'

'What?'

'Judy.'

'She's not my girlfriend, she's my ex-wife.

Amy came out of the shower, dried and switched on the radio, a pop music station, which she knows I hate. She smiled, 'I'll make tea,' she went to the sink, still naked. Tina Turner started singing on the radio, a Sam and Dave number. Amy swayed gently with the soul music, shifting from foot to foot and letting her hips rise and fall as she washed up.

'How can you do that?'

'What?'

'It's freezing.'

'I'm not.'

She clicked the kettle then turned to face me. I moved towards her.

'Don't,' Amy commanded.

'What did she want?' I asked.

'Who?'

'Judy?'

'To talk to you.'

'I've had more fun at the dentist's.'

'What?'

'What did she want?'

'I don't know. She asked for you. She said she couldn't find you.'

Amy had a big, dusty old sofa at the side of the room with a white plastic zip-up wardrobe behind it. For something to do I moved a plaster cast of Amy's previous boyfriend's torso to the floor, then sat on the sofa and shivered. I pushed the cast with my foot.

'Careful.'

'It wasn't me. He nutted my foot.'

'Sorry?'

Amy stood him up and posed him at the side of the sofa. 'Daniel was a perfect specimen,' she said. I couldn't tell if she was joking but decided she wasn't. The French aren't big on irony.

Tina finished and Amy pushed the button.

I said. 'It is *cold* in here.'

The sounds of a hammer on metal echoed from several floors below. A sculptor beating a piece of metal into submission. Amy unzipped the plastic wardrobe.

'Where do you want to go?' She looked at me closely as she said it, holding a plain blue dress to her bare breast. I waited till she was pulling her dress over her head before I replied.

'I thought we were going to stay here.'

'It's too cold. Anyway, I want to go out.'

'So that's why you had a shower.'

'Everything isn't a prelude to something else, Jimmy.'

Satisfied with this gnomic capsule of philosophy, she kissed me on the lips and picked up her coat. 'You had your chance. We'll go out.'

'What about my tea?'

'I hate tea. You can stay here tonight if you want,' she threw the door open and switched off the lights.

'It will have gone cold by then.'

I could hear the soft touch of the rain on the corrugated plastic roof. Amy leaned up and kissed me again in the dark.

'It will keep.'

'Where are we going?'

'To meet some friends. You'll like it.'

'No I won't.'

Amy stepped onto the landing and banged the communal light button with the heel of her hand.

'What's happened?' I asked. 'Twenty minutes ago you were desperate, *"mek luv to me here"*.'

'Well now I'm not. What do you expect? We'd been talking about your wife.'

'Ex.' I hate hobbling down her stone steps nearly as much as I hate hobbling up them. 'And anyway, *I* brought her up?'

'Take your opportunities, Jenner. If not, I'll move Serge in to be my concubine.'

'Serge?'

'With the hammer downstairs.'

'Amy, he's a Neanderthal. He's probably got a string of bruised and pregnant women all over Europe. You'd just be another notch on his club.'

I began to limp down the stone stairs again. When I was a kid in Bermondsey we used to sharpen our knives on stairs like these. You would wet the stone with spittle or a drop of water, then draw your knife across on the cutting side. And so the whole world changes, but not too much at once.

*

Later that evening Amy took me to a concert. Educating 'Cheemee'. Yo Yo Ma plays Beethoven cello sonatas. Yo-yo Jenner listens; feeling hungry again now, thinking about the woman by his side, about the fact the seats are designed for men averaging five-feet-eight, wondering if there isn't anything good on telly, if the cops aren't wandering around even now with my description and my car's index number in all their little black books,

'Where were you earlier, Yo-yo Jenner?'

'Sydenham.'

'Notice anything peculiar there?'

'Not now you come to mention it, no.'

When Yo Yo Ma finished the auburn-haired one announced she wanted to adjourn to a club in Soho to chinwag about art with some of her chums. 'Art' can be translated as 'themselves'. I passed up the chance of spending the night curled round Amy's feet in a freezing Old Ford garret and headed nervously east on a twenty two bus. I can only take so much yo-yo per night-night.

Nine

THE RED EYE winked on the answering machine, 'come and get it'. I pushed the switch. The first message was from my West Indian friend, Leon, 'come and see me, there's someone I want you to meet'. This would be Vaughan, the wannabe detective, no doubt. The second was from my ex-wife, 'come and see me too, only I'm a priority case'.

'Jimmy? It's Judy here. You haven't paid the bill on your mobile or maybe you haven't plugged the bloody thing in again. I've been trying to get you for days. Meet me in the Club Etoile tonight if you can, at ten. Otherwise... well, no otherwise. Just be there. We've just got to have a meet, Jimmy. If you get this message you have to go there. I'll be waiting at the Etoile at ten. You can call me back at NSY if you want.'

I left the phone on the handset. It was ten fifteen and anyway, I try to keep my phone calls to New Scotland Yard down to an absolute minimum.

Ten

THE CLUB ETOILE wasn't a club at all, unless Terry the proprietor a slim, unhappy man in his fifties with long legs and a longer face, didn't like the look of you. Then it was a private club, members only, you need a tie and no sir, membership is closed. The Club Etoile was a wine bar on the Mile End Road, with a big sign saying 'Private' on the door. It had once been called The Star, and was known as a fairly (though not outstandingly, by the standards of the Mile End) tough public house. The Star was once owned by another Terry (Fat Terry, or Fat Tel) who had been a famous gambler, and who had taken the present Terry as a partner when he'd been short of readies owing to a dopey nag's poor performance at Sandown race-course. The second Terry, with the logic of the East End, was called Tel-tel, but never to his face. After only one year of this partnership the Fat Tel was stabbed in the stomach by a customer and retired, hurt, to fritter his money (Criminal Injuries Compensation Board, Royal Ancient Order of Buffaloes, Licensed Victualler's Association, they all chipped in) and his retirement away on obscure northern race-courses. The second Terry bought out Fat Tel and turned The Star public house into a wine bar, a confection, an English designer's dream of a Parisian café. The English designer spent a hundred grand of Terry's bank's money on the decor. I couldn't see a hundred grand in bare sawdusty floors, zinc-covered bars and brass-lined table tops, but Terry could, and he hired young men to wear black trousers and multipocketed waistcoats and wait at the tables. Some of the young men wore suspiciously large moustaches and waited at the tables with something of a swagger, but they were none the worse waiters for that. People said at the time it opened Terry's version of The Star was ridiculous, and no one would be able to pronounce 'Etoile'. People laughed at Terry's black-trousered and big-moustachi-oed young men, and said the East End wasn't ready for this

yet. Terry was right, of course, and 'people' was wrong. The
Etoile was packed every night, and Terry could afford to call
the Etoile 'Club Etoile' and turn away any punters he didn't
like the look of. Also the fact that he had been associated with
some wicked East End villains in his youth had a dampening
effect on the wilder elements of the Mile End's rude boys.
Terry's reputation went quietly before him, and his 'Club' was
a safe and comfortable place in which to take an evening out,
presuming you didn't hang around outside waiting for motorcyclists to take pot shots at you. I didn't after the first time. Out
of the cab, in the club, don't look from side to side, don't look
back. No flinching, Jenner. If you see a milkman, don't meet his
eye. Give him what is known as a 'wide berth'.

*

That night the Club Etoile was busy enough, but Detective
Sergeant Judy Williams, once Mrs Judy Jenner, was sitting
alone at a round, brass-lined table. She had the bottom quarter
of a glass of white wine in front of her. Judy was reading a
Club Etoile copy of *The Standard*, for Terry provided newspapers, too, clamped up in wooden sticks so they could hang,
when they weren't being read, like napping bats from something resembling a hat rack in the corner of the room. Judy was
wearing a little black dress and some immo pearls, earrings
and necklace both. She made me think she was off to a dinner
party, but it was a bit late for that. The dress had a collar and
forearm-length sleeves. Judy's hair looked smooth, combed
and finely cut on her collar. She'd gone blonde again, but
further blonde than natural for her. Maybe it was too blonde
for her complexion. I wouldn't tell her. Judy has blue eyes and
clear skin that makes her look about sixteen, not thirty-six, and
nice, oh very nice legs. Judy seemed to sense my presence
rather than see me. She looked up from the paper and smiled.
I'm a mug for that smile.

'Jimmy,' she stood and kissed me. 'Hello.'
'Hi. What's up?'
'Oh I'm fine. How are you?'

'Don't small talk. I got the phone call, the fire-engine's out-side. Where's the fire?'

She smiled again and a moustachioed waiter came over. For a moment I couldn't work out whether the second smile indicated renewed enthusiasm for me or 'come and get our order' for him.

'Another white wine for me, er....'

'Andrew,' offered the waiter, misunderstanding. Why do you have to have a relationship with the man who serves you in a bar?

'Whisky. Bowmore, no ice,' I cut in, filling the gap Judy had left.

'Can I have ice in the white wine, please, and another Perrier... *Andrew*,' she added, then, when the waiter had left, turned the newspaper round so that I could see the headline.

'Look. Remember him?'

I looked at her. Was she having me on?

'No.'

'Mickey DeWitt. Someone shot him today.'

'Who is he?'

She frowned. 'Mickey DeWitt. The gangster.'

'Oh.'

'Know him now?'

I smiled. 'No. Should I?'

'He was quite famous in his day.'

'Judy, you're a sergeant in Criminal Intelligence, I'm a bloke who's been out of the job for twelve years and when I was in it I wore a uniform. Mickey...' I picked up the paper and read the name off the headline, 'DeWitt... wasn't a figure on the land-scape of uniformed bobbies in Romford in the early nineteen-eighties.'

'Right. All right.'

She smiled at me, usually a dangerous sign. She didn't believe me.

'Romford reminds me. Your name came up today, you know.'

'Only good things, I hope.'

'An old pal of yours, a D.I. Parker rang me, wanted to know what you were up to nowadays.'

'I don't know a D.I. Parker.'

'Used to be a D.S. in Ilford while you were stationed at Romford....'

'Oh Greasy Parker. I thought he'd bought the farm years ago.'

'Well he hasn't. He's keen to say hello.'

I crinkled my fingers at her in a tiny wave. 'That much. What does he want?'

'I don't think he wanted anything. Just to know how you were.'

'I'm fine. What's he up to in Ilford now?'

'Nothing. He has been working in South London somewhere.'

'*Has* been? That sounds as if he's doing something else now.'

'He is.'

I waited.

'Murder Squad. He works with a friend of mine. What are you doing, Jimmy?'

Now she waited.

'Divorce work,' I said.

She gave me that look. At least it was better than grilling me about recently dead Maltese.

'A man's got to live. Anyway it's not hotels in Brighton. It's making sure the husband doesn't squirrel all his money away so the wife can't get at it.'

'It's beneath you, Jimmy.'

'*We* got divorced. *We* hired a lawyer.'

She smiled again, this time her 'you're stupid but I'm not going to argue with you now' smile.

'Was that it?' I asked.

'No.'

Andrew the waiter came back, followed by a tall, sandy-haired man in a dark-grey suit, expensive shirt, red silk tie. Neat freak.

Judy said, 'Here's someone I wanted you to meet, Jimmy. Tom Mack, Jimmy Jenner.'

The tall man held out a hand and I shook it, more by reflex than intended politeness. He was in his mid-forties, but all youthful vigour and crisp clothes. He had that air of deference sometimes put out as a front by powerful, utterly confident men.

'The *famous* Jimmy Jenner.'

'As opposed to?' I asked. He ignored it.

'Em Ay Cee Kay, that's me,' said Tom, beaming 'let's be friends' messages across his freckly face. A bloody Jock as well. 'But don't worry. Everyone gets it wrong and thinks I should be Mack-something... I'll grab a chair,'

Mack turned away. The waiter put his Perrier in front of me. I pushed it to one side and leaned towards Judy.

'Is he your... well, what the hell? Paramour?'

'Yes,' she said firmly.

'You sleep with him?'

'Yes.'

Andrew stared at me. I've never seen a waiter put down a glass of whisky so slowly. I wouldn't have been surprised if he'd missed the table.

'He looks a bit old.'

Judy raised her eyes to a huge, superfluous, lazily rotating fan on the ceiling. Tom came back with his chair, brandishing it like some badge of office. He sat.

'So, face to face with the famous Jimmy Jenner at last. Pleased to meet you,' he said. 'I've heard a great deal about you.'

I could see Terry watching me from his perch at the end of the zinc-covered bar. Terry sat there about six hours a day, drinking Aqua Libra or fizzy water and eyeballing the till and the customers, turn about. He smiled his flat, charmless smile and raised his glass by way of salute. I ignored it.

'Good,' I said to Tom Mack's stupid, vacantly good-natured face. 'My aim is to please.'

'Tom's a Superintendent, East London Murder Squad.'

'*Super*. Done many?'

'New job... the old incumbent retired. Let's not talk shop. Has Judy been telling you about us?'

'Maher. Eamon Maher,' I said. 'You been to Bramshill?'

He grinned confidentially. 'Of course, you knew Maher. Fine man. Retired now. Gone home.'

This puzzled me. 'Tulse Hill?'

'Ireland. He's a great loss.' Tom paused. 'Look, we're going to get married.'

'That's very advanced. Did you have to wait until he retired?'

Tom sat back in his seat and sipped his Perrier. 'I was warned about this. Your drollnesses.'

Judy said, 'Tom thought the only thing was to be straight with you. You would get it from someone; Tom... *we* thought it was better from us. We hoped you'd be *pleased* for us.'

'It's kind. It's very kind. Tom thinks if he's straight off the shoulder, regular kind of fellow, big toothy grin and all that nonsense he'll bluster me into being nice about it. Is that what you do with all the kids on your squad, Tom, give them the 'just one of the boys' act? What do you want me to do, be Best Man, make a speech and buy you a duvet? Come and decorate the bloody flat for you?'

'Jimmy...,' said Judy.

'Officiate at the post-nuptials?'

Tom Mack's toothy grin had gone, at least. 'Jimmy, if I can....'

'Shut your cakehole, Tom. I'm not Jimmy to you. You look all wrong. Your feet are too small to make a detective. You won't hack it in East London. You certainly couldn't fill Eamon Maher's shoes. I give six months before you're Assistant Chief Constable in some far flung part of the realm. What's Judy supposed to do then, give up her job and follow you?'

'You're shouting,' Judy said.

Terry was standing by my side. 'Are you all right, Jimmy?'

I nodded. 'I'm okay.'

'You want me to hook this matey out for you?' He meant Mack. You've got to laugh sometimes, though Tom didn't really see the joke. I introduced them and Terry apologised profusely and professionally but without enthusiasm.

'Drinks on the house over here,' called Tel, backing out of it in the only way open to people in his trade.

'We've got drinks,' Tom said.

'Have another. Line 'em up.'

I patted his arm. 'Tel, who lines up Perriers?' Terry pouted. Even Tom the Jock had to laugh.

When Tel went back to his Aqua Libra Judy said, 'I'm giving the job up. We hope to have a family.'

'Children?' I said, stupidly. We all laughed again, nervously.

'The clock says now or never, Jimmy,' she said, and turned her lovely blue eyed gaze lovingly on Tom Mack. I finished my drink. It was time to split the party up.

'I want to talk to Judy alone,' I said. Tom stared at me. People like him are big on eye-contact. They learn it at college. Tom kept the eye-contact up for about thirty seconds before he spoke.

'I'll wait in the car.'

He raised himself to his full height and swept out.

'You can't be serious,' I said. Judy didn't reply. I ordered another scotch from Andrew, who kept passing with his ears flapping like Nellie the Elephant.

'I am. I brought him, didn't I?'

'There's that as well. He couldn't stick out more if you painted him green.'

'It's your watering hole. I thought you'd feel more at home.'

'It's only my watering hole because Terry comes from Bermondsey.'

'So you stick together. Do you know how much of that you do?'

'Do what?'

'Do 'stick together'. Do 'hang on to nanny's apron strings'. He knew your family.'

'That's a rare thing now.'

'You live in a small world, Jimmy.'

'This sounds like a bit of self-justification here, all prepared for when Bonny Mack gets made Assistant Governer of the Isle of Skye.'

'If everything remained the same for ever, if no one went anywhere or did anything, that'd be about perfect for you.'

'Judy you can't be serious about that clown? What about the big career deal you were always whingeing to me about?'

'I don't whinge.'

It's true. She doesn't.

'I'm sorry.'

'And of course I'm serious,' she looked at her watch. 'We've an appointment. I must go.'

'Nobody has appointments at ten-thirty.'

'I do. We work shifts. How's what's-her-name?'

That's women. When they're cornered, they'll attack.

'Amy. I left her sucking gin in Groucho's to come here when I got your message.'

Which was a lie designed to make her feel guilty and Judy knew it. I lie badly to her.

'Left her alone?'

'We both have our own lives to lead.'

'Hard luck, Jimmy. There'll be another one along soon. Like buses.'

'Amy and I haven't fallen out.'

Judy looked at her wrist-watch and stood. 'Really, we have got an appointment. Drinks with one of Tom's friends.'

'Keeps late hours?'

'He's an MP.'

'Of course he is.'

I helped her put her coat on.

'You've slipped a cog, Judy. In six months time Tom'll be Chief Constable of the Orkney Islands and you'll be up the spout, gazing in wonder at your swelling belly, learning to sprechen the Jock and asking your Lord and Master out there to countersign your application for an Access card. I don't see you as the little housewife-type.'

'Why does everywhere that's not London threaten you so much?'

Which is a point. I'm getting like Leon. We were at the street door now. It was dark outside. Reflections of headlamps shone across the slick surface of the street. There was a big queue of traffic heading east. They get up early and go to bed late in

Essex. Tom was sitting outside the Etoile in a Rover. He was lit
by the beams of passing cars. He didn't look such a happy
bunny now. He was scowling. Tom saw us and forced a smile
at Judy.

'Has the boy wonder been married before?' I asked.

'It's none of your business, Jimmy,' she paused. 'Yes. He has
been. But then so have I.'

'So you have,' I said.

'Anyway, you can never find anyone of our age who doesn't
have complications.'

'Seduce a priest.'

'Very funny.'

'You could, Judy. You could seduce a rock. You could turn a
magnet's head.'

'Shut up.'

Tom wriggled in his seat.

'I hope that's not a company car.'

'He's on call.'

'Of course. He'll have a driver soon, and you'll be able to
solve murders on the way home from *Sainsbury's*.'

She looked at me under long lashes.

'I hoped you'd understand.'

'I understand, okay. That's the trouble.' I touched her
earring. 'Those aren't imitation, are they?'

'They're an engagement present from Tom. We couldn't
have a ring.'

'Of course,' I said softly. She moved her head away from my
hand.

'The business about us, Jimmy, about Tom and me... we're
keeping it to ourselves until I leave the job. I've got three
months. It could be compromising.'

'Who for?'

She didn't answer. Him, of course. She kissed me quickly on
the cheek and ran to the car. I watched them drive away, him
doing all that copy-book stuff of looking in your mirror a
thousand times and sitting there with the indicator on waiting
for a real gap in the traffic. If I did that I'd wait an hour but

sure enough a gap opened and Tom Mack pulled the Rover
into the flow. He was the kind of man who could always rely
on a gap of some sort opening for him. Judy felt she was better
off with him than no one, of course, and she knew she was
better off with no one than with me. The rain fell and I watched
their red tail lights up the Mile End Road till I couldn't see
them any longer, then I watched the red snake's tails other cars'
lights made on the wet tarmacadam. Thousands of them,
thousands of lives acted out. Mickey DeWitt's no longer among
them, since this afternoon.

What was that all about then? 'Meet my fiancé.' That was
very unlike Judy. And all that tosh about Greasy ringing her
and wanting to know how I was doing. Why? He could never
give a toss before. He was working with Tom Mack, she said.
'For' more than 'with', I would bet. Were those two, Tom and
Greasy having Judy on? Had I been spotted sitting outside the
Glass Balloonist after all? No. Judy would spot anyone being
false to her and anyway, Sydenham doesn't even come under
Tom Mack and Greasy Parker's murder squad. A motorcycle
passed and I shivered. 'Someone just walked over my grave',
my father used to say. I stood there watching the traffic for a
while longer, just watching and thinking. After a while I
realised I was wet, too. I went inside to have a drink and a chat
with Terry, who knows what's what and who's who and whose
very stock-in-trade is his ability to listen. He serves very good
whisky, too, which he reserves for pals. Peaty, island stuff; none
of that Speyside rubbish.

Eleven

I AWOKE NEXT morning with the taste of oilcloth on my lips. I opened my eyes and a silver-fish scuttled inches from my face, a monster man-eater in a linoleum primeval jungle. The lino was red, blue, green, and white paisley-pattern. It was cold and sticky against my body and close up it smelled terrible. You don't want to smell any more old lavatory lino than you have to. You certainly don't want to taste it. I lifted myself. I was wearing shoes, socks and trousers, but no shirt. My shoes were scuffed, my trousers wrinkled. My left side, the side I'd been lying on, felt as if a trolley bus had parked on it for the night. I only just remember trolley buses, but their lines are down by my heart. My ribcage had pins and needles, my skin was covered in red weals from sleeping, tyre tracks from the trolley. My head was dull and my eyes sore. Nothing worked. A lorry clunked a gear-change outside and suddenly I could hear the traffic. I blinked a few times and stood. I was in a bathroom near a very noisy road. There was an old-fashioned electric boiler on the wall, a big, polished-copper job. There were old cracked tiles surrounding an old, chipped bathtub, a symphony in ageing white ceramics. By the side of the bath was a little mahogany table supporting an enormous Busy Lizzie. Never has a Lizzie been busier. The harness to my false-leg had cut into me while I'd slept. I sat on the edge of the bath and dropped my trousers. A small, bustling woman of about sixty came through the door, stared at me and at my false right lower leg. Much of her face was hidden by the Busy Lizzie, but I saw her lips purse, and then she turned on her heel and left without saying a word.

*

Tel came a few minutes later, bearing my wrinkled shirt.

'I'd lend you one of mine, but it'd never fit, Jimbo. How do you feel?'

'Ghastly. Did I behave badly, Terry?'

'Nope. You just ordered a lot of whiskies, then you drank them, then you fell over.'

I tried to stand again. I hurt everywhere, especially my head hurt. My brain was rolling around my skull like a doll's eye in its plaster socket.

'Did I talk a lot?'

'Only to me. You frightened my daily.'

'She frightened me. Where's my coat?'

'I put you in a room upstairs. You came down here during the night and fell asleep. Go down to the kitchen and have some cornflakes. I'll fetch it.'

The idea of cornflakes turned my stomach.

'Just a cab'll do. Can you lend me a towel?'

'Go and have a sleep, Jimmy,' said Tel.

'Just call the cab, eh? Twenty minutes on the dot, going to Canning Town.'

'You can't go to Canning Town.'

'Who says?'

'Boycey rang. He wants you to meet him in Epping.'

'How did he know I was here?'

Terry smiled. 'Everyone knows where to find you, Jimmy. You tread a well worn path.'

'I can't go to Epping. What's in Epping?'

'He said it was very urgent and that you had to go. Three line whip. Also he told me to keep my mouth shut about sending you there.'

My brain was working slowly. 'That bad, eh? '

'That bad.'

'Can I phone him?'

'He was calling from a box.'

'Okay. So get me a minicab to Epping. Where?'

'I've got it written down. Er...'

'Er?'

'That bird rang too.'

'Which bird?'

'The French one.' Terry pursed his lips in disapproval. 'The one you're walking out with.'

'Don't you start, Europhobe.'

'She wanted to know where you were. I didn't know what to say for the best.'

'Why?'

'I didn't want to say, 'oh he had a meet with his ex-wife, got rat-eyed and is sleeping it off on my bathroom floor,' did I?'

'Why not?'

'Be sensible.'

'What did you say?'

'I said you could be here, then again, it could be that you weren't.'

'Thanks. That's a big help.'

After he left the room started to sway again. I ran a cold bath and washed myself with coal tar soap which wouldn't lather. I didn't shave nor wash my hair, though I could've done with both. I got out of the bath and switched on an ancient radio Tel kept in the bathroom. The radio was so old I half expected to get '*In Town Tonight*' or '*Workers' Playtime*'. Instead I could only find pop music, or Home Counties women talking earnestly about some iniquity which I didn't quite get. No 'Lillibullero' there. Someone was being really rotten to either the Home Counties women or someone they knew. Middle-aged middle-class women interview each other on the radio so much they've all turned into a stream of Dorking babble. Maybe Winchester babble. The younger ones drop the occasional 'h' to give themselves some cred. I know who you are, you and your dungarees. You and your naked ambition. I sat on the edge of the tub for some time like this, listening to the women's voices saying I don't know what and rubbing my face with the towel and thinking. Then Tel yelled up the stairs saying the minicab was here and I had to slip into the dirty shirt and start making sense. 'Drive me to Coopersale. Don't try to strike up conversation and no pop music.' I practised as I went downstairs. It didn't matter. The driver was a silver haired grouch due for his second retirement and he drove me in silence. Slowly. Out by Leytonstone tube he turned on the news radio. *Good morning to Wilf in Hemel Hempstead. Good morning to you Richard. I have called today to discuss security in the home.*

Twelve

Boycey was in my Ford in a rutted lane near Coopersale. Coming from London Epping Forest is an overblown park, but by the time you get to Coopersale on the one side and Epping Long Green on the other the forest borders onto farmland and you can just – just – imagine Epping as a king's hunting forest where there was something bigger than rats and lost dogs and badly-buried argumentative metropolitan wives to hunt.

The world's oldest minicab driver refused to drive down the lane, so after a brief sputtering argument about 'if you won't drive, how can you call yourself a driver?', I had to get out and limp the last half mile. The ground was covered in squashed and rotting leaf mould and it was wet and I slipped a lot. I'd lost sight of the minicab and I was blundering down a rutted lane miles from nowhere in Epping Forest. With a leg and a half I wouldn't be able to hoof it back to a tube station, leave alone spend the day wandering around the forest looking for Boycey. I didn't even know which was the nearest tube station. I looked up and there was Boycey, right on cue, about two hundred yards away, four square across the lane, arms folded. Boycey was wearing a grey, almost see-through Pakamak, vintage nineteen-sixty-five, and he had the grey plastic Pakamak bag on his head, which is what they were designed for, however queer they look. He looked like a grey plastic leprechaun. He turned, I looked at my feet for a moment, then he'd gone. I tramped on down the soaking rutted road. It took me a long time to cover that two hundred yards and it rained all the time. I rounded a corner and there he was again. Boycey sat leaning against the boot of the Ford, grinning and watching me. When I reached Boycey he said, 'How did you get here?'

'Foot, you pillock. You watched me.'

'Before foot. You didn't walk from Mile End.'

'Taxi. How did you think?'

Boycey scowled and swore. 'You shouldn't have done that.'

'This way. Leave your stick here.'

'Why?'

'Because it'll leave marks everywhere.'

'That bad?' But he'd set off at a pace across country. I stumbled after him, slower, and took my stick anyway. I need it. We rose over a small forested mound and I could hear the motorway, a constant, screaming, belligerent sound. We crossed to a second mound and climbed it. Now the road was below us and our mound became a raised bank separating the forest from the motorway. Below us thousands of cars poured past. On the other side of the bank had been planted with evergreen trees, a pathetic attempt to impersonate the original forest which had resulted in something as unlike Epping Forest as the motorway was. We walked along the raised bank, above the cars and the trees. If they looked up we'd have been silhouetted. We must have looked like madmen on the skyline.

'Is this your idea of a joke?' I called to Boycey. The wind slapped my face as I spoke and either Boycey didn't hear, or if he did he just kept walking. The trees on the side of the bank below us broke briefly and I could see a road parallel to the motorway, separated from our bank by a thick palisade of evergreen trees. We were still above this parallel road and our heads were as high as the tops of the trees. I could still see and hear the motorway. The parallel road would have been invisible from the motorway. I stopped as the trees cleared again. Suddenly revealed on the parallel road there was a Bedford van. It had 'Downtown Borough Council' printed down its side. Boycey went down to the van. So did I. Slowly. The wind and the road noise dropped as I descended, and as I reached the Downtown Borough Council van it seemed to sit in a pool of calmness. The van and its contents were certainly inanimate.

Ralph Purnell was sitting on the driver's side of the van. If his pallor hadn't made me suspicious his eyes would have done it. Ralph was sixty, grey-haired, well dressed. I'd never seen him at the wheel of a Downtown Borough Council Bedford van before. He wasn't the kind of man who'd drive a Downtown Borough Council Bedford van. It would have been below his dignity. Ralph was a fancy dresser. *Had* been a fancy-dresser. The girl sitting beside him had been a fancy-dresser too. Louise. I'd never been that close to her before. The close-ness made me see her anew. Louise was mid-twenties, naturally mousy-haired blonde, much less blonde than her hair looked now. Her roots needed doing. She wore lipstick that was slightly too red too. Robbed of her body's animation, her clothes looked all wrong, as if she'd paid too much for them but had no taste.

I stared through the glass at the bodies inside. Louise's lipstick was too red and now her face was too blue. Once the interior surface of the van's window glass had been covered in condensation, but now that was gone. Instead a thin film of dust marked condensation shapes inside the window. As if dirt had a surface tension. The woman looked like she was asleep. Purnell had his arm around her and her head was rested on his shoulder, as if he was telling her a bedtime story. Only the pallor and her staring eyes gave it away. And of course the blood. His eyes weren't there at all. They'd been shot away by a bullet fired into the temple and across the face. There was a second hole in his forehead and the gun lay loosely in his hand in his lap. I stood up straight. My back ached. I'd been bending and looking a long time.

'You see this happen?' I asked Boycey.

'No. I followed them up the track a bit, then when I realised it was a dead-end I backed up and found the one you met me on. By the time I'd walked back here they were dead.'

'See anyone?'

'No.'

'Hear the shots?'

'No.'

'Wasn't that odd?'

'Well yes, but I wasn't listening for it and I was driving a car and I could have been anything up to half a mile away.'

I walked around the car looking at the ground. Nothing but leaves.

'Go through it,' I said.

'I followed him from his house this morning to work. He didn't go to his office, though. He went straight down to the council yard, signed out this little van. Then I followed him to King's Cross. She was waiting outside.'

'Just off a train?'

'Her bag's in the back of the van.'

'It's not their day.'

'Meaning?'

'It's not the day when they should meet.'

'She never came down on the train before.'

'And they didn't meet in London.'

'Perhaps he'd called her to London.'

'Are we sure she'd come for a dirty week-end?'

'She's a couple of days out for that.'

'It's an expression, Malcolm. I mean she'd come to spend a couple of days bonking Ralph.'

'Apparently.'

'So why did they drive here?'

'Can't say.'

'You followed them?'

'Yes.'

'They come straight here?'

'Yes.'

'Then they had a pre-arranged meeting. They didn't come for a snog, did they?'

'Well, I don't know....'

'They came to meet someone.'

'How's that?'

'... and their plan was, after they met the someone and did whatever they needed to do, they were going to carry on with the midweek dirty week-end.'

'I saw no evidence of another person.' Malcolm shook his head. 'No. The way I see it, it was no murder. Ralph shot her, then himself. Like a suicide pact.'

'So how come he shot himself twice?'

'Like that geezer.'

'What geezer?'

'One of Hitler's generals who did it after the bomb plot. He tried to kill himself and then only managed to put his eyes out.'

'Very good Boycey. You surprise me.'

'You should read a bit more, Jimmy.'

'Did he get it right the second time, this German General?'

'No. He didn't do it a second time. They strung him up with piano wire.' He pronounced it 'pianner'.

'So Ralph Purnell did better than him.'

'How's that?'

'He shot twice. It's a bit off, shooting your eyes out and then having a second bash at it. Shows a great presence of mind.'

'Why?'

'Say the gun dropped out of your hand in between the first shot and the second?'

'It didn't.'

'I expect that's why the German General never got a second shot. Scrabbling around in the dark looking for his gun.'

'Who said it was dark?'

'It would have been for him. It would have been for Ralph, too. If he'd dropped his shooter.'

'It's different,' said Boycey. 'That's a confined space. The German General was by the side of a river.'

'A canal near Verdun. Stülpnagel was his name.'

Boycey looked at me, glared at the bodies again and stepped back. He pointed accusingly at the bodies.

'That's a suicide pact. That is. No doubt.'

I looked at him. Now why would he say that? It was so obviously wrong. Boycey seemed determined.

'Boycey, killing someone and then killing yourself is not a suicide pact. Both parties have to volunteer for it to be a suicide pact.'

'Well they're both dead.'

I walked around the van again, looking.

'What are you looking for?' he asked. I'm afraid I swore at him.

'Why did you park so far away?' I asked.

'This is a dead end. I could hardly park next to them. I followed them up here, they parked. I saw they'd parked and backed my car up.'

'My car,' I corrected him.

'Your car.'

'They see you?'

'They were busy.'

'Doing what?'

'Kissing each other goodbye.'

No cheap joke is too shameful for Boycey.

'You see anyone else?' I asked.

'No.'

I looked at the couple in the car again. I couldn't believe that someone like Ralph, who could live all those years with mendacity, would kill himself. I tried the van doors. They were locked.

Boycey giggled. 'It's an inside job, Jimmy.'

'They were shot by someone else?'

'Who?' He swung around with his arms wide. 'There's no one here.'

'They were meeting someone.'

'I never saw him.'

'Or her?'

'I saw neither man nor woman, Jimmy. I've been all alone here.'

'They met a third person. Maybe more than one.'

Boycey shook his head. 'Maybe a busload.'

'Probably the meeting was planned to be cordial, all pals together....'

'What was it *about*?'

'Returning the gun Ralph took away from outside the Glass Balloonist. Ralph didn't have the bottle to shoot Mickey DeWitt. He carried the gun away for the guy who did it.'

'Who was...?'

'I don't know. But when it came to Ralph handing back the gun, the other person suddenly had a different plan.'

'Like?'

'I don't know.'

'You don't know a lot, Jimmy. This is a lot of guessing.'

'Do you want to hear it?'

He nodded.

I continued. 'They're sitting in the car. They've brought the gun Ralph carried away from the DeWitt shooting. Whoever they've arranged to meet turns up.'

'Maybe he's already there. Maybe he saw them arrive.'

'Then you're in trouble Boycey, because he would have seen you too.'

'What happens in your theory?'

'Ralph offers the gun to the guy who turns up. Ralph's returning it, finishing his business. The guy takes the gun, *'Thank you Ralph,'* and shoots them with it.'

'Why?'

'Change of plan.'

'What change of plan?'

I shrugged. 'Maybe there was something about Ralph that said he was going to do a runner. Maybe having Louise here spooked our man.'

'She'd have seen a gun.'

'Ralph didn't need to hand over a gun. It could have been a parcel. It could have been wrapped in rags.'

Boycey thought about it.

'Say you're right. Say all this happened while I'm driving my car back around to here. Someone turns up. Ralph gives them the gun, then they turn it on him and shoot him and Louise. Why are there no signs of a struggle, Jimmy?'

'I dunno. They're trapped. They're sitting in a car with the doors closed. They can't struggle with someone standing outside the car.'

'One of them could have got away. They didn't struggle and they didn't try to run away. Neither Ralph nor Louise. Why?'

'I think there were two gunmen. Both covering them. Only the one who Ralph gave the gun to did the shooting.'

'How do you reckon there were two gunmen?'

'Because you have to think of the order they were shot in.

Someone has Louise covered with a gun to force Ralph not to struggle. *'Keep still or we'll shoot her,'* so Ralph sits still. The other gunman shoots Ralph. Then Louise.'

'So why did Ralph sit still for that?'

I sighed. The answer weighed on me like a ton. 'Because he loved her. Because he hoped they would let her go.'

'And *why* did these two men, of whom we have seen no sign, no track, no mark and no vehicle, shoot the two lovebirds, Jimmy?'

'That's the problem... I don't know.'

He looked doubtful.

I said, 'Are you sure you didn't see anyone?' I was sure he had.

'Yes.' he lied.

'I'd like to know where they went. I'd like to know where they came from.'

'Anyone see you?'

'No. No one saw me.'

'So go back to the car and make sure no one sees you now,' I ordered.

He hesitated. I looked around, walked back down the lane a few yards. Another car had been there. The tracks stopped just out of sight of the Downtown Borough Council van. The tracks ran over those of the Bedford van, which meant it had been there later. Perhaps the tracks belonged to the vehicle that Ralph and Louise's killer came in. Radial tyres.

'What are you looking for?' Boycey asked.

'Motorcycle tracks.'

'Found any?'

'No.'

'Why motorcycle tracks?'

'It's either that or the brown boots.'

'What?'

'I'm superstitious.'

I walked back to Ralph's van. I picked up a rock and smashed the driver's side window.

'I didn't just see that,' said Boycey.

'Good.'

'You shouldn't be doing this.'

'Thank you father. Am I absolved?'

'I mean it. I can't stand here and watch you do this, Jimmy.'

'So hoppit.'

He walked away, hesitant, turning every few paces to watch me at first but then quickening his pace.

I searched Purnell. Fifty quid, driving licence, credit cards. Nothing. There were some keys. I searched the girl with the same negative result, except she was carrying more cash. She would. I counted. Two hundred and a bit. There were no letters, no suicide notes, no postcards to Mum. Dead, the girl was rather lovely. I'd seen her before but she'd looked hard, almost brassy. Now she was dead I could see a lot of that was tension. It made tight little lines around her eyes and mouth. I looked at Purnell and the girl. There was something wrong with them. Not just being dead. Something else, too. I went to the back of the van, pulled out her suitcase and searched that, too. Fancy underclothes, fancy night-dresses, a couple of cheap novels, a couple of thin day dresses. This girl hadn't come to London to go out much. She'd come to spend her time indoors. Horizontal. There were two more bags. One was undoubtedly Ralph's. I went through it. He'd packed casual clothes too, but he'd packed as if he was going for a holiday. Maybe Purnell and his bint were at cross-purposes. Maybe they had had a late change of plan. I continued searching his bag, methodically, like a customs officer. *'Did you pack this yourself, sir?'* In a side pocket were both their passports and an envelope. *Both* passports. Ralph's in charge. Already they're an old married couple. Inside the envelope was a piece of folded paper. I unfolded it. *Wake. N. 200 lb. 20p. fr bin. 60 * 210°15'.* Directions? There was something else about the handwriting, too. I stuffed the envelope in my pocket. The third bag was a small black nylon one, the sort a certain type of young man takes to the gym. I unzipped it. Krugerrands. Hundreds of them. Thousands of pounds, maybe half a million pounds' worth. There was dust on them. I felt the dust between my fingers, tasted it between my lips. Plaster dust. Slaked, crumbly pieces of plaster stuck to my tongue. Ralph Purnell's bolting money, brought from wherever he hides it. I wet my finger, picked up some more plaster dust and looked at it. Pink. Ralph hid his bolting money inside a wall. I looked about myself. Boycey was gone and all was silence except the steady drone from the M11. I ran my fingers through the gold coins, then closed the zipper on the bag. Leaving the bag was the clearest possible message. The killer didn't want the money. He wanted Ralph Purnell's life.

I quietly closed the van doors, holding the catches back as I did so, as if I was scared of waking the dead lovers in the front. The forest seemed to be leaning over my shoulder, peering at them. I shivered and walked away.

I picked up some branches and made my way back to the Ford. I brushed out my own tracks as I went, like you see in the movies. Brush my tracks out, Tonto. If the police started looking for a murderer they weren't going to find me and my prosthesis.

Lonely Boycey was sitting behind the Ford's wheel with the engine running and the radio blasting, *'News Radio, call this number, we want to hear Your Say'*. Boycey couldn't hear it for once. He stared blankly before himself, lost in thought. I got in. Thinking, thinking. A bit scared. I turned the radio off and he didn't seem to notice.

Eventually he said, 'If that's not a suicide... if that's not a suicide....'

'It's not.'

'Then that's twice in twenty-four hours.'

He got out of the car and strode around agitatedly nearby, slapping his hands and staring at the trees. His normal good humour had deserted him entirely.

I got out too. 'I know,' I said.

Foggy foggy dew blew from our exhaust while Boycey stared at a tree and I waited.

'Jimmy, if the cops place us outside that boozer in Sydenham they'll be a bit upset.'

'Yes.'

'They'll read things into us not going to them or waiting round for the blue lights, eh?'

'I reckon.'

'And if anyone spots us here the cops'll be more than a bit upset.'

'Yes.'

'I mean the two things. First Sydenham and now this.'

'Yes.'

'And they'll think of us as just guns for hire. A couple of guys who'll do what it takes to make a living.'

'Speak for yourself.'

'They'll put us in the frame for the murders, won't they?'

'I reckon.'

'So do I, Jimmy. So do I.'

He paced around a little longer, slapping his hands again. Then he stopped. 'Well, what'll we do?'

'Nothing.'

'Nothing?'

'It's the only safe course.'

His pacing became jerky and agitated. He stopped again. 'We need to report it.'

'Don't make me laugh.'

'What?'

'Boycey, you want to explain to the police what we were doing here?'

'Why not? We were hired.'

'Guns for hire?'

'Not literally. Anyway, *I* never murdered anyone. '

'Have you got anything clever to tell the coppers? Like ideas on who did it or names and faces?'

'No.'

'Because if you haven't they won't believe you.'

'That's not my problem....'

'And if they don't believe you they will take you down the nick and keep you there until you tell them something they will believe. That's what being 'in the frame' means.'

'That's against the law now.'

'*Incommunicado* they will keep you until you tell them what they want to hear. And since you don't know anything to tell them they'll keep getting extensions of detention from simple and suggestible magistrates until you have pissed away a week of your life in a cell. For nothing. Then when they are finally forced to let you go the police will keep you on their brown list for the rest of your life.'

'There's the camera. We could give them that.'

'So then your story is...?'

'The truth. Okay we were there. Okay we were following Ralph. We were taking photos.'

"We were taking photos'; is that all we're going to tell them, Boycey?'

'We could claim legal privilege.'

'How?'

'We'll tell them Menke hired us to follow Ralph Purnell.'

'Why?'

'For privilege. So that our actions fall under Menke's privilege.'

'You're presuming he's going to claim privilege...'

'He will.'

'... and presuming he claims that the privilege extends to us....'

'Of course it does.'

'... and presuming some court will uphold that the privilege extends to us... how will that improve things?'

He was silent.

'Whereas on the debit side, if we tell them we were hired by a notoriously corrupt lawyer....'

'He's not that bad.'

'He's *famous*, Boycey. Every hood in London uses Menke. And *he's* to be our excuse?'

'Yes, why not?'

'Look at it from the coppers' point of view. They'll think, 'that's a bit odd, isn't it?' And you know which thought would plant itself in their ugly little minds next?'

'Go on.'

'That we'd gone to Menke and fixed an excuse when we needed one. That we'd gone to him *after* it had happened. Like all the other villains who go to Menke and ask him for alibis and excuses and dodgy defence tactics to get them off the hook. If we tell the police Menke hired us to spy on Ralph Purnell it will absolutely convince them, *convince them* that we have something to hide.'

Boycey thought about this in silence.

'Where's the film?' I asked him.

'There are prints in the boot of the car. Down the side of the spare wheel. I had them done last night in an all night chemist in King's Cross. There's an unfinished film still in the camera, too.'

Boycey screwed up his face.

'Why are you so sure it's a suicide, Malcolm?'

'The way I see it, Ralph had no way out... so he talked Louise into joining him in a sort of final, desperate lovers' pash, shot her then shot himself.'

I waited. He didn't go on. After a while he said, 'Well?'

'Way out of what?'

Boycey nodded excitedly, plastic hat bobbing in the rain.

'You listen to the news radio?'

'Do I have a choice?'

'It's him they described. The police believe Ralph Purnell killed Mickey DeWitt.'

'You were there, Boycey. What do you believe?'

'He walked past us with a gun. He was there.'

'We were here.'

'It's not the same.'

'Only to us. You still haven't said; what didn't he have a way out of?'

Boycey rolled his eyes. 'His situation. He'd have been *wanted*.'

'I thought that was the point of modern society. Everybody wants to be wanted. Few achieve it.'

'Capital 'W' Wanted, Jenner. You saw him in Sydenham and so did I, wandering along with a gun in his hand and an empty look in his face. The cops would have got him soon enough.'

'Why the suicide?'

'That's easy. Spite.'

'Spite? As in "malice"?'

'It's the only way of taking your insurance money with you. Ralph's suicide was pure malice against his Missus.'

'*This* is thinking? This is what you've been cracking your brain over while I've been wandering the byways of Epping looking for you?'

Boycey nodded again. Rain ran down his acne scars. Irregularly. 'If anyone cops our number here Jimmy, and we haven't reported the shooting to the police, we're going to be in the chocolate, know what I mean?'

'I love you Boycey.'

'Sure. I've got the scars.'

I got in the car. Boycey got in too.

'What were you *doing* in Kings' Cross?'

'Following him, what do you think? I wish I'd never seen him.'

'Last night, I mean.'

There was the briefest pause before Boycey said, 'Getting the pictures done. There's a place there that does on the spot developing, twenty-four hours a day.'

So there we had the source of Boyce's amazing attraction to the female sex. It was the subject of commerce.

'Isn't King's Cross where all the prossies hang out, Malcolm?'

'How should I know?'

How indeed. I said nothing.

'We should just hand all this over to the police.' He said, without enthusiasm.

'We've been through all that.'

He put the car in gear. It gave that old auto lurch. As we left Boycey gunned the accelerator, spinning the wheels across the muddy leaf-strewn lane, just for good measure. No tyre tracks from us.

'Someone might have seen this car. Or me.'

'You were miles away, Boycey.'

'Still.'

I didn't answer.

'We should call Menke,' he said.

'I will.'

'Now. We should call him now.'

'This is a forest. Do you see a phone box?'

'There's this thing.'

He held up the mobile. I took it and pocketed it.

'If I report any murders Boycey, it will be from a phone box with a handkerchief over the mouthpiece, preferably one that'll accept four penny pieces and require me to press button 'B'. I may slip a note under the police station door, I may give a kid ten pee to take them a note or even use Interflora. But I am not, repeat *not* reporting multiple murders from a mobile blower with my moniker stuck on the bottom of the highly traceable phone bill.'

'Last time. I think one of us should stay by that car and the other should go and call the police.'

'Now which is it, the lawyer or the police?'

'Either. Both. We should do it now, Jimmy. Straight away.'

I didn't answer. He didn't argue on, either, which was a bit queer. I would've. I'd have said, *'Why are you behaving so, Jenner? What's in it for you?'* Whatever else you'd say about Boycey, he's not usually slow to grasp changes and attribute motives to them. Why's he suddenly gone stupid now? *'Why are you behaving so, Boycey? What's in it for you?'* I thought, but I didn't speak either. Now *that's* a paradox.

Thirteen

'WHAT ARE WE going to do?' He'd asked. Boycey had looked weak when we parted.

'Behave as normal,' I'd said. But 'normal' for the last couple of weeks had meant following Ralph and Louise around. Now Ralph and Louise didn't exist we weren't going to do that any more. I set Boycey down at a tube station so that he could resume the rest of his life as if nothing had happened. He asked me to get his money from Menke. Ever practical.

I went home and changed my shirt. Only one message on the machine this time, *'Chimee, call me, where have you been?'* I took the film out of the camera and developed it in a 'Community Photography Centre' in Dalston, the sort of place where people talk Trotskyist in-between sipping tisane and eating carrot cake. I don't speak the political 'yeah man right on' language, but I've got a disabled bus pass and an appealing face when I want to, so they let me in, one of the huddled masses. The pictures were no good, but that was my fault, not Boycey's. Taken through the rain-spotted windscreen of my Granada the snaps looked as if they were covered with silver nitrate measles, or maybe they were pictures of a cloud of flying saucers that just happened to be in Sydenham on the day I was snapping. The ones Boycey had taken came out fine because he'd done them through a wound-down side-window and had them developed professionally. There's a lesson.

Boycey had taken a beautiful snap of the man in the blue wind-cheater. Good old Boycey. I looked at my literally measly photographs and wondered if I shouldn't have asked him to take all the pictures. There was only one good picture of Ralph Purnell and none of Mickey DeWitt, before or after bullet holes. I relaxed in the Salvador Allende Community Photography Project Coffee Bar with a cup of decaff and looked at my prints and laughed at myself. Why laugh? Because it's a black joke. I'd been hired to stop Ralph abandoning his marriage with all his loot. I'd never met Ralph's wife. Menke told me I was looking for evidence first that Ralph Purnell was having an affair and second that he had a great deal more money than his official income tax form would reveal. I'd managed that. It was all that had been intended. The black joke was what came next. The things you find when you're not meaning to. First Mickey DeWitt got shot. Now Ralph and Louise were sitting in Epping Forest, each with more orifices than would be natural and normal and a frosty silence between them. If that wasn't enough the car carried a hundred grand in loose change in the boot. It was the kind of back-handed success you have to see the funny side of. I noticed the roomful of coffee drinkers and photographers had fallen silent. A little black girl with plaits approached me and said, 'What's funny?'

'Oh, I just thought of a joke.'

'Why have you got a stick?'

'Because I keep falling over.'

Her mother came over and clutched the child to her bosom. I clutched my photographs to mine and staggered out into the screams and roars of the street.

Dalston, I love you.

*

I came back from the Dalston Dreamers Community Photography Project still clutching my measly pictures but now also a plastic bag full of plenty of Railton Road salad.

The communal door to Defoe Mansions was open. This annoyed me. What's the point in all the answerphones and security if people forget to shut the front door?

Because of where I live, I have invested in some special heavy duty front door locks, 'Made in Switzerland'. Unfortunately I failed to invest in a special heavy duty Swiss doorframe to go with them, so when I reached my floor there was a copper and a charming little clutch of neighbours standing round my front door, which was hanging off its hinges, like a drunk on a good Saturday night. The policeman turned and the crowd followed his gaze to me.

'This is 'im, this is 'im. Johnny Jenner,' the woman down-stairs said, and the policeman and I went into my flat, closing the door behind us as best we could, excluding and disap-pointing the neighbours.

The policeman was about thirteen, with such a big adam's apple I'm surprised he wasn't in a zoo, or in a glass jar full of formaldehyde in Guy's medical museum. He had a great big notebook from which if he was called upon he could presumably tell whopping lies.

'What's nicked then mate?' he asked airily, as I put down my bag of salad and mooched around the room, turning my possessions over with the tip of my walking stick, wondering for myself.

'It's hard to tell,' I said. 'I've never taken everything out of the drawers and thrown it into a pile like that before.'

'You're lucky, they never crapped on your carpet.'

'I've always thought of myself as the lucky type too.'

'What line of work are you in?'

'Enquiries.'

'What, divorce, that sort of thing?'

I stared at the spotty face below the coal scuttle helmet. He ducked behind the notebook.

'No. Directories. I work for British Telecom.'

'Right.' And he wrote it down.

He stalked the pile of broken possessions.

'I reckon this is down to the Brown Brothers, don't you, John?'

'*Who*?'

'The Shades.'

I have noticed before that you have to be very current to keep up with young London coppers' slang.

'Do you smell anything?'

He sniffed and shook his head.

'Do you smoke?'

'A bit. What am I supposed to smell?'

'I don't know. An old fashioned smell. Lime oil. Why do you believe my burglars were black?'

'Why, John, have you got an house full of Swiss locks if you ain't scared of black kids coming round here and turning the drum over?'

I put the salad down.

'Have you seen any black kids wandering around Stoke Newington with crowbars and sledgies?'

'No.'

'Well next time you do, you nick them. They're your men. Meantime keep your eyes, ears and mind open or you won't even catch a cold, leave alone a burglar.'

He mooched in his turn around my pile of broken possessions. 'Did you have anything of value then, John?'

'Jimmy. Jimmy, Jimmy, *Jimmy*. And 'no'. Not nicked, anyway. They left the answering machine.'

'Keep your hair on. There's no need for all that.' He examined the answering machine, poking it with his pencil as if he was Perry Mason afraid of disturbing fingerprints. 'It's a crap answering machine, Jimmy.'

'It works.'

'And they never nicked nothing else?'

'As far as I can see, they didn't steal anything else.'

'You sure?' Was he winking? 'You know, videos, televisions. Sort of thing you might need to make a claim on your insurance for?'

'Aided and abetted by a friendly report from my local policeman?'

He broke into a smile. 'That sort of thing. I don't think there's enough points here for a detective.'

For a moment I half-thought he said 'pints'.

'Points?'

'That's how they're measured as worth investigating. So many points for the cost of the goods, so many points for the nature of the crime, so many points for an aged or single woman complainant, so many points for a repeat offence...'

'So many points for living in Kensington?'

'But you don't live in Kensington.'

'They probably get a better class of Brown Brother over

there, worth going after.'

'You could be right. Gangs that travel to expensive districts to burgle can sometimes rate a team of detectives.'

'An entire team? Complete with door-buster. And all I rate is you?' I said.

'I wouldn't put it like that, Mr Jenny, no. It's just a question of matching resources with needs.'

'How many points do you reckon I rate then?'

He was suddenly glum.

'Nearly none.'

'I won't bother locking up in future then. No point. I'll just leave me clobber out on the landing with some carrier bags and some red stickers, so the burglars can let each other know which pieces are spoken for.'

'Don't be like that, Mr Jenny...'

'*Jenner.*' I spelt it out. 'You'd better write it down. Or don't I have enough points for that?'

The young policeman wrote my name down, then smiled.

'Look on the bright side, there's always the new video that'll come from the insurance company.'

'What video?'

'With camera,' he said, and ducked behind the notebook again. I went to the kitchen to see which pile the coffee tin was in and whether they'd left me a pot to put the coffee in. What I needed was Wilf from Hemel Hempstead. You need a lock on all your windows and a couple of six foot men with machetes outside your front door, mate. Now that's what I call secure.

Fourteen

NOTHING WAS STOLEN. When he'd gone I checked. Definite, nothing gone. I phoned a locksmith, abandoned my swinging front door to the surveillance of a couple of old lady neighbours and took the Granada for a drive. If there was nothing missing from my flat what they wanted was either in my car or my head. My car was full of crisp wrappers and week old newspapers. That left my head. I'd only made one recent acquisition in the knowledge stakes. Mickey DeWitt went for a drink in a boozer in Sydenham. He was shot and I saw Ralph Purnell walking away with a gun in his hand. Now someone had shot Ralph and his floozie as they made their break and tried to make it look like suicide. All people with new lives. Mickey had been a Christian too, a believer in rebirth. Mickey had got his new life, Ralph was just about to get his new life with Louise. Ralph was entirely secular, at least as far as I knew. But Mickey... if Mickey's Christian sect had known just how unreconstructed Mickey was he'd have had to have been born again again.

Whoever shot Mickey knew him, hence all the stuff of doing it somewhere public and shooting his eyes out to boot. Mickey's death was a warning. It was something which could be interpreted, a deadly message aimed at those who needed to know what it meant. The size of the audience didn't matter. Only what it meant mattered. Ralph Purnell didn't shoot Mickey. When he walked past me in Sydenham he didn't look like he'd just blown the eyes out of an old associate. I don't care if he had the smoking gun in his hand. In fact, nothing about Ralph suggested he shot people. His life had not been that of a man of action. His demeanour in the days before DeWitt's murder and his own death gave no sign he was pre- paring to change this sleepy life of paper shuffling, of putting his signature on the bottom of planning applications and

taking backhanders from developers. Ralph wasn't the sort of
man who'd kill someone, least of all his beloved Louise. I
stopped the car in Haggerston and took out Ralph's envelope.
Wake. N. 200lb. 20p. fr bin. 60 * 210°15'. What is it? I copied the
code from the folded sheet into my notebook. What does it
mean? I tore the page out of my notebook and stuffed into my
prosthesis' shoe, then motored down to Shoreditch.

I put the negatives for the measly pictures in a black
japanned tin box I keep in the bank, also the original of Ralph's
envelope. Normally the japanned box just holds some pictures
of me, Joe and my parents, a thousand quid in Harry Houdini
quick getaway money if I ever need it. You have to remember
to change the notes every few years otherwise you could find
yourself trying to buy a ticket to Ireland with huge white fivers
printed out in scrawly Bank of England official handwriting. I
flipped the money with my thumb and put it back. Also the
box contains wedding spoons from the failed marriage with
Judy. Why do people give you spoons when you get married?
As if you'll suddenly develop a passion for boiled eggs. I made
a mental note to buy Judy and Tom Mack some really ugly
spoons as a wedding present, ones that went green after a
week alone in the cupboard or black if left out on the shelf.
Now *my* wedding spoons would nestle next to something
worth wrecking my flat for; the pictures of the people coming
and going to the Glass Balloonist plus Ralph's envelope. *Wake.
N. 200lb. 20p. fr bin. 60 * 210°15'*. Also I kept Joe's Smith-and-
Wesson 38 in the box, a crusty old wartime shooter from the
look of it. I found the gun among my father's things when he
died and decided against submitting it to Probate. Some
enthusiastic detective would have dug the old fellow up and
made him do six months in Pentonville for possession of an
unlicensed weapon. I took the gun from its thick, opaque
plastic bag. Twenty-five years oiled but unloved, un-polished,
unopened. God knows what it had done for a living before Joe
came by it, and God was keeping his mouth shut about what
Joe had done. I handled the gun, then wiped it on my shirt-tail
and slipped it into my waistband, at the back, under my jacket.

I wiped my oily hand on my shirt-tail too. I took a last look at the pictures before I locked the box.

'Everything all right sir?' said a twenty-year-old Uriah Heep with a grey waistcoat and stovepipe legs when I handed him back the box. Where do banks get them from?

'Spiffing. I was getting out my Russian Railway bonds. Rumour has it they're about to pay out.'

He smiled, 'Believe it when you see it sir.'

'My very motto.'

'They're not stable, sir. The Russkies.'

'Who *is*?'

'We are sir.'

'The British?'

'The bank sir.' Was he laughing at me? No.

'Steady as she goes, eh?'

'Our very motto, sir.'

I left the bank and looked for a phone box. I made a call to Leon the mechanic, then wandered round Shoreditch, worrying. I sat on a bench in the churchyard but ended up sharing it with a foul smelling and rather woozy drunken bookend. It wasn't any black kid who broke down the door of my flat, it was a professional housebreaker, the sort that doesn't care how much noise he makes because he's brought a gun, or a big tough friend with a Staffy on a leash. Or maybe even a warrant card. Then there was the problem of Boycey, who'd been a long way from telling me the truth the whole truth and nothing-but-the about what he'd seen this morning and what he knew about what. If he was so keen on calling in the police why didn't he do it? He didn't need my permission to do anything else – why start asking with that? There was also the question of what he'd seen – or more to the point, heard. If he hadn't heard the gunshots that killed Ralph and Louise, Boycey must have been dead rather than deaf. He was neither when I saw him an hour after. Boycey was hiding something. Like me.

I bought an afternoon edition of the evening paper, went to a Greasy spoon for a cup of tea and a bit of quiet. A notice on the door said 'No Soiled Clothing', as if to emphasise it wasn't a laundry. If I wanted my shirts washed I'd take them somewhere cleaner than Old Street. I ordered tea and two toast and sat on a hard bench with my elbows sticking slightly to the oilcloth surface of the table. A small, fat, dark-haired woman working behind the counter noticed me sitting with my elbows in the air and came and sloshed lukewarm water on the oilcloth with a dirty dishrag, then wiped it dry. Ish. The tea and toast arrived and I sat sideways on the hard bench and opened the paper. On an inner page it said, 'Downtown Borough Surveyor found shot dead – Police link to Sydenham gang murder'. I took my time over that headline. No mention of the money, no mention of a passing citizen (me) stoving in their window. I leaned down and took the piece of copy paper from my shoe. Wake. N. 200lb. 20p. fr bin. 60 * 210°15'. Didn't mean a thing.

Why was Ralph Purnell's motor full of gold? It could only be because he was doing the great escape. What from? The police nicking him for shooting DeWitt? Hardly. How about him being spotted at Sydenham and being questioned by the police. Perhaps he was frightened of what he'd have to tell them. Ralph undoubtedly knew who had done the shooting – he carried the gun away. To clear himself Ralph would have to tell who had used it.

I sat and cracked my brain over this for a while. Ralph reckons he's on a short leash from the police, and that once they find him they're either going to accuse him of the murder or squeeze the name of the murderer of DeWitt out of him. So Ralph uses a pre-arranged couple of days of sauciness with Louise-the-bint to spring a departure on her. Darling, I'm going to take you away from all this. Now. But first we have to make a meet with an old pal of mine somewhere nice and quiet. I give him the gun back, re-assure him of my intentions for the future. The pal listens politely, patiently even, then we depart.

Only that hadn't been the ending. You need to swap the 'then we depart' for 'then he shoots us both. Have I let you down, Louise?' This last impassioned.

You let her down, Ralph. Oh have a heart, Jenner. How was I to know he'd shoot us? It was someone I'd known for a long time. It was someone who trusted me, and I trusted him. You trusted him too much, Ralph. How could you believe you could just give a gun back to a murderer and tell him you're leaving? How could you have believed nothing would happen? Unless... unless you had held some other secret over him in the past, and hadn't let him down. Ralph had no fear when he arranged to meet his killer and hand back the gun. Experience had taught him he didn't need to fear the man. I thought back to the girl's face in the van. It was the first time I'd ever seen her looking calm and peaceful. Poor Louise. Was the Porsche worth it? Louise had tasted the good life, after a fashion, but paid dear. What did Ralph have that was so special it was worth killing him and Louise for?

Ralph was carrying his valuables with him; Louise, his hundred grand or so. The code on the piece of paper must be one of his valuables too. *Wake. N. 200lb. 20p. fr bin. 60 * 210°15'.* What is it? Something important. I put the paper back in my prosthesis' shoe. I thought about it. Now I knew why the couple had looked odd. Someone had searched them first. Before I did. No one had searched the back of the van, though. I was certain I was the first to go through their bags. Why had someone searched the bodies but not the bags? Because Boycey had disturbed the killer.

This tells me something worrying about Boycey, something he has not, so far, revealed. Boycey must have seen the killer.

So much for theory. I needed to clear up the enigma of Ralph. I looked at my watch. I just had time to talk to the lawyer.

Fifteen

I DON'T LIKE doorstepping, but some people are so dodgy it's the only way of being certain of getting hold of them. Ernesto (Ernie) Menke was just such a person. Officially an Englishman born of a Spanish father, Ernie Menke's genes had done the rounds of Europe and the Middle-East for the last couple of hundred years. He could've (and did) come from anywhere and nowhere, all at once. What is certain about Ernie is that he'd passed the necessary examinations to become a solicitor (in his day, of course, it hadn't been absolutely A1 compulsory to have a degree; mere deviousness would do fine as a qualification) and had immediately set up in sole practice. Ernesto was considered by police and criminals alike as the dodgiest solicitor in the East End. This is no mean accolade, and both groups found it useful to have a character who was generally accepted if not as a fair dealer at least as a well-known negotiator between the two sides (three, if you include insurance companies) of the crime game.

I do the odd bit of work for Ernesto Menke, for which he pays too late and too little. But Ernesto is a good contact for anyone (me) who needs to know what's what and who's who on the dark side of the street. It was for Ernesto that Boycey and I were baby-sitting Ralph Purnell. Our task had been to demonstrate, in an informal way, that Mr Purnell had an awful lot of loot. Too much for a council employee.

Ernesto lived quietly. He looked like a sixty-year-old Armenian or Ashkenazi doctor, right down to the coat with the persian collar and the black homburg hat. Ernesto had dry, wrinkled skin which was heavily mottled with huge pale brown blobs. He had dark brown eyes and wore heavy hornrimmed spectacles. Ernesto had a distinguished grey-white beard on the end of his chin which more or less matched the distinguished-looking dab of grey-white hair he revealed on the other end of his head when the homburg came off.

Ernesto's face and hands were very wrinkled. He had a house in Hertfordshire, but during the week lived in a modern, smart-looking flat on the better side of Clissold Park... better than my side, anyway. Every morning at eight Ernesto would walk his Jack Russell in the park, take it to a neighbour for the day, then get in his big grey Volvo and motor the mile-and-a-half to his office in Clapton. Once installed in the office, he would be protected behind a battery of dragon-like secretaries, and unobtainable for interview except at his choosing. Then, in the evening, he'd fetch the Jack Russell and take it for another spin round the park. The trick was to catch Ernie during the dog walk, either before he got behind the secretaries or after he'd come out. This being the evening I had to wait for the after, which is less predictable, in terms of when your man will come. Imagine being a dog with a bursting bladder. It beggars belief. I tucked the evening paper under my arm and waited for Ernesto on a wet bench in Clissold Park. I waited for a hour. So did the dog.

*

'You shouldn't let him do that. People's kids have to play here.'

I did it in my best policeman's tone. Menke turned guiltily, jerking the Jack Russell as he did.

'Gotcha, Ernesto.'

'James.' He recovered quickly, the result of years of practice. 'What a pleasant surprise. I don't often see you here... out for a stroll?'

'No. Out to catch you. You're late.'

Menke flinched. 'Well, you know where my office is, if it's a question of accounts... '

Some black kids went by on in-line roller skates, whirr whirr. They were young and supple and dressed in bright colours, designer roller-skaters. They were three and the last of the three whirled on his heels to look at us, still skating, only this time freewheeling backwards. The skater grinned. We must have looked an odd couple, me with my walking stick and Ernesto Menke with his homburg. The dog yelped at the end of his leash.

'Oh it's a question of accounts, okay. But not money.'

'I'll give you five minutes.'

'You'll give me as long as it takes, chum. Do you read the paper?'

I waved my evening paper at him.

'It's a bit early for me.'

'You should.'

We strolled. The ground underfoot was wet and the trees were wet. A pale autumn was slipping out of view. The polarised light made the mass of leaves under the trees seem solid. Red, black, white, white. I squeezed-up my eyes to see it.

'Ralph Purnell.'

He nodded solemnly.

'Ralph Purnell. Mm... he is who?'

'Oh knock it off, Ernesto. He was a Downtown Borough Surveyor, right? And the way I had it you wanted to settle his dough on his wife by way of a friendly divorce, right?'

'No, I had no desires in the matter. *She* did. I merely acted for her.'

'And the way you put it to me was that Mister Purnell earns, according to his publicly stated salary, thirty grand a year, which is more than most citizens but still breaks down pretty badly compared with the living costs of two late middle-aged people running separate establishments. No "official" savings, I expect?'

Ernesto shrugged.

'The thirty is all he was going to admit to in court... or so you'd been informed. And you had strong information from Mrs Purnell that he was reckoned worth a lot more in cash value by way of dodgy connections, backhanders, bunce for the boys, sweeteners, topping off money and all the other dirt that goes down in the construction trade, and especially goes down in the direction of borough surveyors. *Certain* borough surveyors.'

Ernesto pulled at his lip but said nothing. I went on.

'The way I was given to understand things, given to understand by you, Ernesto....'

'By my *clerk*, James....'

He moved half a step sideways, as if he wanted to physically slide out of it. I took his lapel between finger and thumb.

'Your clerk was acting for you, sport.' He looked down at the finger and thumb, but I didn't let go at first, only when he'd got the point. Then we walked again, we three. Menke, the Jack Russell and me. I carried on speaking.

'Mrs Ralph Purnell believed her husband was one of these characters. But that isn't all, Ernesto. There were implied promises in it, you'd had your clerk tell me. That's what she'd found so disappointing.'

'You believed, she believed, my clerk believed... I can't be responsible for what other people believe.'

'*This* is what the wife had been led to believe, over all the years of their happy marriage; that in the fullness of his retirement she is going to partake in all this hidden dosh, which dosh Ralph the Dodger has been forced to put to one side lest it show up to any public scrutiny. And the source of Mrs Purnell's disappointment is that, with the imminence of Ralph's retirement, with some light visible at the end of her particular tunnel, with Ralph having less than two years of measuring and writing and yelling at his chain boy to go, she suddenly finds herself out of a job... or at least out of a bed, out on the street and out of the aforementioned dosh.'

Menke stopped to let his dog snuffle at a park bench, then pee on its painted leg. When he began to walk again, I went on.

'Ralph the Dodger was discovered to have found himself a floozie, a twenty-something bimbo with knockers out to about here and a skirt up to about here.'

Ernesto looked at me.

'I've seen her,' I said. 'Louise is a very good looking woman, in her way. I've seen her in the flesh and I've got a photograph of her. I've seen her as recently as this morning. She's quite striking. I've even seen the Porsche she drives. How long has Ralph the Dodger been putting subventions her way?'

He allowed himself a smile.

'I don't know. Nobody knows.'

'So, with the advent of the floozie, La Purnell saw her plush future slipping away. Maybe Ralph *wanted* to be caught, who knows? Maybe he was so used to having things his way after twenty-odd years of Mrs Purnell doing her doormat imperson-ation that he didn't think it would matter. She wouldn't do anything. But Ralph was wrong. Mrs Purnell had iron in her soul, and was not going to be walked upon this last time. The floozie could have Ralph, there was no question of needing his physical presence. Mrs Purnell *herself* would be satisfied with the loot. Correct?'

'That's what I understood.'

'And the newly bitter and twisted Mrs Purnell did not mean the pension. She did not have it in mind to go the Family Court route and be allotted half of the two thirds pension Ralph was about to come into, i.e. ten thousand quid....'

'Very good James.'

'I worked it out while I was waiting for you. If La Purnell wanted to keep the matrimonial home she would have to get a mega mortgage to realise enough cash to give him his half of the value of the house. She'd end up giving all the money back to Ralph in repayments on the mortgage... which mortgage no one will give her anyway because she's too old and doesn't have a job and has been impoverished by a Family Court which will have offered her the ten thousand quid per annum. Can't support much of a mortgage on six grand per annum and you well and truly on the wrong side of fifty, eh Ernesto?'

'What six? You said ten.'

'She isn't giving up eating till after she's dead. Six, eight or ten, it wouldn't support much mortgage by the time she's eaten, clothed herself and paid her bills, eh?'

'I wouldn't have thought so, no.'

'Or she could move out. That was another choice. That's about the only choice. Go to some rented room somewhere. La Purnell wanted the dirt on Ralph to stop him doing the dirty on her, eh? Am I accurate so far?'

The black roller-skaters were approaching again. Menke dropped his dog lead, slipped his hands under my mackintosh and patted my buttocks and back. The black kids went past with eyes wide. This time all three turned, stared and free-wheeled backwards.

'Let go Ernesto,' I said, 'You're scaring the saucepan-lids.'

He glared after the kids until they turned again and skated away.

'Since you are not wired for sound, Jenner, and since we are not broadcasting the fact; yes, that is my understanding of Mrs Purnell's position, though I would add it's only my understanding of it... not a definitive statement. She thought Ralph might have had quite a bit more money than he was admitting to and that was the money she wanted. But you knew that. It was your brief.'

'*Which money* he'd acquired by illegal means. Aren't you required by some professional organisation to hand over evidence of a crime to the proper authorities? I mean Dodgy Ralph was Dirty Ralph, too.'

Menke picked up his dog lead and walked on.

'Under English law, Jimmy, there's a general duty. Everyone is so obliged. Not just solicitors. You too. If, while undertaking your investigation, you had discovered evidence of a crime, you would have been obliged to report it to, as you so quaintly put it, the proper authorities. But the truth is that I had no evidence of a crime and neither did you find any.'

'Dirty Ralph, money stashed, jam on his hands? You have my report and you reckon you don't know a thing about this? Or is it that taking backhanders from building contractors isn't a crime any more?'

'There's no evidence. Only a supposition by a bitter woman and a little evidence from you and Malcolm Boyce that Ralph Purnell went to pubs when he should have been working and drank in the company of.... '

Here Menke's step faltered. I stopped with him but went on talking.

'Ponces, pimps, robbers, criminals of all sorts. The scum of London. Bad company for a public servant, I should say.'

'But not a crime, James. Drinking with them, that in itself is not a crime.'

'Owning a whopping great house in Yorkshire with the floozie installed and swanning around in her cabriolet....'

'*Is – not – a – crime.*' Ernesto Menke said it very deliberately, pausing between each word. 'Perhaps he'd inherited some money that no one knew about, perhaps he had an evening job, perhaps he'd saved very hard for a long time. There's a general duty to report crimes. There's no duty whatsoever on the general public to *investigate* them.'

'On his pay? He bought the Porsche and the floozie by saving his pocket money?'

Menke stopped.

'Your five minutes is up.' He lifted and resettled his homburg, as if he was being polite. 'Now I must go.'

'Mickey DeWitt was shot last night.'

'I know.' He stood his ground, smiling politely. He replaced the hat.

'You're a cool bastard,' I said.

He nodded acknowledgement.

I went on. 'DeWitt was the one we thought greased Ralph's palm. Bribed him.'

'Is this something else you know?'

'Guess. Am I right?'

He nodded but said nothing.

I continued. 'I saw Ralph Purnell with DeWitt when DeWitt was shot.'

He raised the hat again, this time to wipe his brow in exasperation. The dog looked up adoringly.

'I've got photographs,' I said. 'And I need to know what to do with them.'

'Do what you want, Jimmy.'

'I'll take them down the nick then, shall I?'

'Look, Jimmy, as I remember it, you were paid twelve hundred pounds to follow Ralph Purnell. Boyce was another... er...'

'Seven fifty.'

'You've a head for numbers. Mrs Purnell paid you two nearly two thousand pounds to get her some information. If Ralph Purnell was having a drink with DeWitt it's his problem.

Maybe you should tell the police you saw him there. That really is a duty. What's your problem? You were do a straight-forward and legal if covert job. You got the information, you got your money.'

I laughed. 'Not yet.'

'Will get. She got the information, she will get her money... now *what's* the trouble?'

I slapped him in the midriff with the evening paper. 'Read that. Dirty Ralph is now Dead Ralph. It's not only DeWitt who's dead. Ralph Purnell is too.'

For the first time in all the years I've known him, Ernesto looked shocked. He walked a few paces and sat on a green painted bench. Parts of the paint had flaked away to reveal other incarnations, dark blue, dark grey, red oxide. I sat beside him, grateful to take the weight off my leg. Ernesto didn't look like he would ever speak, then suddenly he did.

'How?'

'Shot. Boycey found him and the floozie in a van up in Epping Forest this morning. Both dead with bullet holes in their heads.'

'Shot himself?'

'Maybe. It *looked* like it.'

'Meaning?'

'I don't think so,' I said.

'No? Who did then?'

'I wasn't there. You got any suggestions?'

'No. I've no idea. It's shocking.'

'So are pink knickers. Let's try and keep our minds on things which are practically useful. Why did you hire me and Boycey both?'

'Because of your.... ' He pointed at my leg.

'No, no. Why *me*? You hired me and suggested to me that I used Boycey. Why not just hire Boycey in the first place?'

'Because I needed you. She needed you. Boyce on his own is too stupid, he'd muck it up. You on your own... well, you can't run around.'

'Is that it?'

'And there's your face.'

'Ah. Ralph might smell a rat if he saw me hanging around his house.'

'His wife said they both knew your face.'

'I've never met them, Ernesto.'

'So you've said. She obviously didn't think so. And you've been in the papers a lot.' He rubbed his face. 'What are we going to do?'

We were sitting by a rubbish bin. I turned its contents over until I found a plastic bag. There were some empty orange juice cartons in the plastic bag. I tipped them back in the bin and kept the bag. Menke watched me. 'It won't have been his wife,' he said.

'She was browned off with him. She wouldn't be the first wife to get her husband shot. Or even to do it herself.'

'I think you'll find those are *femmes fatales*, Jimmy, not matrons from Chigwell. Anyway, she won't have had him shot during the period she paid you to watch him. I doesn't make sense. She *knew* you were watching him.'

'I'll have to talk to her.'

'I don't know about that.'

'Well it would be better....'

He nodded. 'What about the police?'

'Even the Metropolitan Police are clever enough to find his wife.'

'Are you going to tell them you were following him?'

'What would it achieve? Will *she* tell them?'

'I'll advise her not to refer to the matter unless someone asks her directly, 'were you having your husband followed?' I'll tell that if the question comes up she should refer them to me.'

'Meanwhile,' I said, 'What do I do?'

'I don't know, Jimmy. I'll need time to think.'

'We may not have time.'

'I know. Do nothing till you hear from me. Okay?'

'It'll have to be.'

We both stood and began to walk again, the Jack Russell trotting happily around Ernesto's heels, trying to trip the hand that fed him. Me too.

'How much is outstanding on your bill with us?' And Ernesto Menke lifted his wallet out.

'And then I woke up, Ernesto. Don't go flashing that about in Clissold Park. You won't make it home.'

'It's not so bad round here, Jimmy.'

'I was burgled this morning.'

'The schwartzes?'

'No. Unless it was a black copper.'

'The police?'

'Or a professional burglar. Took nothing. Read everything. Must have been a detective.'

'Why?'

'Metropolitan policemen in tall hats are not noted for their devotion to the written word.'

Menke sucked his teeth. 'What's the world coming to?'

'I was wondering myself. How long have you been a divorce lawyer?'

'I'm not a divorce lawyer.'

'That's my point.'

'You know I was doing it for another lawyer.'

'Who just didn't happen to know any enquiry agents of his own. He's a bleeding funny divorce lawyer, isn't he?'

No answer.

'Where does the money come from?'

'What money?'

'The two grand. Nineteen nine-fifty. If she doesn't have resources of her own....'

'Who said that?'

I took Menke's dog lead from his hand and gave him the plastic bag.

'Okay. Tell me this, do you know a geezer, about sixty-five, wears a blue wind-cheater? Very confident looking. Silver grey hair, slim, fit looking.'

'Can't you do better?'

'Like what?'

'Race, colour of his eyes?'

'English, Irish or Scottish. I don't know about the colour of his eyes. Blue. Grey, maybe.'

'You sound as if you could find out.'

'Meaning?'

'You have a photo?'

I didn't answer.

'Where did you see him?'

'He went into the Glass Balloonist just before Mickey DeWitt was shot.'

'You think he had something to do with it?'

'Yes.'

Menke considered. 'No. I don't know him.'

'How about a big bloke, aged about thirty, polished brown boots, mousy coloured hair. Jeans.'

'That's a description?'

'Sometimes rides a motorbike, sometimes drives a lorry. A white box van type.'

He shook his head. 'No.'

'How well did DeWitt know Ralph Purnell?'

'Know what? That he's cheating on his wife?'

'Are they in something together?'

'Like what?'

'I don't know. Some sink of corruption. Were they about to redevelop Rainham Marshes together as a shopping centre? Build a new Thames Tunnel lined with the bones of their enemies? Were they white slaving out of Wapping Wharf?'

'There hasn't been a ship on Wapping Wharf since the sixties,' said Menke. 'What's this for?' He held up the plastic bag.

'You'll see. Just walk on another couple of yards. Do you know a woman, mid-twenties, blue grey eyes, pointed features, dresses like she's in some kind of profession, but definitely not a doctor or something? Maybe an accountant. Wavy dark hair down to here.' I put my hand on the base of Menke's persian collar. It had a silky feel.

'No.'

'Could have been you saw her with Ralph Purnell. Maybe Ralph runs two bints.'

'I've never met Ralph Purnell at all. Never seen him, only passed his name to you on his wife's behalf.'

'Or with DeWitt, maybe. Maybe she's DeWitt's sin? Don't tell me you've never met Maltese Mickey, you of all people.'

Ernesto Menke just looked at me.

'Is Boycey still working for you, Ernesto?'

'No.'

'Sure?'

'Certain.'

'In that case he asked me to ask you to settle his bill.'

'Consider it done.'

'Look. We're back where we started. Notice anything?'

'No again. What's this for?' He held the bag up again.

'It's so you can clear up after your dog. I'm going to walk on with him a little further while you do it.'

'No. Don't be stupid.'

'I'm not being stupid, Ernesto... you are. If you don't clear it up I'll go straight to Stoke Newington nick and turn you in. It's my duty to report evidence of crimes... you just told me so.'

'Don't be ridiculous.'

'I'm not. We'll go to court together. I'll be chief witness for the prosecution. It'll cost you a hundred quid fine, plus a day's wages for me, plus you'll get blackballed from the Rotary.'

'I'm not in the Rotary.'

'You never will be at this rate. Clean it up.'

I never knew he swore before. Then he said, 'You would.' It was a statement I didn't need to confirm. 'It'll rain soon. The rain'll wash everything away.'

'It can't rain, Ernesto. All the water's down here on the ground already. Some of it's got to evaporate before it can rain again. Could take days. Clean it up.'

I put my hand on his silky wool collar again, only this time I grabbed and pushed him down. The dog watched impassively. Some friend. Menke knelt.

'What's all this for, Jenner?'

'It's my new campaign of public spiritedness. You're my first volunteer. Scrubby scrubby.'

Sixteen

I LEFT HIM to it. When I walked away the roller skaters had returned, and were standing round Menke watching him. I walked down to the Stoke Newington Church Street gate and tied his dog to the iron railings, a good strong round turn and four half hitches, in case anyone tried to steal the little darling. Then I walked along the road towards Defoe Mansions, Château Jenner. I stayed on the Clissold Park side of the road. There was heavy traffic and I didn't want to take my chance skipping through it. My skipping is indifferent. I walked towards a pedestrian crossing. An over-powerful floodlight shone down upon an old lady as she tottered across the black and white tarmac stripes. A grey Vauxhall separated from the flow of traffic and glided though the light. Darkness was falling. Darkness is always falling in the English winter. By December it's hardly worth getting up. In June it's hardly worth going to bed.

I looked across at the courtyard to Defoe Mansions. The bin men had called since I'd gone out. They'd thrown our rubbish all over the courtyard. Saves putting it on the lorry. I could see the lorry down the road, four burly young men on overtime, tipping dustbins vaguely in the direction of its steel jaws. Maybe I should go and scrag them, too, just like I did Menke.

Maybe not. Brave Jenner.

I could see a black BMW Five Series in the yard in front of my flat. A couple of black men were sitting in it. I couldn't see their faces, but one had a huge bunch of dreadlocks tied with a green and yellow band at the back of his head.

A voice beside me said, 'Get in the car.'

I half turned but his hand on my shoulder stopped me.

'Don't look round. Don't make a sound. Just get in the car.'

I just saw enough. It was the fellow with the white box lorry, only today he seemed to have left his white box lorry at home. He'd brought his Browning though. I could feel it sticking into my side. The black men in the BMW had turned and were looking at me. Leon and another fellow. I didn't know him. I looked down. A pair of polished brown boots stood behind my worn-looking, black Oxfords. Why are London street shoes called Oxfords? I thought. Why does my brain go onto a parallel plane whenever I'm in danger? It's a self-protection mechanism. The brain wants to disassociate itself from the flesh. *With him? No. I'm not with him. I don't rely on all that blood and bone and oxygen.* A disappointing if understandable response on the part of the brain. What else should it do? Formulate a plan, brain. *Such as, Jenner? He has a gun sticking into your side.* The ultimate in aversion therapy, a gun in your side. I thought about resistance, about revenge, about the fifty-year-old Smith-and-Wesson in my waistband; a useless, empty-chambered lump of gunmetal.

'I said, get in the car.' His voice was cockney-but-not. Estuary. It wasn't an unpleasant voice, and his tone was firm but polite, like an over-insistent taxi driver who'd already loaded your bags.

He stood with his head behind mine and pointed past my shoulder to a grey Vauxhall parked at the kerb. The nearside door of the Vauxhall was open. There was someone at the wheel. An older white man. I couldn't see him clearly. I supposed it was Blue Windcheater.

Across the yard, the two black men got out of the BMW and began to run towards me. Leon and the guy with the combed back Rasta haircut. They were wearing suits and crombies, and as they ran they had their hands inside the crombies, across their chests. They looked like Yardies in a film, just about to draw their Uzis and get their man.

'Get in the car. This is a gun in your side,' the man in the brown boots said. 'I'll shoot you if I have to.'

'No you won't,' I said. If I wasn't already dead I had nothing to fear. If he hadn't already pulled the Browning's trigger, why should he now? Brown Boots had his opportunity to kill me outside the Etoile. He missed. Now, with a magnificent opportunity, a literally unmissable chance, with the gun stuck in the back of my ribs, he wasn't pulling the trigger. Commanding me to get into the car meant only one thing. New instructions had been issued. Brown Boots wasn't to shoot me. Why? I knew something? No. Pulling the trigger would fix that. I *had* something. That's more likely. That works. What have I acquired recently that Brown Boots might want from me? Photographs. Leon and the big chap in dreadlocks were getting ever closer. Brown Boots shoved me towards the Vauxhall. I resisted. Leon and dreadlocks were closer still. I felt Brown Boots tense as he prepared to push again. I twisted so that he rotated past me as he pushed, falling against the open door of his own car. He rolled and lay off balance against the car

'Get in!' screamed Brown Boots, composure all gone at last. 'In or I shoot!' He waved the Browning at me. I swung at him with the walking stick. He held up his arm to defend himself. The stick connected with his forearm and he dropped the gun. He stooped to pick it up and I swung again. This time I connected with his face. Blood gushed from his eyebrow. The black cavalry vaulted the wall outside the flats and began to cross the road. Brown Boots tried again to pick up the gun. I swung with the stick again. Leon and his big pal were almost on top of us.

'Grab him!' Leon shouted, as if I needed telling. I tried. Brown Boots threw himself inside the Vauxhall car and it accelerated away towards Newington Green, door swinging, Brown Boots boots scuffing until he managed to drag himself in and close the door. I picked up the Browning. No doubt we could have walked down there and caught up with them, the traffic's that bad in the evening on Newington Green. We didn't try. Leon called after them, 'Come back here and we'll blow your blinking brains out!' Or something like that. Leon took his hand from his pocket, revealing it was empty. Dreadlocks did the same, only he withdrew a *Guardian*.

'Deadly,' I said.

'*You* can talk,' said Dreadlocks, pointing to some red blood spots on the ground where we stood. 'You should have a licence for that stick.'

Leon introduced his friend. 'Vaughan, this is Jimmy. Jimmy, Vaughan.'

'Thanks, Lochinvar. It was like being rescued by the Fugees.'
Vaughan blushed all the way down to his Reebok Classics.

'You didn't need rescuing,' said Leon.

We walked back to their BMW.

'This is the person I wanted you to meet, Jimmy.'

'Sorry?'

'You know, when you didn't ring me back.'

'I was busy, Leon.'

'Too busy to shake the hand of the man that would save his
life.' Leon put on his worn-down, philosophers face.

'I shook his hand. I'm glad I met you, Vaughan. What were
you going to do with the *Guardian*, by the way?'

'Punctuate him to death,' said Lochinvar. 'We weren't worried.
Leon said you had a gun.' We got in the car.

'Two now.' I put the Browning in the dash. 'I don't have any
ammunition.'

'None at all?'

'That's the point of us coming,' Leon told him.

'So what are the suits for?'

'I'm not just some scruff,' said Leon. 'A fellow doesn't have
to spend his life dressed in oily overalls.'

'Sorry. Did you, um, get what I asked for?'

'Not here,' said Leon. 'Later. We don't drive round with it in
the car in case we get a pull.'

Lochinvar gave me a big, toothy smile and started the
Beemer's engine. We drove away, crunching the uncollected
and redistributed rubbish under the tyres of the BMW.

'Who was the guy outside your flats, Jimmy?' Leon asked.

'I don't know.'

'Never met him before?'

'Meaning?'

'He wasn't the bloke who shot up the milko, was he?'

'Hm.' I thought so.

'Hm.' Leon thought so too. 'Hm. I got here a bit earlier this
time.'

'That *is* an improvement.'

'What does that mean?'

'Nothing.'

'We're not picking a fight, are we Jimmy?'

'No. I just feel a bit testy.'

'Look on the bright side.'

'I'm trying to.'

'He didn't shoot you.'

Leon stroked his chin.

'Have you figured out what he wants yet?' asked Leon.

'It's something to do with that divorce work I was doing.'

Leon smiled. 'Told you so.'

He took a mobile phone out of his pocket and made a call.

'What is it with you blokes and black BMWs?' I asked Lochinvar.

'What is it with you and the crappy Ford?' Lochinvar laughed. 'I've seen your car in Merlin the Mechanic's garage.' He nodded at Leon, who was busy parleying Jamaican patois down his One-to-One phone. Leon closed the phone and smiled.

'Okay?'

A couple of police cars passed us as we drove towards Stamford Hill, sirens blaring, heading for Defoe Mansions. No doubt they were armed response units. They'd spend an hour setting up and another hour sitting around in back-to-front blue-and-white check caps, yelling through loudhailers, threatening a dustbin with deadly force unless it came quietly. We stole away, meeting no one's eye as we drove.

*

Leon directed Lochinvar to the side of the River Lea. We rolled slowly down a concrete road set between two pre-war housing estates. The estates looked as if Hackney council had forgotten their existence since nineteen fifty. The road sloped towards the river. Waiting at the bottom of the road, next to the green lane that ran beside the River Lea was a smooth-looking black girl in her early twenties. She was sitting in a black Mini Cooper correcting her lipstick in the rear-view mirror. Her lips were enormous, luscious, voluptuous. You could tuck yourself in

them and get a good night's sleep. As Lochinvar rolled the
BMW to a standstill the smooth-looking black girl tucked away
her lipstick, got out of the Mini and tiptoed to the boot of her
car on very tall red shoes.

Leon leaned out of the window and waved at her. 'Rosie.'

She opened the boot of the Mini and lifted out a small but
heavy packet wrapped in brown paper. She handed it to Leon,
who was still inside Lochinvar's BMW. Leon ripped the packet
open just enough to fetch a couple of rounds out. He showed
them to me.

'Where's the gun, Jimmy?'

I wriggled it out of my waistband. When Leon saw it he
whistled.

'Where did you get this? The Science Museum?'

He pushed the rounds into the gun. They fitted slickly.

'There you are. Give the girl her money.'

'How much?' I asked.

'Two hundred,' said Rosie.

'I haven't got two hundred quid,' I said. 'In fact I don't hardly
have any cash at all. I don't suppose you'd take a cheque, Rosie?'

Rosie was deadpan, unresponsive. Her lip curled in. I
wanted to plead with her. Don't do that. Leon looked disap-
provingly at me. He sucked his teeth. Rosie looked at him,
waiting for a lead. Leon looked at me, looked at the dashboard
locker, looked back at Rosie again, then gave his verdict.

'You give her the other one,' he announced.

'Which other one?'

'The Browning.'

'No.'

'What's the matter with you, Jimmy? You're not Wyatt Earp.
You don't need two. Fair exchange is no robbery.'

'No, Leon. Just no.'

Leon allowed the silence which followed to mature, hoping
I would change my mind.

'Okay,' said Leon to the girl, 'trust him for it.'

'You're a sport, Rosie,' I said. She looked through me.

Leon opened the door and climbed into Rosie's Mini.

'Vaughan will take you home,' he said. Lochinvar looked solemn.

'I didn't ask anyone to look after me.'

'So look after him.'

'Say I don't want to?'

'Rosie will have her ammo back.'

Now she grinned, baring huge white teeth within the luscious lips. She licked her lips self-consciously. Leon noticed me watching.

'You had a visitor at your flat while we were waiting,' he said.

'Who?'

'Foreign woman. Said she'd been round the Etoile looking for you.'

'Oh. How did she sound?'

'I didn't speak to her. Vaughan did.'

'Vaughan?' I asked.

'She sounded pissed off,' Lochinvar replied.

'Oh.'

'She said you had an appointment for lunch.'

Rosie was laughing at me. I pointed into the Mini's footwell.

'Make her take those shoes off, Leon, or you'll both end up on a slab.'

Rosie swore and drove away.

Lochinvar did a three point turn in the BMW. Very smooth, no bumping the kerbs or other cars. Very impressive. The sort of thing which would please a driving instructor. He didn't find it hard to irritate me. He stopped the car facing back up the hill and put the handbrake on.

'It was his gear,' he said, 'His money. She was keeping it for him.'

'I know,' I said.

'You knew?'

'He's too kind.'

'You reckon?'

The young have little sense of irony.

'All right. Let's try another tack. Why does Leon think I need you to look after *me*?'

'He doesn't. But maybe you'd be better off being driven round in a black man's BMW for a couple of days.'

'Why?'

'It's both more and less predictable, Jenner.'

He was laughing at me. Scratch that comment about the young and irony.

'So why *your* BMW?'

'Because I'm Leon's nephew.'

'Good for you. What do you want from me, nephew?'

'I want to learn the trade.'

'Don't start that crap again or I'll have to ask you to drop me off right here.'

'Think about it. There would be good money to be made for a black private detective.'

'Why?'

'Imagine all the people who'd come to me but wouldn't come to you.'

'Hair-stylists?'

'Black people....'

'Not necessarily a mutually exclusive group.'

'... won't necessarily trust a white private detective.'

'If they've the wits they were born with....'

'But often people haven't. And think of all the places I could go that you couldn't.'

'Are you just burning off excess petrol or are we waiting for a reason?'

'I was waiting for Leon and Rosie to get clear.' He put the car in gear and pulled away.

'I'm right, aren't I? I would do good business.'

'Maybe.'

'But?'

'But I don't give lessons.'

'Fair enough.'

We rumbled back up the concrete road and out of Amnesia Estate.

'But you won't mind if I drive you around and pick up any hints I can from simple observation?'

I didn't answer.

'Bearing in mind it's free. Chauffeur and his BMW both for no charge. Better than struggling with your crappy Ford.'

'Your BMW?'

'My sister's, since you ask.' Rosie was his sister. The Mini she drove had been one of Leon's mixed fleet. Leon could lend you a fire engine or a Sherman tank if you asked nicely enough. 'You want me to take you home?' he asked.

'No. Let's let the armed response coppers sweep the area and take statements before I go home.'

'Then... ?'

'Mile End.'

'What about the French woman?'

'What about you minding your own business?'

'Sorry.' He drove a little further. 'Why wouldn't you let him have the Browning?'

'Lochinvar, we've only just met. You seem like a nice bloke and you may have saved my life.'

'It's nothing.'

'I really don't want to be rude to you.'

'Good. That's nice.'

'So do me a favour. Shut up and drive the car.'

'Who *is* Lochinvar?' he asked. I held my finger up, like a conductor with his baton.

We made the rest of the trip in silence.

Who says a man can't learn?

Seventeen

I HID THE guns and ammunition in a Tesco's plastic carrier bag. I hid it among other carrier bags of mixed parentage which were on a small flat roof at the back of the Club Etoile, above the kitchen. The carrier bags were full of newspapers. The newspapers could only be reached by someone in the spare room of Terry's flat, in other words me, or by seagulls. The newspapers had originally been placed there as part of a recycling drive by a vaguely green woman Terry went out with for a while. Since she'd recycled herself to her ex-boyfriend the bags of greenish old newspapers had stalled on the flat roof above the kitchen.

I washed, then went downstairs and bought Lochinvar an apple juice in the bar. Lochinvar wouldn't take a drink-drink because he said he 'trained'. He wouldn't take an orange drink because it might upset his acid balance when he trained. He wouldn't take an iced drink because he said you never knew what people made ice out of. Apparently 'water' wasn't the right answer. A man in his gym had told him there was sugar in the Aqua Libra Terry loved so much, so Lochinvar didn't want that. He wouldn't take any refined sugars. It felt like a game I couldn't win; I'd only offered him a drink. He took an apple juice after reading the label for a long time and being reassured by the ever patient barman it was definitely not, under no circumstances carbonated. I listened to a lot of bullshit about his training regime. Lochinvar made himself sound like a cross between Daley Thompson and Red Rum, but was unspecific about which sport he was preparing for. After another apple juice he conceded there was no sport, except if being admired by women was a sport. Terry's moustachioed waiters seemed rather keen on him. Maybe they 'trained' too. They didn't look any more like imbibers of unrefined sugars than Lochinvar. Eventually, on his third apple juice, Lochinvar went all maudlin about how his life had gone wrong since his woman threw him out so that now he's got nowhere to live and what a pain in the arse it was because he'd he never had a job anyway. I never knew apple juice could have that effect on people. I thought he was going to cry. Did I know how difficult it is for a black man to get a job in London? Well, actually I did, but getting work as a self-employed private detective presents a similar challenge. He would be doubling his problem rather than halving it. The fun would be in finding clients. He said he expected he'd pick that stuff up from me. Your *professionalism*, as he called it. Lochinvar liked the word, 'professional' and squeezed it into sentences wherever he could. I told Lochinvar that if he really wanted to be useful and professional he should drop the pimp-mobile back at Leon's, rent a black cab and stand-by outside my flat the next morning. I borrowed a monkey from Terry's till and gave most of it to Lochinvar to use as a deposit for renting the cab. Then I packed him on his way and went out to use the pay phone between the bar and the lavatories.

I rang Amy. She wasn't there, but her answering machine had somehow become frigid, as if she'd re-recorded the message but in a bad mood. Next I rang Boycey. I wanted to warn him about Brown Boots. Boycey didn't answer. He was probably in a call box phoning me. The message from his answering machine droned round and round in my head but I didn't want to talk to his tape. 'Watch out Boycey. If anyone approaches you wearing brown boots, duck or run.' Leaving a message like that on Boycey's answering machine would be a hostage to fortune. I didn't know who would listen to it. Next I rang Judy. She wasn't at work, but a grumpy man in her office said he'd pass a message. I didn't believe him but left one anyway, then put the phone down and went back to the bar. Andrew waltzed around the room, doling out drinks, picking up tips. He gave me a look as I went back to my seat, nodding towards a large man in his mid-fifties who had taken my place. Warning me. Terry was nowhere to be seen.

The man in my seat had black-dyed hair slicked down with

so much cream it looked like patent leather. Greasy Parker. I almost turned away. I could have just left the bar. I didn't. I leaned across him to get my drink. Greasy smelled of lime pomade. He turned.

'Jimmy. Jimmy Jenner. Long time, eh?'

I clutched my jaw and made a show of not knowing him.

'Er... don't tell me.'

'I won't.'

'I'll get it in a minute. Er... D.S. Parker, Ilford, nineteen seventy five.'

'That's me.' He looked pleased. He was almost as false as me.

'What are you up to?' I asked.

'I'm a Detective Inspector now.'

'*No*? Just how many years service can you do?'

'I'm retiring in six months.'

'Think, Greasy, if you could do a hundred years service you'd make Chief Inspector.'

'People don't call me Greasy any more.'

'Old habits die hard with me.'

'Still the joker. Can the humour and I'll buy you a pint.'

'They don't sell pints here.'

'Tell me about it. What do you make of this lemon bollocks?' He pulled a slice of lemon out of the top of a bottle of Spanish beer and aimed it at the barman, who caught it low like a one handed slip-fielder, then binned it.

'Bravo,' I said and applauded the barman.

'Give him one too,' Commanded Greasy, holding up his bottle of beer.

'I'm not desperate,' I said. I waved 'no' to the waiter.

Parker stood and pushed the stool towards me. Terry was still nowhere to be seen.

'Sit down.'

I sat.

'You see the class of person that gets in here?'

'What do you mean?'

'Jungle bunnies in suits.'

He wasn't laughing. I don't know why I even waited for him to crack into a grin. He was dead serious.

'I just don't know what this country's coming to, Jimmy.'

'You haven't been giving lectures in Stoke Newington nick, have you Greasy?'

'Why?'

'I met a PC from there. Reminded me of you as a young man.'

He looked around the room, admiring his image in a mirror. He turned back to me. 'What were you doing smarming up to uniformed policemen, Jimmy?'

'I wasn't. He was smarming up to me. Some dirty slag of a burglar had turned my flat over and the PC was after a back-hander for fixing the insurance report. *I* just don't know what this country's coming to.'

I smiled. Greasy winced. He asked, 'What was his name?'

'The burglar?'

'The copper. If you knew the burglar's name you wouldn't need a copper.'

'Is this a wind-up?'

'No. You may want to make a complaint against police. If you do, I want to be in the clear. I don't want you going round telling anyone DI Parker gave you crap advice.'

'So what's your advice?'

He grinned. Triumph. Greasy had got a fish to bite. He leaned back and looked serious. Greasy oozed fake-gravitas.

'You need to be sure of your facts,' he said. 'That's my advice.'

'Come off it Greasy. I'm not a simpleton.'

He stared closely into my eyes. It was like being given a bath by Haigh. Greasy lifted his glass to drink and Andrew, my personal waiter, leaned under his arm and dabbed with a cloth at the faint wet ring Greasy's glass rim had left on the counter. Andrew mouthed 'hello' at me. Greasy turned and looked at him.

'What a dump, Jimmy. Full of poufs and ponces. Why do you come here?'

Andrew had gone.

'I sometimes ask myself that very question. Though not for

the same reason.' I looked around the room. 'You know, you're a very old-fashioned man, Greasy.'

'Just old.'

A silence. Was he waiting for me to contradict him? I didn't. Eventually Greasy spoke.

'You know, there was recently a drive-by shooting outside this very boozer.'

'No?' I looked shocked. 'I thought that was a foreign phenomenon. You know, America, South Africa, places like that.'

Greasy waggled his beer bottle. 'Something else they've imported.'

'*Criminal*.' I said. 'Anyone hurt?'

'No. Put your hands together and give thanks is what I say.'

'Do you?' It seemed unlikely. He sucked his bottle of beer as an answer.

'Witnesses?' I asked.

'Nah. Don't make me laugh. Look at this place. People don't want to get involved.'

'Is that so?'

'Yeah. You wouldn't know it had happened, except the bloke had bullet holes in his windscreen.'

'Couldn't have been caused by gravel chips?'

Greasy gave me a withering look.

'He said... '

'Who "he"?'

'The driver of the car. Are you listening to this story?'

'Riveted.'

'*He* said there were a couple of witnesses. A spade and a bloke with a walking stick.'

He looked me up and down, with meaning. I blanked him, smiling, and asked, 'What were they like?'

Greasy nodded towards a black man. 'They all look the same to me.'

'Give it a rest, Greasy.'

'Oh... the other bloke. The bloke with the stick? According to the witness, the guy with the walking stick looked like you.'

'Witness?'

'Witness. Victim. Man with holes in his car. It's all the same. He said the guy with the walking stick drove the spade away in a white car.'

A silence.

'What colour car have you got, Jimmy?'

'Rust. It's this year's colour. We're calling it Autumn Red.'

He waited. I said nothing more. Eventually he said, 'It wasn't you, was it?'

'No.'

Another silence. I broke it by asking, 'You working in the local nick?'

'No.'

'So what's your interest in this case, Greasy?'

'Nothing. I'm just making polite conversation. It's been a long time, Jimmy.'

'Since?'

'Just a long time.'

Beads of sweat had formed on his forehead, a glistening counterpoint to his shining, slicked-back black hair.

'Hot?'

'No. Why?'

'You're sweating,' I said.

Greasy wiped his forehead with the flat of his palm, then looked at his palm. I half-expected him to sniff it.

'Last person I knew with lime-flavoured lard on his bonce was my old man,' I said.

'That's right. He did wear hair cream. They all did then.'

Now I stared at him.

He smiled. 'Have that drink, Jimmy.'

Eighteen

A FTER GREASY HAD gone Terry re-emerged. He didn't meet my eye. Bastard. I took up station at a table facing the door, drinking Aqua Libra, just like Terry. I moved partly to get away from the smell of fake lime, partly because I wanted to buttonhole Terry about Greasy, cowardice and friendship. Not now though. All in good time. I would save the conversation until there was no till to attend, no waiters to distract, no kitchen for him to withdraw to.

I waited and read. Lochinvar had left me his *Guardian*, once a newspaper but now with so many pages aimed at women, the media and schoolteachers it doesn't take long to get through the news pages. I read meeja and wimmen pages for half an hour, then the sport, then what's on telly though I had no intention of watching it, then I went back to the news pages and started again.

'You want another paper, Mr Jenner?' asked Andrew the waiter, who seemed to have adopted me as his personal client.

'Any different news in it?'

'I dunno. It's an evening paper.' He fetched it. The dead couple in Coopersale were on the front page, pictures lifted from their passports.

'Look at that. Murder,' he said. I couldn't work out whether it was 'murder' a statement or 'murder' an exclamation. I decided not to pursue it.

'Thanks Andrew.'

'S'okay.' He smiled but didn't leave. 'Er....'

'Go on?'

'Your friend said you'd pay the bill.'

'Greasy? Bastard,' I said. Andrew giggled. I counted out the money.

'What's his real name?' asked Andrew.

'I think he was baptised 'Greasy'.'

He laughed. 'What did Greasy want?'

I glanced over at Terry, who was looking away.

'Did someone put you up to asking me that?'

Andrew frowned. 'No. Just making conversation.'

'I thought you lot were like doctors and lawyers, you know, professional ethics and all that.'

'Us lot?'

'Waiters.'

'I'm sorry. He was just such a queer cove to find in here.' Now Andrew didn't even smile. 'Should I go away?'

'No. You're right. He was a nasty piece of work. What did he want? He was just trying to set a worm in my brain.'

'Did he succeed?'

'I hope not.'

'So do I, Mr Jenner.'

Andrew went away. Then I read the story in the Standard. Plenty of detail. I knew the journalist. These fellows have their sources. I wondered who had given him all that detail.

Judy walked in. Andrew was passing with a tray and flinched as she came through the door. It's not just me she has that effect on.

'Gin sling,' she said and sat.

'I'll have a whisky.'

'You sure, Mr Jenner?' asked Andrew, with 'you don't want no whisky' written all over him.

'Of course.'

He left, shaking his head. Andrew approached Terry at the bar and whispered to him. Terry shook his head too, slowly, sadly. He plucked at the collar of his shirt, as if to remind me of my lost night.

'This had better be good,' said the ex-Mrs Jenner.

'People are angry with me, Judy.'

'They'll have to wait in the queue.'

'I mean it. Someone took potshots at someone-else, thinking they were me. Someone burgled my flat, then someone tried to kidnap me.'

'Serious?'

'Serious.'

'Call a policeman.'

'Well that's another subject I wanted to ask you about. You said Greasy Parker was on the Murder Squad?'

'I did.'

'Sure?'

'I'm sure.'

'So why would he ask me a load of questions about someone shooting-up a milko outside here?'

'Milko?'

'Don't worry. They didn't hit him.'

'Greasy?'

'The milko.'

'So far, Jimmy, this conversation bears a close resemblance to a confused phone call. I expect you have a good reason for getting me to run halfway across London?'

'I ran for you, can't you run just a little bit for me?'

She sighed for an answer.

I said, 'Greasy Parker burgled my house.'

'How do you know?'

'How do you think?'

'You caught him?'

'Not in so many words.' I leaned forward. 'I'm going to tell you something.'

She rolled her eyes. The drinks came. 'Do I want to know what you're going to tell me?'

She looked so lovely. I changed my mind, just for a heartbeat.

'I'm in love with you,' I said, candour personified.

'Oh Jimmy for God's sake... '

Andrew was lurking. I raised my voice a little. 'I've been a fool but I'll change all that. I'm in love with you and I wish I'd never done any of the things that upset you in the past. I want you to come and share my home, put up curtains, make babies... '

'Jimmy.' There was warning in her voice.

'You can't marry that big booby while I'm begging.'

Andrew left, walking on eggshells.

'Jimmy, I gave up a perfectly good dinner engagement to answer your call. Is this what was so urgent? Taking the mickey out of us?'

'I promise not to become the Chief Constable of anywhere.'

She started to stand.

'I'm off.'

Her drink was untouched. People were staring. Terry and Andrew were staring. I held her hand. I whispered, 'Please don't go.'

She whispered back, but forcefully, 'Stop buggering about, Jimmy.'

'Please.'

'Why should I stay?'

'I *know* Greasy Parker burgled my flat today.'

'Know?'

'Know.'

She sat slowly. Terry and Andrew smiled at each other, misunderstanding.

'How?'

'In a minute. You said Greasy was working for your intended.'

'That's a secret.'

'That Greasy works for him?"

'The intention. How do you *know* Greasy Parker burgled your flat?'

'It smelled of lime pomade.'

'*Jimmy*. You *can't* be serious.'

'And he came round here just now and gave me a grilling. Tried to ply me with filthy Spanish beer with lemons in it while he asked me questions about some guy who got pot-shotted outside here a few days ago. And about Sydenham.'

'Sydenham? What about Sydenham?'

'Later. You know why Greasy was grilling me?'

'Do I want to?'

'It's obvious. Your jealous intended wanted to see me off.'

'So he gets his D.I. to turn burglar? I don't think so.'

'What else do I have in common with Greasy? What other interest would a Murder Squad Detective Inspector have in a private detective with no money and a milko with holes in his white Ford?'

'What *about* Sydenham?'

'Well, actually there's a story.'

'Tell me,' she sipped the gin. I leaned under the table and looked at her legs.

'What are you doing?'

'I wanted to see your stockings. If you're wearing police-woman stockings I can't tell you.'

'These are civilian stockings.' But she crossed her legs and clamped her knees tightly together, very much the police-woman.

'All right. You know Maltese Mickey was murdered last night?'

'Yes.'

'In Sydenham?'

'Yes. In Sydenham. What do you know about it?'

'Outside the Glass Balloonist?'

'Get on with it.'

'I was there.'

She looked away, irritably. I waited. She turned back. 'Jimmy... Jimmy....'

'Outside. I was outside.'

'You waited for the police to arrive, of course?'

'Are you taking this seriously? Who's going to wait for the police? Everyone was out of that street in sixty seconds flat.'

She moved her head closer to mine, elbow on the table, hand on her brow, hiding her eyes, like someone fending off a headache. I watched her lips part.

'Go on.'

'I'd been following someone... '

'Who?' She cut in, eyes still hidden behind her hand.

'In a minute. I was following *someone* who was about to get divorced only he didn't know it. That's what I was doing. Being a private detective. He had a trull on the side and he'd been salting away drab money for himself and her. I was hired on behalf of the wife, who had decided to pre-empt any problems

during the actual divorce process by gathering evidence about
him first.'

'And DeWitt?'

'DeWitt came later. I was sitting outside this pub waiting for
my man to emerge when all the shooting started.'

'You saw it?'

'No. I wasn't in direct line of vision.'

'And the police?'

'I didn't wait. I hadn't seen anything. I didn't tell the police I
was there because I had nothing to tell them.'

'You saw nothing?'

'Not while it was going on. I heard the shots and I walked
over there to the pub forecourt. There was a woman screaming
fit to burst and DeWitt lying on the ground with holes in his
chest and his eyes shot out.'

'A superstitious assassin?'

'No. I think it was a warning.'

'How do we get from there to you thinking Parker burgled
your flat? My Tommy's squad doesn't even cover that ground.'

'Her' Tommy. I'll kill him.

'Well...'

'Well?'

'I did see *something* in Sydenham.'

'What?'

I drew breath. 'I saw the man we'd been following walk away
from where Mickey was murdered. And he was carrying a
gun.'

'The one that did the shooting?'

'How do I know? I don't suppose every third person on
Sydenham Road packs a shooter.'

'So you were a witness.'

'But I didn't see this man shoot anyone.'

'You should have stayed, Jimmy. You should have stayed
anyway but if you saw a man with a gun then you were an
important witness and you should have hung around,' she
thought about it. 'I wish you hadn't told me this.'

'Judy, the bloke I saw with the gun is a low-grade money-

grubbing crooked surveyor. A local government officer. He'd
no sooner shoot out someone else's eyes than his own. Which
brings me on to my next point.'

I turned the *Evening Standard* round on the table so that it
faced her. Dead Ralph and Louise looked out from its front
page, reproachfully. I tapped his head with my finger.

'Ralph Purnell?'

I nodded.

'Was he the person you saw walking up Sydenham Road?'

'Correct.'

'He's the man you were following?'

'Correct.'

'And he's the one who committed suicide with his girlfriend
in Epping Forest.'

'Incorrect. What suicide? He took two shots at it.'

'That's been done before.'

'You're not going to start talking about German generals?'

'No,' she looked puzzled. 'Which German generals?'

'How did you put that together so easily.'

'You gave me clues,' she replied. I waited for the true
answer.

'I work in criminal intelligence. People are guessing. People
are talking. Purnell and DeWitt go back years.'

'Purnell is dead, people presume he shot DeWitt?'

'Yes.'

'That's a bit of a leap.'

'It's not my leap. I'm sure they have their reasons.'

'Yes. Which reasons?'

'Who cares? It's not my business. It's definitely not yours.'
Judy sat back in her chair. 'Jimmy, you have sailed closer to the
wind than ever before, and if you want my opinion it is 'don't
ever do that again'. But I think you will have got away with it.'

'What about Greasy?'

'What about him?'

'*Burgling my flat.*'

She looked away.

I went on. 'I am genuinely browned off. *That's* why I called you here. Imagine how surprised I was when Greasy turned up instead.'

'Co-incidence.' But she thought for a second. 'Why do you think *anyone* would have burgled your flat?'

'Now you're starting to sound like the PC who came round.'

'Answer.'

'We took photographs.'

'You and...'

'Malcolm Boyce.'

'What are you doing with Boyce?'

'We were following Ralph Purnell. Aren't you listening to this?'

'Where are the photographs?'

'Boycey's got them,' I lied. You have to sometimes. 'I think somebody was looking for them and he broke into my flat. He wore pomade, just like the someone who came round to this bar this evening bending my ear about how he wished we hadn't fell out of touch, what a great old mate I was really and by the way could I give a detailed account of my movements in the last forty-eight hours? What do you reckon?'

'Which? Parker had your flat burgled because Tom is jealous of you or because you have some photographs?'

'So you admit it?'

If we hadn't been in such a public place I'm sure she would have hit me. A champagne cork popped behind us.

'Also, 'I said, 'he made a crack about my old man.'

'Who?'

'Greasy Parker let it drop he knew my father.'

'On purpose?'

I shrugged.

'How else can you know someone? Anything less is acquaintance-ship.'

'Let it drop, I mean.'

'Yes.'

'And you're not getting paranoid, Jimmy?'

'On the house!' cried Terry and slapped the bottle of champagne and two glasses on our table. 'From the Club Etoile a celebration of romantics everywhere. Now you have to kiss him.'

'Why?' Asked Judy with a glare that would go through sheet steel. Terry grinned back.

'I'll call you Jimmy,' she left our table, all folded coats and business-like looks.

'Cheers, Tel.' I said.

Her hips swung and her shoes clicked as she walked to the door. Click click click. Hips swi-ing-ing. She was wasted on that dopey copper.

'Have a glass of champagne.'

He poured it. I drank. Andrew brought Terry his Aqua Libra.

'Terry, do you remember my Dad?'

'Yes. Of course.'

'Did he know any gangsters?'

Terry laughed. I did too. A silly idea.

'Only your brother; and frankly *he* could have had a better shot at it.'

'Do you remember him wearing lime pomade?'

'The old man? Yes. Lots of people did then.'

'Of course they did. Like that git Greasy Parker who was in here earlier.'

'Never heard of him,' said Terry. It was unconvincing.

'He was here.'

'I didn't see him,' said Terry.

'How do you know?'

'Know?'

'How do you know you didn't see him if you don't know him? This place must be full of people you don't know personally. It must be full of people you don't recognise. So how do you know you didn't see him?'

'I wasn't here, that's what I meant.' He looked guilty.

'You could see it in their hat bands,' I said.

'Hat bands?'

'Lime pomade. You don't see it now.'

Terry composed himself. 'People don't wear hats now, Jimmy. No one does.'

'Nearly no one.'

'If you like. Have another drink, Jimmy.'

'No.'

He looked at me for a few seconds. 'I never asked the bastard here.'

An admission, at last. I asked, 'Why did you hide in the kitchen?'

'Greasy Parker's bad news, Jimmy.'

'Scared?'

'Yeah.'

'He said he knew my Dad. Did he?'

'I don't know.'

'He knew my brother?'

'I don't know. Really. I don't know. He may have done. Have a drink, Jimmy.' Terry stood at the bar and smiled. His face beamed, 'trust me'. I felt weak. Judy was gone, the night was yet young. Terry was older than me and could remember Bermondsey as I couldn't or as I thought I should. Trust him. Why not? Terry always lies but if you push him he'll tell you the truth, unlike other people who always claim to tell the truth, no matter what. No one always tells the truth, especially those claiming to, who always lie. Who *invariably* lie. I used to love sinking a few drinks with Terry when I was younger, and do now, except of course he doesn't drink. But he tells a lovely story while you do the sinking. I took the glass from him.

'Lose much?' He asked.

'Lose?'

'In the burglary.'

'Sod all.'

'There you are. Every cloud has a silver lining.'

'And every silver lining its cloud.'

'Drink up and cheer up, sport.'

I only carried out the first of his commands. I could feel the headache coming on and I hadn't drunk it yet.

Nineteen

BUT I DID. That night the penny dropped. I was in the rain on the street, the Mile End Road where they're doing the roadworks. New traffic lights, so we've all got something to watch while we sit in the traffic jam. Red, red and orange, green, but still you just sit there, jammed. It wasn't a penny that dropped so much as a wily coyote's anvil, a safe, a heavy metal object. It missed my toes, it missed my nose, it only grazed my scalp but it hit me, hit me full fair square in the brain. Clunk. Not the memory but the bit you use for rational thinking. Clunk.

Terry was with me.

Looking back on it, he only wanted to make sure I didn't get into trouble. I'd left his pub. What for? I don't know. To wander. To wonder. To walk. I was walking in the road because trenches cut the pavement. I was drunk and fell in the muddy trench just as Judy turned up again. That's my luck. She'd come back to make sure I was okay, having dumped me in the Etoile. She found that I wasn't. The Scotch git Tom Mack watched us from his Rover, sneering while Judy bent over me. Perhaps he wasn't sneering, but why hold back on your feelings? Your true feelings. Even if he didn't sneer I smelt it. I was upright again. I turned from him and stared into the shallow trench. Clunk. When Judy left I watched the rain falling into the trench. My clothes clung to me. I wiped mud off my trousers.

'Bleeding trench,' I said. I leaned on my recovered stick, suddenly sober now, soaked and freezing and gazing into the shallow trench. Terry stood close by my side.

'You all right?' He asked, quietly, almost reverently.

'I'm all right. Dangerous things, trenches.'

He shrugged. I watched the rain falling into the trench. My clothes clung to me. I wiped mud off my trousers.

'Yes,' Terry said at last, with a dry sounding voice.

'Even shallow trenches. You don't need to get much bigger than that to swallow a man.'

'Thinking about Joe Boy?'

'Thinking about the trench, too.'

'I knew you were.'

And we were silent for a long time, staring at the trench before I spoke again.

'I know people say you can drown in a couple of inches of water... but who's ever known someone who's done it?'

'She's right,' said Terry, 'Too much thinking boils your brain. You want to try to relax a bit.'

Which is a good bit of advice, if you can follow it. I can't.

'Was it raining when he died?' I asked.

'Don't you remember, Jimmy?'

'No. I was sixteen. I never knew I'd have to remember it in twenty five years. Was it raining?'

'No.' He paused, waiting for me to dismiss him. I did not. Terry waved his hand at the ground, accusing it. 'You know what it's like down there. It hadn't rained for weeks before and it didn't rain for weeks after. But you know what it's like down there.'

I do. The very rivers of London run under our feet. Dig a hole and it fills with water. Dig a *big* hole and it caves in, if unpropped. Stand too close to the edge and you will cave in with it. Only a thin tarmacadam surface keeps us from plunging into the sticky clay below. As my brother had slipped down the dirty bank of the long buried River Neckinger, I had fallen from the side of the Black Ditch. Every hole in London fills with water. Pass your glass and I'll show you.

Part two

God is love

Twenty

THAT NIGHT I slept at Terry's Club Etoile again, this time preferring sheets and a bed to the bathroom floor. It wasn't just drunken convenience. There was a touch of the cowardy custard about it. I didn't want to take any non-voluntary rides in Vauxhalls with men in brown boots. And there was the problem of Greasy Parker. He wanted something from me. He might have decided it would be easier to find with me in the flat. I didn't want my beauty sleep ruined by teams of coppers with or without warrants to search. Also there was whoever had searched the babes in the wood. Brown Boots? Blue Windcheater? Maybe they'd want a second go at renewing our acquaintanceship. Nah. I'll sleep at the Club Etoile tonight.

I got up early, washed, shaved. Outside the window a diesel engine rattled. I pulled up the blind. Lochinvar was down there in a smart-looking London cab. I found a plastic Waitrose bag, recovered the guns and ammunition from under Terry's pile of newspapers and transferred them, wrapped in a couple of newspapers, from the Tesco's to the Waitrose bag. Call me a snob, I don't care. I went downstairs, looking as clean as I ever would, and let myself out of the Club Etoile. The cleaner was coming in, the same one who'd caught me in the bathroom, a hard-faced woman of about sixty. We passed in the doorway. She gave me the glare. I smiled.

'More taxis?' She asked.

'I'm amazed you recognise me with my clothes on.'

'It's the smell.'

London women. Outside it was slashing down. Rain on me, what do I care? I got in the cab.

'Where to, guv'?'

Lochinvar had been practising his cabby act.

'Chigwell. You been waiting long?'

'Not unless you include the drive to your flat.'

'How did you know I was here?'

'Leon suggested it.'

'Where did you rent this?'

'Leon's.'

Where else? He pointed at a notice. 'Sit well back in your seat for comfort and safety.'

I did as I was told, clutching the plastic bag full of guns, newspapers and ammo to my knees. 'How was the flat?'

'Still there.'

And the cab lurched forward.

'How's Rosie?'

'Carrying a torch for you.' And he laughed. 'Here, this was pinned to your front door.' He passed me back a piece of crumpled paper. I uncrumpled it. 'Ring me, you bastard', was written on the piece of paper in angry, round and decidedly French handwriting. Her handwriting was like an accent. Ring me you bastard, Cheemee. I will ring you, Amy, I replied in my head.

I pushed the glass open and called to Lochinvar. 'If you're going to Chigwell you'd better head for Stratford or we're never going to get there.'

Taxi drivers. Even amateurs go in for all that, *'oh dear we'll have to go right round the one-way'* caper.

'Right,' said Lochinvar, cheerfully.

'And you'd better put the meter on, otherwise you'll look like the most generous cabby in Britain.'

He clicked the meter over like an expert. It doesn't take long.

Twenty one

RALPH PURNELL HAD lived, when he lived, where London ends. His was a modern 'executive' style house in an estate full of cul-de-sacs just where Chigwell runs out to the country. Around each cul-de-sac was a cluster of houses; each house with sweeping lawns and intimate garages which, opened, would reveal matching black shopping Golf GTi's. Hers. I was driven around the estate looking for the Purnell's house by Lochinvar the Friendly Cabby, windows open on account of drizzle and the wipers groaning. The roads had names like 'The Coombe', 'Tithedale', 'Staneway'. The houses had names like 'Five Ashes', 'The Barn' or 'The Old Dairy' though there were no ashes, no barn and no dairy, old or otherwise. Purnell's 'Blue Remembered Hills' was in The Mead. Lochinvar parked at the end of the cul-de-sac on a shallow slope, then I walked back a hundred yards across winter-faded but manically neat lawns to Blue Remembered Hills. A curtain lifted opposite the cab. I strode purposefully across the soaked grass of Purnell's place and pushed the doorbell with my walking-stick. The bellpush was set in the centre of a mock Georgian sapele door with smoked glass panels. A tiny old woman wearing a long black dress tottered along the hallway behind the door, peered through the smoked glass panel at me, then clicked the latch open. She had a balding head and a grey moustache. She looked like nothing so much as a country parson in drag, though her greeting was less friendly.

'What?'

'I've come to see Mrs Purnell.'

'She's bereaved. She ain't seeing no one.'

'She'll see me.'

'I'm her muvver and I say she ain't seeing no one.'

'How quaint, a local. Give her this.' I held out my card. The old woman took it in arthritic fingers and squinted at the print. I pushed past her while she read.

'You got a condolences book?'

'What do you think we are, peasants?' She indicated a fake Georgian side table with a tall imitation-leather bound book on it. Next to the book was a tortoise-shell Parker. I took out a biro and opened the book. The old woman turned the squint on me, waved the card and said, 'Jenner?'

'James.'

'Do we know you?'

'Why don't you go and find out?'

She did, reading my name aloud again as she walked, as if 'Jenner' was a bar of soap she might let slip through her fingers, or a complex formula, easily forgotten. I wrote in the tall bound book. *James Jenner, Defoe Mansions, Stoke Newington,* and the date. The biro left blue sticky ink between my fingers. I wiped them on the handset of their phone. She came back with another much taller and tubbier woman wearing another long black dress. It reached from her ankles to her throat, where she wore a large black ribbon and a piece of what I presumed was garnet. Mock Victorian. Her hair was white dyed black and she had a painted beauty mole on her cheekbone. Mock modest. She stared at me from behind the dark glasses. I knew her immediately.

'Mr Jenner?'

'Himself. Mrs Purnell?'

'Yes. I didn't really expect to see you.'

'Really really?'

'Really. Come in.'

The accent came out of Brent Cross Shopping Centre via Marks and Sparks lingerie and Safeway's delicatessen counter. It wasn't a bad effort, though if Mrs Purnell really wanted to carry off a change in class she'd have to gas the old lady or nail her up in a cupboard. I followed Mrs Purnell into the living-room. The old woman followed me too, but stopped and stood in the doorway, not so much framed as supported by the jamb. Mrs Purnell sat and smoothed her dress. I stood awkwardly before her, without a plan. I'd had one before I came but seeing her had emptied the cupboard. She looked up at me.

'Sit down.'

'In a minute... my leg.'

'Do you want some tea?'

'That'd be nice.'

The old woman had gone.

I looked around the room. Department store furniture. Thousands of pounds worth of velour-covered foam seats. It wasn't the taste so much as the quantity. One wall was covered with a huge and modern fake elm 'fitted unit' bibliothèque. It carried the usual; family photographs, a bowl of fruit, a lot of booze, some cut glass, twenty or so videos and one book. An intellectual. *Slim Your Own Hips*. Who else's hips would you slim? Next to the bibliothèque a panoramic window gave onto a wintry garden, guarded by a row of tall and grisly variegated Leylandii. Through the glass the garden was a picture of drooping branches dropping rainwater. Mrs Purnell sat in silence, watching me looking out, then said softly.

'My husband was going to cut them. They need a lot of cutting.'

She said it with enough pathos to make a stone cry. I didn't.

'It's a bad time.'

'Yes. Don't mind my Mum.'

'Do you know why I'm here?'

'Mr Menke rang.'

'Of course. I expect you've got a lot of questions to ask me, Mrs Purnell.'

She said nothing. Eventually I said, 'You know who I am?'

'Yes. You're a private detective.'

'Why did you hire me?'

'I didn't.'

'Well somebody did.'

'I didn't hire you in particular. I asked for a detective. You're what I got.'

'What about Menke? What did he say?'

I waited. She said no more. The tea came. The old woman put a glug of milk and two lumps in mine unasked, then scowled and left. Mrs Purnell clasped her cup on her knees, trembling slightly in her fingertips, eyes damp and red, as if she'd been crying. A good act. Mine was nearly as good.

'What did Menke say?' I repeated, gently. I didn't feel gentle.

'He said you'd been in Sydenham. And that you'd seen Ralph there.'

'Yeah. It was a bit more than that, you know. There was yesterday, too.'

'None of it matters.'

'Did you give a statement to the police?'

'Just the bare facts.'

'Being?'

'He came home from Sydenham agitated.'

'Did he tell you what had happened there?'

'No.'

'Did he tell you why he had gone there?'

'No. I don't know why he was in Sydenham, or even that he was there until Menke told me.'

'Then?'

'When he came home? He made himself a drink. He phoned someone. I don't know who. He was downstairs. I was in bed. Then he came to bed.'

'Was it his girlfriend?'

She pulled a sour face. The girlfriend. She who must not be named.

'I don't know.'

'Then you and Ralph went to sleep?'

'I don't think so.'

'Don't you know?'

'We were in separate rooms. But it sounded to me as if he hardly slept.'

'That implies you hardly slept.'

'I didn't sleep at all. I don't sleep much now. I don't think it's going to improve in the short term, Mister Jenner.'

Those eyes behind the dark glasses. I wanted to see them, to look deep into them.

'What happened in the morning?'

'He got up and went out. That was the last we saw of him. I can't say I'm sorry he's gone. I can't say I'm sorry at all, except the hurt he left behind him,' she cried a little. She didn't seem to put much into it.

I went and sat next to her, very close. She put the cup down. She held me in a steady gaze behind the dark glasses, her eyes on my face, examining me. Her face was calm and composed now, her hands unmoving on her lap.

'What's your first name, Mrs Purnell?'

'Lola, if it's important.'

'Lola. That's nice. Just how well did you know your husband, Lola?'

'How well does anyone know anyone?'

Philosophy again. Please, leave me out.

'You weren't bothered he was sleeping with other women until you thought he was going to leave you?'

'That's it.'

'Just like that, you weren't bothered, then you were?'

Suddenly there was controlled venom in her voice and she hated me. Suddenly she wasn't simply a tubby, middle-aged woman living in a neat-freak bad-taste house.

'What *do* you want?'

'I don't know, Mrs Purnell. You were the one who did the hiring. What do *you* want?'

She didn't reply.

I stood, walked a couple of paces to the bibliothèque, began to look at the photos. The first showed a man in his late thirties. He wore a black Italian suit and was leaning against a Jaguar. Beside him stood Janice, or 'Lola' as she preferred to be known now. It wasn't Joe. Too old. The next was of Ralph and Lola Purnell when they were younger, with a child. Then the child, a girl, alone; then a woman with a baby, then with a child, this time a boy. The woman was in her mid-twenties, tall and dark-haired. The eyes would be grey. She was very elegant, with a thin face, full lips and sharply cut features. If she wasn't clever she looked it. The girl from Sydenham, with the briefcase and the suit. The smart-looking girl as she grew up as Ralph and

Lola's daughter, then had a child of her own. The photos on the bibliothèque told a little family story.

'Who's this?'

A grumpy voice, an admission. 'My daughter, also Lola. This is when she was a kid.'

'And the other?'

'My grandson.'

'She's married, Lola?'

'It's a modern world. No.'

'So she's Lola Purnell still? Just like you?'

No answer. I tried again. 'What does she do for a job?'

'Why do you want to know?'

'She looks professional.'

'She's an accountant.'

'Where does she live?'

'You're behaving as if you're the policeman investigating Ralph's death.'

'If only I were.'

'Exactly what is the point of your visit, Mr Jenner?'

I persisted. '*Where*? Not Sydenham?'

'No. My daughter lives in Epping. Just down the road....'

'I know where Epping is.'

'Good.'

'It's not far from there to Coopersale.'

'It's not far from here, either. Next to the M11 isn't far from anywhere, if you've got a car.'

'Do you drive?'

She smiled.

'No, Jenner, I don't drive. What's the matter, didn't we pay you enough?'

'I was well paid. And you got what you wanted.'

'I didn't want Ralph dead. I just wanted what was fair in what was left of our marriage.'

'You were married for a long time. Over twenty years, isn't it?'

'Nearer thirty.'

'Did you ever feel the need to hire a private detective before?'

'No.'

'But Ralph had plenty of other women.'

'We all make our compromises. What are yours?'

'Doing divorce work. Do you know what your husband was doing in Sydenham?'

'When?'

'When? When do you think? When Mickey DeWitt died.'

'Who's he?' She smiled, warm and polite.

'Are you serious?' I said.

'Of course. You're very aggressive Mister Jenner.'

'I'd like to talk to your daughter.'

'No. Definitely not.'

'Why not?'

'She's upset.'

'But you're not?'

'I'm desolated.'

'You look it.'

'Some of us are stronger than others. Again, tell me... what exactly was the point in you coming here? I hired you, you've done the job, I paid up. What do you want?'

'Good question,' I said, as much to myself as her.

She stood and held out her hand. 'If there's nothing more.....'

I shook it by reflex.

'There's lots more. I'll see myself out.'

I did. I was angry when I left, and stalked across her rainy lawn again, as much as a man with only one and a half legs can stalk.

I slumped in the back of the taxi and refused to answer Lochinvar's questions. We waited in icy silence for about forty minutes.

Now another taxi, a blue Sierra minicab, came to the Purnell house. Lola came out of her house, wearing a brown tweed suit, black stockings and brown brogues. She had a rainmac thrown over her shoulders and it twisted as she slipped her tall and ample figure into the back of the Sierra. They moved off. We followed. They didn't go far. Cross country. A quick jaunt past Abridge, now into narrow, high-hedged lanes and along an escarpment. Stapleford Tawney, turn off for Navestock, turn off again into what seemed like the tradesmen's entrance to a big country house. Lochinvar dropped me and I walked down a scruffy gravelled drive, past a sign, 'Nomadic Golf Club, Trade Entrance'. The Sierra was by a little van, 'Nomadic Golf Club Functions'. The minicab driver was munching a torpedo sandwich and swinging his head lazily. When I got closer I could hear his radio. Easy Listening. I thought Ray Moore was dead. I walked around the side of the country house. Part of the ground floor was a bar. I peered over a window ledge. There, in the bar, was Lola Purnell. She took her coat off and sat next to a man. He wore smart leisure clothes now, a green roll-neck jumper with the sleeves pushed up, but there was no mistaking him; Greasy. Lola and Greasy didn't look all that pleased to see each other, but they talked anyway. Stilted-looking. I couldn't hear them and I couldn't go in. I stared at them through the window. A pleasant young female voice beside me said, 'Can I help?'

'I've lost my ball.'

'Are you a member?'

'You need to be a member to lose a ball?'

I turned. My interrogator was a woman of about thirty wearing Barbour everything and carrying a plastic bag and a steel tipped stick. The stick had a couple of pieces of paper lanced on its steel tip.

'I'm afraid you'll have to leave,' she twirled the stick. 'I'm responsible.'

'You see that man?'

She looked at Greasy too. 'I see him.'

'Have you seen him before?'

'No. Who *are* you?'

'Department of Social Security. He's supposed to be on the dole. What do you reckon?'

She peered over the window ledge again.

'He doesn't look like it.' Her brow furrowed and she turned to me again. 'If you're from the DSS where's your pass?'

I showed her.

'This is a disabled bus pass Mister...,' she went to read the card again but I snatched it away. She twirled the rubbish stick.

'You'll have to go. This is private property.'

We may raid these premises if we believe unemployed people are lounging around here, not being available for work.'

'Leave.'

I left. Lochinvar took me round to the front entrance of the golf club and we waited for half an hour. From the road you could see the golf club car park, but only if you stood. I spent the half hour leaning on the cab's bonnet, blinking rainwater out of my eyes. Then Greasy came out of the golf club, walked over to a nondescript blue Vauxhall. It had two aerials. I climbed back in the cab. The Vauxhall flew past us. Lochinvar turned the cab around as if he was taking his test with a particularly pernickety examiner.

'Lochinvar. For god's sake get on with it.'

But he kept turning e-v-e-r so slowly. The Vauxhall was out of sight. Lola's taxi passed. I ducked in the back of the cab but I'm sure she saw me.

I gave her twenty minutes, then we found a phone box and I dialled her number. The old woman answered, polite as ever.

'Yeah?'

'Can I talk to Janice?'

'There ain't no Janice here.'

'Janice Conkey, used to live down the Southwark Park Road.'

'Who is this?'

'A friend from Bermondsey. You must be old Mrs Conkey. How are you doing?'

'You've got the wrong number mate.'

'I don't think so. I want to talk to Janice Conkey and I reckon she's on this number.'

'Well she ain't.'

'You sure?'

'I'm sure.'

She rang off, doubtless looking at the blue biro ink on her fingers too. I spat on mine and rubbed them with my hanky but the blue biro ink stuck, stuck faster than Janice Conkey's name had stuck to Lola. But she was Janice, okay, and soon she would know I knew it.

I dropped the phone and walked back out to Lochinvar.

'Yes?' He smiled. 'Now what?'

'Take me home.'

'I'm learning lots, Jenner. Lots.'

'If you don't want to do the job, sod off. No one's forcing you to stick around.'

Lochinvar slammed the glass closed and drove me home. He'd cheered up again by the time we got there.

Twenty two

I DON'T BELIEVE in Kismet. Fortune has two faces. Fate is there to be resisted. If we have a destiny it is to be the one who resists. The chance would be a fine thing. I saw Lola Junior – the woman with the business suit and the wavy dark hair – less than two hours later and I believe it was an accident.

*

When Lochinvar and I got to Defoe Mansions Boycey was opposite my flats, parked at the wheel of a brown Morris Ital, circa nineteen-seventy-eight. Apparently the motors are so good they outlive the bodies. This certainly seemed to be the case with Boycey's Ital. The man himself was dressed in a Terylene suit, dark brown wig, a pork-pie hat and black immo Ray-ban glasses. He was reading *Sporting Life* as if his depended on it. I got out of the cab and ostentatiously handed Lochinvar a fiver, then gave him instructions to poodle up and down Stoke Newington Church Street with his orange light on but under no circumstances to take a fare.

'Who's the spade?' Boycey asked as the cab pulled away.

'He's a getaway driver for the Darby and Joan club.'

'What?'

'He's a taxi driver, Boycey. What do I know about who he is?'

'So why were you talking to him so long?'

You get nothing past Boycey.

'Why are you wearing dark glasses, Boycey? It's November.'

You get nothing past me, either. What a couple of aces. I took him up to the flat and gave him a cup of coffee, once I could find the pot and some cups in the wreckage. Boycey leaned on the window-ledge so he could watch the road outside and pulled his best sulky face, then turned and looked over the ruined room.

'You had a visit too.'

'Let me guess... from a copper called Parker?'

'I don't know who it was.'

'Big geezer in his fifties, smells like a harlot's handbag.'

Boycey pouted, yes. 'I came round last night but I couldn't get an answer. I reckoned you were already a-bed.'

'I stayed at Terry's.'

'I know. He told me.'

'What did Parker want from you?'

'He said we'd been spotted in your motor taking pictures in Sydenham.'

'What did you tell him?'

'That he'd made a mistake. Then he hit me. So I gave them to him.'

'You're a brave man, Malcolm.'

'He said he'd already asked you and you said I had them.'

'And you believed him? You're very suggestible for your line of work.'

'He says I have to give him the negatives or he's going to fit us up for the murder.'

'Ditto.'

'He said that to you?'

'No. Ditto, you seem to have come over gullible all of a sudden.'

He talked for an hour, all the time looking down at the street below, every few minutes looking at his watch and fidgeting. Boycey complained that we'd been let down by Menke, by DeWitt for getting killed in front of us, by Purnell for 'committing suicide' in front of Boycey.

'What did Menke say to you, Jimmy?'

'Just what I'd expect. *'Keep your hat on, sit still, do nothing till you hear from me'.'*

'Did he say when we're going to get paid out?'

'You skint?'

'No.'

'So what are you getting at, Boycey?'

'Well all bets are off, since Ralph's dead. Presumably the widow will inherit all and Menke will pay the rest of our bill. That's all.'

'Case over?'

'Never was one.'

'You want to just pass Greasy the negatives and get out of it.'

'Very astute, Jimmy Jenner. This is my first corpseless day out of the last three and I want to keep it that way. I'm not a bloody undertaker. I'm back to the repossessed cars and the divorce work from today.'

'Ralph Purnell was a divorce, remember?'

'Well Ralph's dead so there's no divorce case.'

'If I'm to follow your logic, why did Ralph kill DeWitt?'

'How do I know? Thieves fall out. We know Ralph was at it.'

'Taking bribes from property developers?'

'So Mickey doesn't pay him one over.... '

'You think Ralph and Mickey were up to something. Mickey fails to pay out. Ralph has a personality transplant, grows a backbone, for once in his life becomes a man of action. He acquires a gun, arranges a meeting in a public house in Sydenham with Maltese Mickey and observed all by diverse persons, Ralph shoots Mickey in the back, front, both eyes. Then he calmly walks away with the gun in his hand....'

'The police think that.'

'... then has another personality transplant in a fit of grief, calls down his strumpet from jam-butty land, shoots her, then shoots himself. Twice.'

Boycey screwed his face up.

'The police believe that story.'

'Course they do. And in the tooth fairy.'

'Thieves fall out. Ralph and Mickey could have fallen out.'

'They could. What exactly was the purpose of coming here, Malcolm?'

'To deliver a message.'

'Being?'

'Greasy wants the negatives, then that's that. He doesn't want us to be witnesses, he won't cause us any more problems.'

'That's big of him. Why is he so interested? It's not even his case.'

'Is Greasy bent?'

'Of course. It doesn't explain his nerve, does it? He is either being reckless, going after those pictures or....'

'Or?'

'He's very confident.'

'He's that all right.' Boycey touched his face, the fleshy part of his cheek above the bone.

'How am I supposed to deliver the negatives to him?'

'You have to give them to me. Then he'll arrange a meet with me.'

'Why does he want to do that? Why not get them direct from me?'

'Do I know how his mind works? He told me to get the negatives off you, meet him some place to be advised in the West End and hand them over and there would be a good drink in it for us as sources of information. Otherwise he's going to fit us up.'

I said, 'You know, I've been thinking about the girl. The dark-haired one, the gorgeous one.'

'No? What girl?'

'You *do* know Boycey. The one we kept seeing. With the formal suits and the attaché case. The one who had you shaking your nutty slack and boasting about you were going to do this and do that, like you do with all your dream girls....'

'That's not boasting.'

'So you know her?'

'No.'

'The one whose photo we took before DeWitt was shot.'

'Oh yeah... that one. What about her?'

'I was wondering who she was.'

'I dunno. Why?'

Actually I was just wondering if he knew she was Janice's daughter. Boycey looked dumb. Well, maybe he didn't know. He slurped the last of his coffee.

'I say give Parker the photo negative and duck your head under the sheets. That's what I say Jimmy.'

'I'll see you out,' I replied. He put down his cup and glanced out of the window.

'That spade's still patrolling Stokey in that black cab.'

'Who are you that you can tell black cabs apart? Tonto? That's a different spade in a different cab, you pillock.'

I saw him to the door. I gave him a minute's start then went down to the street and hailed Lochinvar. I had to have a row with an old man and his wife who said they'd hailed him first and were going to complain to the Hackney Carriage Office. Like most retirees, they had more pressing business than the rest of us.

'Where we going, Jimmy?'

'I don't know, I just said, follow that car.'

'Follow that car. Like a film.' He laughed and slammed the glass between us. The old man and his wife stood at the kerbside cursing like navvies.

*

This is how come I'm under Bond Street with a gift-wrapped silver napkin ring in my pocket. Lochinvar and I followed Boycey in the taxi through an hour and a half's worth of London traffic jams to the underground car park behind John Lewis's Oxford Street branch. Lochinvar couldn't mooch around there not taking fares so he dropped me while Boycey was underground parking.

I took the Browning from the plastic bag and stuffed it in my waistband. I shoved the rest of the package, including the Smith-and-Wesson, down the side of Lochinvar's spare tyre. I put my mobile phone down there too. Something else I didn't need to carry.

I told Lochinvar to report back to Defoe Mansions at midnight with the cab.

'What are we going to do?'

'Break into somewhere,' I said sarcastically.

'Cool. Anything else?'

'Yes.' I scribbled on a card and gave it to him with some bank notes. 'I want you to buy as many roses as you can with that and deliver them to a woman called Amy Dupont. This is her address.'

Lochinvar puttered away in the cab, looking like he'd found his vocation. I followed Boycey into the ground floor of John Lewis's. He'd no sooner gone through the door when I lost him. I can't walk all that fast. I blundered round the haberdashery department looking for him. It was like looking for a haystack in a needle.

Out on Oxford Street the world is there with a carrier bag. 'I bought it here', 'I bought it there', 'I bought it every-bleeding-where'. I looked around their hard shopped-out faces for Boycey. Gone. A boy in a cheesecutter hat stood very close to me, eating a hamburger while a small man stood across the street, 'Eat less Protein' on a board he carried.

I asked the boy, 'Did you see a man come out of here?'

'About a thousand in the last five minutes, not including you.'

Smart arse. The crowd poured past. It can't be true that there are so many people in Oxford Street and you don't know any of them. Of course not. You might know a dozen people there at any one time, it's just a question of walking down the same section of pavement when they do, of looking up and seeing and recognising them. Didn't I have an office job with you in nineteen-sixty seven? We worked in a Dickensian import/export. I was a messenger. You typed. Rats ran amongst the stock. There was a Palestinian guy there who drank the milk from his tea cup each time I poured it in. How the hell was I supposed to make tea for him? It was my job. Eventually he was sidetracked by your legs, which, excuse me, were quite a lot less like piano legs then than they are now. I turned my attention from matronly women to a shop window, deciding that Boycey wasn't going to present himself. I went in. I knew that I had to do better than send a bunch of roses to ingratiate myself with Amy. But what? Then I saw the antique silver napkin ring. I bought it, slipped it into my pocket and went outside to find a telephone.

'Amy, cheree.'

'Cheemee? How are you?'

'Wonderful.'

'I am. I'm going to have a show.'

'Of?'

'What do you mean, 'of'? My art.'

'You haven't done any.'

'It's situational,' she said, with exaggerated patience. 'With a video.'

'Like a 'happening'?'

'We don't call them that.'

'I'm sorry.'

'It's okay, Cheemee. It's not your subject. I'll teach you.'

'When?'

'Tonight.'

'Okay – we'll celebrate. We'll go and have dinner together. You can choose any restaurant you want in Brick Lane. Price no objection. I just need to be home by midnight.'

'Wonderful Cheemee. I am shaving my body for you.'

I can never quite fathom out whether she's serious or not.

'Video?'

'No video. What do you take me for?'

'Don't get all in a lather, Amy.'

'Gros bisoux, Cheemee.'

Gros bisoux to you too.

*

Amy, Amy, why am I always late? It wasn't my fault the train wouldn't come. Anyway, I had a surprise on Bond Street tube station... let me tell you Amy; I saw the woman there. Lola Junior. This is good fortune indeed. Or this is the person Boycey was meeting. I couldn't believe my eyes as I bought my ticket and she strolled past in the booking hall. It was her, okay; mid-twenties, tall and dark-haired, long dark hair past her collar. She was smartly dressed in a dark-blue, well-cut business suit. She carried a ruby red leather briefcase. I just knew there would be a ruby red leather Filofax inside it. She had high cheekbones, blue-grey eyes, clear skin, a pointed chin. She carried herself as if she thought about it. Everything about the woman in the dark-blue business suit was elegant. Lola Junior, Lola Junior. How could she be Fat Lola's/Janice's daughter?

I followed her down to the eastbound platform. So we were both eastbound. Now we were bound for the same destination. I watched Lola Junior make her way to the far end of the platform. Men watched as she passed. Then I lost sight of her. The platform had been filling up, but suddenly there was a real mob waiting, as if all the Oxford Street shoppers had decided to go home at once. After another five minutes the station supervisor made a mumbled apology over the loudspeakers, rolling-stock, vandalism, staff shortages, signal failure, inclement weather over Iberia, the management regrets to announce... but still no train came. I craned my head forward, nosey Jenner. Where was that woman? I daren't lean further forward. I'd fall on the track and about a thousand people would fall with me. We were jammed close; no train approaching and about three trainloads of humanity crammed onto the platform, sweating, heaving, each person not feeling very well disposed towards the others. Bond Street tube was seriously crowded. There was a suburban lady by my right side, standing with a lot of shopping bags pressed against me. On my left stood a boy with a nodding head, ting ting pop music sounding through his earphones. You'll be deaf soon, ting ting ting. In front of me was the painted line and the edge of the platform. I don't like standing by the edge of the platform in big pushing crowds. It makes me nervous. I'd rather be somewhere else... outside the station, for example. I'd rather pay for a cab. I'd rather walk, however long it'd take. Once you've started on that train of thought there's no stopping it. I started pushing and shoving my way to the back of the crowd. People resisted, squeezed back. I was stuck, jammed among them. Now I couldn't breathe, too. I pushed again.

'Mind your stick, mate.' The boy with the nodding head spoke slightly too loudly. I moved my lips but said nothing. He kept nodding, but now smiled amiably. Once I reached the wall the going was easier and I began to shove my way towards the exit. What I wanted was some air. I stood in the first current of air I came to, still in the crowd but with the fresh cool draught running across my face. Some people began to push their way out of the station, but I stayed for a few more seconds, enjoying my draught. Now Lola Junior passed me. I could have reached my hand out and touched her. She walked right by me, slowly, stumbling in the crush. She looked as ill as I felt. The train rumbled into earshot and the yellow indicator board showed Epping 1 min and Hainault 5 min. There was the rush of thick air as the train approached, the sound of thunder from its wheels. I took half a pace towards the exit again. The train entered the station with a blast of air and a steel scream from its brakes. A thousand people breathed a sigh of relief and prepared to elbow their way aboard. Lola Junior changed her mind and turned to join them. I followed, grinding my teeth.

Twenty three

Epping is a long way from Bond Street. The red geometric snake stretches east and north, all of the Central Line, a two-newspaper journey. I didn't take even one newspaper. By the time the train pulled into Epping I'd been reduced to reading the soles of my own shoes. Loakes. Sale, sole, seal, soak, kale and (almost) Koalas. Between Loughton and Debden I tried to read those of the woman opposite, but she tugged at her skirt and left at Theydon Bois with a snooty look and a flash of Dolcis. You can't do much with Dolcis. Solid. Sold. Soil. Clods. Coils. Cisd. Only one more stop to Epping.

Lola Junior, daughter of Janice Conkey, now-known-as-the widow Purnell, lived near the station. I followed Lola Junior uphill to her house through the rain. Hers was a neat, spacious street full of neat and spacious nineteen-thirties semis. Accountant culture. The long twilight had started hours ago. Darkness was falling as Lola stepped into her drive. It's hardly worth turning the lights off in the English winter. I waited some distance away. It's hard to hide on a street like that. Then I saw a large middle-aged man get out of a dark car and follow her up to the front door. I recognised his bulky figure. I gave them a couple of minutes to get inside before I approached the house. I slipped into the front garden.

Some earlier occupant had cultivated the garden. Mature trees shaded the red brick bay-window from the view of passers by. The winter bare trunk of an old passion flower framed the bay. I walked a few paces into the short, gravelled drive, then squeezed between a couple of trees, pressing myself against the ever-wet body of an evergreen honeysuckle. The stem of the honeysuckle was as thick as a fist. I could see through the bay window now. Inside the front room of the house a man sat in the bay extension. He sat at a dining table and he was banging his fist slowly up and down for emphasis. There was no violence in his movement, he was just putting

full-stops on his sentences. I couldn't see his face, nor to whom
he was speaking. As if to answer me the lights came on inside
the bay-windowed room. Greasy Parker lowered his fist again,
was emphasising something to Lola Junior. What? She looked
neither convinced nor scared. She was a very self-confident
young woman. Greasy got fed up emphasising, stood and
pulled on an overcoat. She stood patiently while he finger-
wagged, then saw him to the door. I pressed further back into
my gloomy evergreen Lonicera. The front door opened and
Lola Junior bade farewell to Greasy on the doorstep, a formal
shake of the hands. He was pressing the case for something to
her, but she just listened politely and shook his hand and her
head. A side door opened in the living room and I saw a man
come in, moving slowly and carefully, as if he wanted to be
sure not to be heard by Greasy. It was Brown Boots. The man
stood in the living room, lit like a goldfish in a bowl. Greasy
stood in the doorway wagging his finger and his tongue,
oblivious to Brown Boots a few feet away. Then Greasy gave
up suddenly. He strode past me into the gloom of the
afternoon, jamming a hat onto his head. Greasy must have seen
me if he turned. He passed inches away. I could have touched
him. Even if he'd turned he wouldn't have seen Brown Boots,
who concealed himself from the window as Greasy left the
house. Lola carefully closed the door as Greasy's footsteps
crunched in the drive. After a few seconds Lola came back into
the living room and pulled the curtains; heavy, red jobs;
refugees from a Victorian pub. She'd gone for the whole house
make-over. After a minute or two Brown Boots left the house
too. No doorstep farewells for him. No lover, then. A messenger?
He stole across the road to a Range Rover. I followed, playing
grandmother's footsteps. Brown Boots pointed his keyring at
the Range Rover and the car's alarm beeped in response. I
shoved the Browning into his ribs but he made no noise at all.

   'Hello, sweetheart. It's me. Jenner. I've got your gun trained
on your heart and I'm fed up enough with you to pull the
trigger. So get in the car and keep your movements dead simple.
Any fumblings or turning around and I'll fire. Understood?'

'Yes.'

I wasn't kidding. I wasn't feeling very generous towards him. We got into the car. I sat in the back seat.

'Drive.'

'Which way?'

'Forwards, arsehole.'

He drove. We slipped out of the town towards the forest. At Ivy Chimneys we turned off and found a lay-by hidden from the main road.

'Stop.'

He stopped the car. A car passed us, seemed to pause for a second though his brake lights didn't come on, then drove on.

'What's your name?'

'Peter.'

'Peter what?'

'Kay.'

I leaned over his shoulder and pushed my hand into his jacket. No gun. I reached into his inside pocket and took out his wallet.

'Turn on the light.'

He did. His eyes watched me in the mirror as I went through his wallet. Credit cards, Southwark Council library card, driving licence, Peter Kay, Peter Kay, Peter Kay. He lived in Carter Street, the site of a famous but now defunct police station. I shoved the library card in front of his face.

'Read much?'

'They rent out CDs.'

I threw the wallet onto the front seat.

'Okay Peter Kay, take me to Tommy Slaughter.'

He picked up the wallet and looked at me in the mirror again.

'How am I supposed to do that?'

'You can do it.'

'He's *dead*.'

'Yeah, I know, he's propping up the Westway.'

'So how am I supposed to take you to him?'

I pulled the trigger and shot out the side window next to his head. We were deafened by the sound. The acrid smell of the charge filled the car for a second. The window burst out but a few cubes of broken safety glass fell back upon Peter's shoulder.

'Peter, I am not joking and I do not want you to sit there thinking you can pull the wool over my eyes. Take me to Tommy Slaughter or you're going to have one more hole than you know what to do with.'

I shoved the barrel of his Browning against his temple. He flinched, trying to move his head away. I could feel his temple trembling down the barrel. I brushed the few shards of broken glass off his shoulder and spoke again, very softly.

'Take me to Tommy Slaughter.'

'He died thirty years ago.'

I shot out the other window. This time he went. He wobbled, he pouted, he shouted, he screamed. When he'd finished babbling he breathed, 'He's in the forest!' like a child confessing.

'Where, Peter?'

'Under it.'

'Who put him there?'

'Maltese Mickey.'

'When?'

'Not long... not long. A few weeks ago.'

'Who do you work for?'

'I can't say.'

I tapped him on the cheek with the shooter.

'Don't tempt me, Peter.'

'I can't say because I don't know.'

'Who is the old guy with the blue eyes and the windcheater?'

'Who?'

'Tempting me....'

'Just some guy who was in Slaughter's gang.'

'His name.'

'I don't have his name!'

'But you and he killed Ralph Purnell and the girly, didn't you?'

'No.'

'Yes you did.'

'I don't have his name. He just calls me and tells me where to meet him, what to bring, what to do. I don't have his name.'

'I don't believe you.'

'It's the truth.'

'Where did you meet him?'

'In a pub in the Old Kent Road.'

'What, he just spotted you for a prospect, strolled up to you and said, *'I won't tell you my name, but how about joining me in a career of assassination? Good pay with the prospect of eventual advancement in the business.''*

'Mickey DeWitt introduced me.'

'But you took him the gun he murdered Mickey DeWitt with.'

'That was months later. Anyway, I didn't know he was going to do that.'

'But you knew someone was the target in Sydenham?'

'Yeah.'

'So who did you think it was?'

'You.'

It was getting cold. November is no time to put your windows out.

'Why did he want to kill me?'

'How the hell do I know?'

'You were willing to do it.'

'He gets what he wants. He pays.'

'Is he Tommy Slaughter?'

'No.'

'How do you know?'

'Because he's fucking dead!'

'Don't swear at me, you saucepot. I'm the one with the gun.'

'I'm sorry. I'm sorry. I just know.'

I shot out the windscreen. He's lost his calm completely now. He was quite right to. I was going to put the next one in him. I said very slowly.

'Where is Tommy Slaughter?'

'I don't know.'

'How do you know the grey-haired man was in Slaughter's gang?'

'DeWitt told me. He said they'd been in it together. He said they'd known each other for years. Ralph Purnell too.'

I leaned back in the seat and took careful aim at his head. He could see me in the rear view mirror.

'Where's Tommy Slaughter?'

'I'll show you. I'll show you.'

'You do that.'

He started the engine. He knocked out half the shattered windscreen and drove again. Not far. Just as well. It's too cold in the English winter to drive with all the windows open. We headed towards London. He turned into the forest again before we reached the Wake's Arms, then turned onto an unmade road running right into the forest proper. After a hundred yards or so the road was blocked by a tree trunk laid across it. After that the road became a muddy track. Peter Kay got out and rolled the tree trunk out of the way, then we continued. The dead leaves were thick on the ground. The trunks of bare-limbed trees loomed towards our lights, like the souls of lost Londoners. The forest is an eerie place at night. The car rolled and groaned down the muddy track. We stopped. Why do I have the feeling I've been here before? Peter got out of the car and fetched a lamp and a shovel from the boot.

'He's here,' he said.

'Where?'

'Under the earth.'

He oriented himself from a couple of big oaks, then began to pace out a distance across the fallen leaves. I followed him. Limping. Holding the gun before me. Eventually he found the spot and scraped the leaves off the surface.

'This is where Tommy Slaughter is.'

'How do you know?'

'I put him here. With Mickey DeWitt and Ralph Purnell.'

The black night seemed thick, tangible. I could put my hand on it. Our lamp was puny against it.

'How come you put Slaughter here?'

'He was walled-up in a house in Leytonstone. Behind a plasterboard stud wall. He'd been there for years. Sort of dried-out. Mickey took me there to move him with Ralph.'

'Was there money in the wall, too?'

'Krugerrands. How did you know?'

Was he serious?

'Was there a dispute over the money?'

'No.'

'It was a lot of money. Thousands, maybe hundreds of thousands of pounds.'

'There was no dispute. Mickey didn't need it.'

'And you?'

'It wasn't mine to worry about. I was already being paid. Well paid. I was on to a good thing. I didn't want to upset Mickey.'

'Does the man in the blue windcheater know about the money?'

'No. He doesn't even know I went and helped Mickey. He mustn't.'

'Why?'

'Mickey told me.'

'So Mickey didn't mind that Ralph took the money?'

'Who told you that?'

'A little bird. And you still don't know who this old, grey haired guy is?'

'I swear I don't.'

'Why did Mickey and Ralph want to move the body of Tommy Slaughter?'

'The house was going to be knocked down. Haven't you noticed? They're building a motorway in Leytonstone. All those gimpys up in trees demonstrating. The builders would have found the body.'

'And the Krugerrands?'

'I don't think Mickey and Ralph knew the Krugerrands were there.'

'Hadn't Mickey and Ralph been responsible for walling-up

dear old Tommy in the first place?'

'I don't think so. We had to tear down half the house before we found him.'

I thought for a minute. If Mickey and Ralph didn't know where to look for Tommy it meant someone else immured him. Not Peter Kay. He was learning to walk at the time. I dug him with the shooter.

'Dig.'

Peter dug.

Twenty four

THERE USED TO be a popular game show on television which was split into two halves. The part where the contestants played the game proper, won prizes, laughed, cried and provided all the rest of the ersatz drama television needs, was the second half. But the first half was much more exciting. In this part the contestants competed to be the one winning or losing, laughing or crying later. The first half competition consisted of a tall, bald, scrawny fellow rapid firing questions at each contestant until they were unfortunate enough to say the magic word, which was 'no'. Then a small, bald, fat fellow, who'd crept up behind them, would bang a big gong for all he was worth. Bong! You're out. As a child, I had often sat on the linoleum floor in our council flat watching this game on television, and had even more often wondered what it felt like to be the one who received the shock.

'Are you a girl?'

'No.'

Bong!

Now I know.

Peter had been digging for about ten minutes. He'd excavated a couple of feet. It was easy going. The earth had been dug recently. By him. He stood in the hole he was digging. It came up to his knees. I stood above him with the gun and lamp. He hit something as he dug.

'What's that?'

I leaned forward to peer into the trench.

'Can you see?' he said.

I leaned again. 'No.'

Bong!

Or so it went in my head. My ears rang, my eyes were heavy, my tongue felt a size too big for my mouth. I couldn't support my own weight. I couldn't support my own consciousness. I think I pitched forward. I felt as if I did. It was like

going into a darkened room when you're very tired. I brushed
against Peter Kay as I pitched. I would have clutched at him
but my hands were full. The darkness, the quiet, the comfort of
the darkness again was welcome. I lay on the bed and sunk my
head into the pillow. At first it felt quite good. I dreamt for a
while of a barbecue grill, of game chips and salty sauce. Then
the dream turned sour. I dreamt of prison bars, of steel grills
with my fingers stuck through them, I dreamt of eating cous-
cous but strange tasting stuff, like no tabouleh I'd tasted before.
I didn't like it. I dreamt that the carpet was over my face, that I
was chewing my pillow, building sandcastles, slipping under
the spuming sea on Clacton beach. When I tried to open my
eyes I saw only darkness. My eyeballs hurt. What kind of
darkness *hurts* your eyes? When I tried to sit up I was pinned
down. My ears were plugged, my mouth full, my fingers were
still stuck through the prison bars. I was suffocating in the
dark. I couldn't call. My mouth was full. No one would have
heard, anyway. I realised where I was. Under the earth. My
brain worked very quickly. I'm under the earth. Where? I was
in the grave Peter had dug. Epping Forest yawned above me
while I gasped below its roots. How far to the surface? How
long have I been here? I was buried alive, but not for long. I'd
breathed my last lungful of air. I couldn't guess where I'd get
my next. Not from this stuff. I knew how Joe had felt. I
wondered how long this breath had lasted. I wondered how
long his last breath had lasted him. I was amazed, confused by
how fast my brain was working. How long had I felt like this?
How long is now? How long did I have left? My head hurt, my
pulse banged around inside it. My lungs felt as if they had
been packed hard with cotton. Stuffed. I must breathe. I must. I
struggled furiously to lift my arms, but they were trapped.
Then I felt a weight on my back. It was a surprise. A weight on
my *back*? It meant I was face down. I tried to twist but couldn't.
I tried again to scream but couldn't. I opened my mouth as best
I could but nothing happened. Then there was darkness for a
brief eternity, and I'd lost the fight. I was dull and tired and
dying. Then air hit my mouth and I was gasping, gasping,

gasping. The earth fell away. I was almost free. Strong hands lifted me and I sneezed. My breath came as if someone was jumping up and down on my chest. As if all my ribs were broken. The sensation subsided. My ribs didn't hurt, my lungs no longer felt as if they were a couple of well-kicked footballs. My head hurt sharply at the back, where I'd been hit. Are you a fool, Jenner? No. Bong! I rolled on my back and blinked in the light of a torch. I smelled lime pomade.

'You pratt, Jenner.'

Greasy. I didn't speak. I lay there, just enjoying breathing. He shone the torch beside me. I rolled back and looked where he shone it. I'd been in a shallow grave. The bones of the previous occupant were mixed among the earth I'd churned in my struggle to escape. The bones were in no particular order, or so it seemed. Except that the head was at the top, where heads should be. Thin, desiccated skin stretched over the skull. A clump of hair remained attached. I still held a rib in my hand. I dropped it.

'Look at that,' said Greasy. 'This bloke's a mummy. I've seen that before, a cat that got stuck in an attic.'

I coughed and spluttered god knows what off my chest before I spoke. 'He hasn't been here long.'

'No, Jimmy. This guy's well dead. He's a mummy.'

'Not in Epping bloody Forest he's not! It's wet!'

Greasy leaned back from me and waved his hand in front of his face.

'Ooh. You smell of earth.'

'He's only been here a couple of weeks. He was kept in a plasterboard hidey hole for thirty years. That's what dried him out.'

'Amazing. I never knew it happened to humans.'

'Greasy, what the hell are you doing here?'

'That's a nice way to treat me. I'm looking after you.'

'Thank you....'

'Ungrateful wretch.'

'But how did you know I needed help?'

'You're not invisible, you know. I saw you outside young

Lola's place, standing in the shrubbery. I saw you hijack that young herbert. I must say, I thought you'd done him in when you were parked in the lay-by. Bang bang. Brown underpants. I bet he was pleased, wasn't he?'

'I never asked.'

'You still got the gun?'

I felt around myself, then around the grave. No gun.

'No. Did you see the second man, the one who hit me?'

'No. When you turned off the main road into the woods I went back to the Wake's Arms, parked the car and walked here through the forest.'

'How did you find us?'

'Lights. No one else was showing lights in the forest. I just followed them.'

'What did you see?'

'Two people burying you.'

'Did you disturb them?'

'No. I didn't know what was going on. I just crept up and watched. I thought it was you and the young bloke filling in the hole. Then I saw them walk away and I knew it couldn't be you. No limp, you see. And the second bloke was smaller than you.'

'Did you get a look at the second bloke?'

'No.' He waved his arms, appealing. 'It's dark.'

'Young, old? Tall, small? Could he have been a sort of fit seventy-ish?'

'Could have been a twenty-year-old tart, mate. I don't know for sure.'

I was starting to recover. The difference between life and death is time. That's all. Not much time needs to pass to get you from one absolute state to the other. Since I hadn't died I was alive. A burial which doesn't destroy you improves you. I rubbed some of the dirt off my face.

'Why did you burgle my flat?'

'I didn't.'

'I smelt your pomade.'

'I went there after someone had burgled it. I looked around.'

'Who burgled it?'

'The person I was following at the time.'

'Who was?'

'Peter Kay.'

I stood.

'Why did you go there?'

'I was following him.'

'Why were you following him?'

'Someone told me he'd tried to kill you. Outside L'Etoile. With a pistol.'

'Who told you that?'

'Who do you think? Terry. Your friend.'

'Why would he tell you?

'He cares for you, Jimmy. He wants to protect you.'

'Did you know Peter Kay was in that house in Epping?'

'No.'

'So you weren't following him?'

'No.'

'Why did you visit young Lola?'

'I can't tell you.'

'You don't want to?'

'I can't tell you. Official police business.'

'And this isn't?'

I pointed at the shallow grave. He didn't answer. I tried to brush the dirt off myself. I didn't have much success.

'So what now?' I asked him.

'I'll drive you back to town.'

'What about this?' I pointed at the grave.

'Who is he?'

'I can't tell you,' I said.

'Don't push it, Jimmy.'

'Well, Peter reckoned it was Tommy Slaughter.'

There was a tell tale gap. I could see his brain working in the darkness. The gap was too long.

'Tommy who?'

I swore and staggered away, unwilling to listen to this crap any longer. In the distance I could hear traffic on the roundabout.

I had no stick now and fell over often. My leg was killing me, ghost pains below the knee and real ones above it and on the stump. Once I reached the road I paused for a moment. I remembered Ralph's note. *Wake. N. 200 lb. 20p. fr bin. 60 * 210°15'.* Two hundred yards north of the roundabout was a lay-by. The note contained instructions for finding the grave. That was Ralph's insurance, but the man who shot him never found it. I headed for Loughton Station. It's downhill but a long way on one foot and a knee. After about fifteen minutes a couple of police cars passed me, going in the other direction, blue lights flashing, sirens screaming. Greasy must have called-in the local plod.

I continued down the hill towards Loughton. I walked for a long time. The trees came right up to the edge of the road, crowding me out towards the cars. I slipped and tripped as I walked. I was exhausted. Shadows loomed at me through the forest. Car headlamps flattened me against the great fat tree trunks. I tried hitching. Not many people want to pick up muddy limping scarecrows who stink of the grave. I wasn't surprised no one stopped. Then I was surprised when someone did. I kept walking. He rolled the car along the gutter, just beside me, with the window open.

'Come on. Don't be so picky.'

'Shouldn't you be back there, calling for SOCOs and tying plastic bags to your feet, Greasy?'

'I'm not setting myself thirty-year-old murders to solve. I called it in from a phone box outside the pub. The local police can come and stumble over it.'

'I just don't trust you, Greasy.'

'Jimmy!'

'I mean it. Buzz off. Sling your hook.'

Greasy fumbled by his feet and lifted out my stick.

'Take this at least.'

Loughton was a mere sodium glow in the darkness and I was knackered. I was never going to make it without help. I stopped stumbling down the hill. He pushed open the passenger door. I got in.

'Where do you want to go?'

'The Savoy Grill.'

'You need a reservation.'

'Then you'd better make it my place.'

He drove. I turned my back to him and slept like a baby, hands and head curled around the crook of the stick.

I woke when we were nearly home, turning off the Seven Sister's Road towards the reservoirs. Every muscle and bone in my body seemed to ache. I stretched. All around us London was teeming with life. I felt surprised by it. I felt like a man who'd never seen it before.

'The joint is jumping,' I said.

'Back from the grave, Jenner.'

I didn't answer at first. I watched the cars and the people of North London. I'd never liked them so much before. Greasy was smirking, full of himself.

'You know, I never mentioned thirty years.'

'Thirty years?' He frowned.

'When I asked you about Tommy Slaughter back there, you said *Tommy who?* But when you talked about the dead body, you described it as a thirty year old murder. If you didn't suspect it was Slaughter why did you start talking about *'thirty years'*?'

'We wouldn't be able to prove whether or not that body is Tommy Slaughter, Jimmy.'

'DNA?'

'You need something to compare it to.' Then he clammed up. After thirty five years as a rozzer, open-ness and confessions were just against Greasy's nature.

We were in Stokey Church Street. He stopped the car.

I said, 'You know, we worked in the same nick as each other for a year and you never mentioned you'd known my Dad.'

'Would it have mattered?' he asked. 'Would we have become friends?'

'No.'

'That's my point. I called-in the dead body anonymously. No one knows you were there. No one knows I was there. It's too complicated.'

I tried once more. 'Why did you visit young Lola, Greasy?'

'Official business.'

'You do some bloody funny official business.'

'I know.'

Did I see a glimmer of shame in his eye? If I did it was fugitive. I couldn't find it at a second glance. I got out of the car and strolled across to Defoe Mansions. My leg ached, my head hurt, my eyes were sore and I just hoped I was imagining the putrid taste in my mouth. I wasn't. I stopped and breathed deeply a few times, trying to clear the taste from my mouth with some good old dirty London air.

I walked on. My stride was slow and confident. I affected nonchalance.

There's a limit to how many times you can die.

Twenty five

I SHOWERED AND found some clothes from the untidy pile the burglars had made in my bedroom. Maybe life is better like this. Creased but convenient. Ten million slatterns can't all be wrong. I rang Amy and said I was sorry, this was yet another night I wasn't going to make it. She didn't seem upset.

'You are angry, Chimmee.'

'I've had a bad time. I'll tell you all about it when I see you.'

'Okay.'

'Did Lochinvar drop off the roses?'

'Who?'

'Vaughan. The black guy.'

'Oh yes. He brought me roses. Thanks Chimmee. I forgot. I'd better go. I've got the shower running.' Amy likes decadence as long as there's hot water and a fridge full of Chablis. Tacos and a guacamole dip wouldn't go amiss, either. She put the phone down. No time for gros bisoux and just as well because I wasn't in the mood. I rang Boycey but got an answering machine. 'This is Clean Air Contracts....'

I put the phone down. The red lights were flashing on my own answering machine, but I had more urgent business. I was angry. Back from the grave and angry. I went downstairs and got that Ford to work. Abracadabra. Vroom. It didn't dare resist. I drove the Ford to the Mile End and parked it round the back of the Etoile. I felt the skin creep on my neck as I got out. Fear. Why? What am I scared of? Force of habit. I had nothing to be scared of. As far as brown boots Peter Kay and his nameless ancient killer in the wind-cheater were concerned, I was dead and buried in the Epping Forest. Tonight I slept with the cadavers, with the hastily buried remains of suburban arguments.

Terry was in the usual spot, sipping the usual non-alcoholic brew.

'Tel.' We shook hands.

He smiled. That flat smile of his was half the trouble; Terry looked like some gangster's hit man. Tel was a thin, mean-faced man. He had a full head of steel-grey hair, cropped short, and a grey-looking, lined face to go with it. Terry might have looked like a killer but he was a pussy-cat.

'Drink?' he asked.

'Whatever you're having.'

'Well, you know I don't drink booze, Jimbo.'

'So give me some of that muck.'

The waiter brought a glass and Terry poured me some of his Aqua Libra. Tel sipped the non-booze. I downed mine in one, then poured another from the bottle.

'You'd better watch that stuff.' Flat smile again from Terry. I pulled a face.

'Tel, did you know someone called Peter Kay?'

'No.'

'Young bloke. Well-hard. Dresses like a gay lorry driver, all check shirts and faded denim.'

'Is he a pouf?'

'How the hell do I know?'

Conversation stopped in the room.

'Keep your hair on.'

People began to speak again. But they watched us. 'Do you know him?'

'Not from your description. No.'

'And you didn't tell Greasy this Peter Kay shot at me outside here?'

'No I didn't. How could I if I don't know him?'

'Why does Greasy Parker keep going on about my Dad?'

Terry sipped his Aqua Libra and stared into the polished wood of his bar. Thinking. He stood suddenly and went behind the bar, then through the doorway to the kitchen. A few seconds later he craned his neck around the doorway, then beckoned to me with a finger.

I went round the counter too. The kitchen was a modern one with stainless steel ovens and counters. A plate of steaming mussels stood on the counter in the centre of the room. Terry was at the sink, washing his hands.

'I've sent the cook out the back for a fag.' He turned to face me, shaking the water from his hands. 'No towel.'

I threw Terry a tea towel.

The swing-door behind me opened a fraction.

'Out!' Yelled Tel.

A moustachioed face appeared round the door. Red face, red moustache, red hair. 'The *moules*, Mister Terry.'

'The *moules* are off, tell them.'

The red face looked desperate. 'I've already said the moules are on. They've been waiting ten minutes.'

Terry jerked his head and the waiter came in for the mussels.

'*Moules* only take a minute to cook,' I said.

'People pay for work,' said the waiter, happily. When he'd left Terry said, 'You know that Joe and me were bad boys. But you probably don't know the details.'

'I don't.'

'When I was a kid, I did a few banks. I was never caught. Your brother did them with me. This was the sixties, don't forget. It was easy. You just ran in, shot out the ceiling and had them fill your sack with money.'

'How many?'

'We did it half a dozen times. We made a couple of grand each time.'

'Joe robbed banks?'

'Only a few.'

'Oh well that's all right then.'

'But it went wrong.'

'I'll bet.'

'Joe left a fingerprint outside Barclays in the Rotherhithe Road. And he'd been nicked for thieving when he was a kid.'

'He was bound over for that. And he was a juvenile. They're supposed to throw the fingerprints away.'

'Sometimes you amaze me, Jimmy. They have to say they throw the fingerprints away. That's the law. It doesn't mean they don't keep a copy somewhere, just for reference.'

'Go on.'

'Your brother left a fingerprint outside the bank and got lifted by the Rozzers. But he wasn't charged.'

'Why?'

'I haven't finished. He was lifted in his girlfriend's house down the Blue. Southwark Park Road.'

'Janice.'

'Exactly. So he's nicked in Rotherhithe, the robbery took place in Rotherhithe. We expect an appearance in Rotherhithe nick and Rotherhithe Magistrates Court for a pre-trial hearing. But it never happened. They never took him to Rotherhithe nick. They took him to Tower Bridge. And no sooner does he get to Tower Bridge nick than they take him into a side-room and talk to him. It becomes clear he's not talking to Robbery Squad. He's talking to some coppers from this anti-gangs squad. And they make him an offer. '*Keep your freedom but work for us. Specifically, give us everything you can on Tommy Slaughter*'.'

'How do you know all this?'

'He told me.'

'Why did he tell you?'

'Because only three people knew we'd done that job in Rotherhithe. Your brother, me and Janice Conkey. As soon as they nicked him Janice ran down to the phone box and told me he was in custody. As soon as he was released Joe rang and told me he was out.'

'When did they release him?'

'The next day.'

'And what did Joe boy have to say for himself?'

'A lot of crap at first. A big spiel the anti-gangs coppers had given him. Well, they knew he'd have to have a story. The guys from the anti-gang squad told anyone who'd listen there hadn't been enough evidence against him. Joe did the same. They'd even provided him with a lawyer who could 'spring' him.'

'Don't tell me. Menke.'

'That's right.'

Someone tried the kitchen door. Terry put his foot against it for a second.

'Joe was a terrible liar.' He held his finger and thumb so that they nearly touched. 'It took about this much pressure to get him to tell me they'd let him go on the basis he helped them put Tommy Slaughter away.'

'Or?'

'Or?'

'It's a dangerous course of action. There must have been a threat over Joe. So, 'or?''

'Prison.'

'Not enough.'

'That's what he told me.'

'And you just accepted it? You must have been a lot dopier when you were young.'

He made no reply.

'What about my Dad and Greasy?'

'Greasy was a young DC on the anti-gangs squad. He was the copper who convinced Joe to do it.'

'That bastard.'

'He was doing his job, Jimmy. Just doing his job.'

'Haven't we swapped roles here? Aren't I the ex-copper with right wing tendencies and you the kind-hearted bar keeper?'

He didn't reply. The door opened again, the waiter looked at us and left again without a word. The gas in the ovens hissed behind us. Terry had a proper kitchen. The back door opened and a man in a long white apron came in. Liam the chef. He pointed accusingly at the table. 'Who's took my *moules*?'

Terry clapped him on the back. 'You're a suspicious man, Liam, that's your trouble. The waiter's had your *moules*. Presumably he was the fellow who asked you for them in the first place.'

Liam went back to his stove muttering about parsley.

'Let's go for a walk, before the chef kills me.'

'In the street?'

'Jim, you're getting like Liam. You worry too much. I'll bring us an umbrella each.'

So we went for a walk.

Twenty six

THE STREETS WERE cold and dark and wet and I felt it. We needed the umbrellas. Terry talked as he walked with me, and he seemed to walk me for miles. I was suddenly tired and my limbs were heavy. My head hurt and my eyes stung, my steps were leaden. My limbs ached, present or not. Terry talked and talked as we walked. I listened.

'When Joe died, Greasy and your father met.'

'How?'

'I introduced them.'

'Why?'

'Because your Dad thought Joe was weak and useless. Your Dad could never see any good in Joe.'

'It hurt him when Joe died.'

'Of course. Twice as much as it should have done.'

'Because he felt guilty over his useless elder son.'

'Yes. I introduced your Dad and Greasy so that your Dad would know there was more to it. So that he'd see there was good in Joe.'

'I don't believe you,' I said. 'What did Greasy know about it?'

He sighed.

'If only you two had come along in the right order.'

'What does that mean?'

'You were the stronger son. Your Dad knew it, Joe knew it. The whole bloody world knew it.'

'If Joe was weak and useless so were you.'

'How's that?'

'How else would you describe robbing banks? Rushing in with your shotguns and balaclavas. Terrifying teenaged cashiers into crapping their trousers and handing over the lolly. It's not very brave, Terry. It's not all that clever, either.'

'We were hungry...'

He held up his hand as I went to interrupt. We weren't hungry.

'... for success. For change. It was the sixties. The affluent society. London was swinging. Why couldn't we join in? Everyone was having a whale of a time, except us. We were just a couple of stupid bastards from Bermondsey. A couple of yobs. If Harold Wilson's wonderful bloody white hot techno- logical society had belly fluff, we were it. How else would we get up there with the others? Study hard and get a degree in medicine? Start up a business? What with? Shirtbuttons?'

'You've done it now.'

'I got the chance to change.' His voice was passionate. 'Joe didn't.'

There's no answer to that. Not only do those who die young miss out on old age and frailty, they evade the opportunities for self-improvement the rest of us have to bear. So Joe was smart for once. Good old, nineteen-sixties, forever-young-man, un-reconstructed Joe, true to his own nature. In his way.

But I wasn't satisfied with Terry's story.

'How did the police get Joe to spy on Slaughter for them?'

'Threatened, I suppose. Not prison. He wasn't scared of that, and frankly you'd have been a big man if it was known you'd gone to prison rather than split on Tommy Slaughter. He'd have made his reputation, in our world.'

'So?'

'I don't know. I thought we might get an answer here.'

'What's here?'

'Maureen Nicolson.'

'Never heard of her.'

'Mobile Maureen. Ring any bells?'

We were outside some modern council flats off the Cambridge Heath Road.

'Nope. Should she?'

'You'll see.'

He pressed half a dozen entry-phone buzzers at once, announced himself as a social worker trying to get in to help an old lady and sure enough someone let us in. It never fails.

The flats looked like they were one-bedroom jobs occupied by houseproud old people. The stairs were clean and the front doors had their small square neat brass knockers polished. The place smelled of Harpic. Clean round the bend. There was no loud music and none of the smell of urine I associate with the stairwells of Bethnal Green council flats, just disinfectant on the stairs and landings and the soft chatter and weak-brained music of television commercials behind drawn curtains.

'Maureen is famous for two things,' said Terry as we mounted the stairs, 'One is for running a mobile knocking shop around Salmon Lane in the nineteen-sixties.'

'A mobile *knocking* shop?'

'Hence 'Mobile Maureen', as she was called. Two girls and herself in a big camper van, a converted Commer ambulance done out like a Tuareg prince's idea of heaven. Red velvet, tassels, big plumped-up cushions, Arab rugs and all that caper. She used to lurk outside a phone box. Somewhere she never did any business. Then people would give her a ring and she'd bring the camper van and the girls round to them. Kerb crawling done in reverse, so to speak. It was her way of defeating the Street Offences Act. 'Camper vans' are not 'premises' by any stretch of the imagination.'

'And as long as she did it herself too no one could prove she lived off immoral earnings.'

'Clever girl, eh?'

'Why did she go out of business?' I asked.

'Everything has to end.'

We'd reached the top of the stairs. Terry caught his breath. I'd never thought of him as middle-aged before. He's well over fifty now, so, why not?

'Are you all right?' I asked.

'Fine. It's just over there.'

'You said she was famous for two things.'

'Well, actually it's the other thing she's really famous for. You see, Maureen's little idea was driving the Vice Squad nuts. You can imagine. They all knew who she was and what she was up to but they couldn't figure out a way to collar her. So they put on uniforms and started breathalysing her about three times a week. The idea was that if they couldn't collar her they could at least ruin her business. Breathalysing was all the rage then with the coppers because it hadn't long been introduced. Mobile Maureen was very cautious, of course, but eventually they copped her for excess alcohol on a New Year's Eve. This must be oh, about twenty five years ago. More. Thirty maybe. Now comes the thing, the second thing mobile Maureen's famous for. Maureen develops a plan. Comes the day of the court hearing and she sacks her brief, to whom she has described the plan and who is down on his knees outright begging her not to do this to herself. Maureen won't listen. The brief is so impressed he goes into the public benches just to watch the amazing events he knows are about to unfold. Maureen goes into court, explains to the magistrate she's sacked her brief and will do her own pleading. The top-Johnny magistrate laughs, 'Are you experienced enough to shoulder this burden, Miss?' he asks. They know Maureen well in the magistrate's court, you see. Well enough that they don't need evidence of character. So they're all sitting there, nearly sniggering with pleasure, and Maureen's up on her hind legs defending herself. Normal people had a lawyer, Maureen was a fully-paid-up member of the awkward squad, she had to do it herself. She pleads not guilty to the Magistrates, saying she hadn't taken one drop of alcohol all that day nor the day before nor the day before that.'

'That's common. Lots of people claim that.'

'And it doesn't cut any ice. Of course. But Maureen hadn't finished. What she *had* been doing, Mobile Maureen told the Magistrates, is giving blow-jobs to drunken clients all evening. More than a dozen. She reckons she got the alcohol from there. From giving blow-jobs to drunken punters. You can imagine the scene in court. Their Honours the Magistrates, when they got back on their chairs and done a lot of coughing and blowing and sneezing into their handkerchiefs, take a glass of water each and have a little conflab with the Magistrate's Clerk before telling her this is anatomically unsound. Can't be done.'

We had walked along a landing. Bright lights of Bethnal Green shone below us, inky black streets between. I could hear a siren in the distance but I couldn't see the blue light.

'And Maureen, all part of the act, looks downcast, as if she's thinking, *'drat, another good defence gone for a burton'*. So, highly amused, the top-johnny Magistrate straightens his face out with some difficulty and, feeling rather pleased with himself since he's such a wag, as legal people often see themselves, asks her out of interest where she got a dozen drunken clients from, one after the other on the trot like that.'

Terry stopped and rang the bell at a door. It didn't look very different from any other front door, certainly not exciting enough to be the door of Mobile Maureen.

'And, looking as if she's realised all of a sudden that she's going to take a caning here, and honesty would be the best policy with such a grandee as the top-Johnny magistrate, Maureen pipes up, *'Oh, easy. I did the entire night shift at Tower Bridge nick, Your Honour, one after another. And the Vice Squad put me up to it'*.'

I laughed. We waited. I shivered again.

'I'm bloody freezing.'

Terry put his finger to his lips. After a while a bolt slid and the door opened. I was confronted with a woman in her early-sixties. Her hair was dyed black and piled on top of her head. She wore patent, sling-back shoes and a body-hugging slinky black dress. Considering her age Maureen had managed to keep the body the dress hugged in pretty good shape, but discretion might have dictated a looser fit. Her dark eyes flashed with some sort of proprietary liquid glitter. The fresh bright-red lipstick explained the delay in opening the door.

'Oh,' she said, disappointed. 'I was expecting a friend.'

'What's that supposed to mean?'

'Whatever you want it to mean, Terry Crisp.'

'I *am* a friend.' He sounded genuinely hurt. Maureen stepped aside.

'Come in before someone sees you.'

We went in. We followed her through a flock-lined hallway and into the living-room. There was deep carpet underfoot and enough musk in the air to make me want to gag. The living-

room walls were lined with something very like thin, gold-
printed red leather and along one wall was a brown leather,
deep-buttoned chesterfield almost as long as the room itself.

'Jimmy Jenner, my friend Maureen Nicolson.'

'Jimmy Jenner,' she looked at me. She leaned on the 'Jenner'.
I looked back, straight back. She took my hand for a second.

'Jimmy is ... '

'I know who Jimmy is.'

'Of course you know who Jimmy is. He's a friend of mine,
Maureen.'

'And?'

'And he wants to know some things about his brother Joe
and the late Tommy Slaughter.'

'So you tell him.'

'I don't know what you know.'

Maureen looked at me for a second, then decided. 'No. I'm
busy.'

'So's he.'

'I have a life you know.'

'I know.'

'Say I don't want to tell him?'

Terry was unmoved.

Maureen wrinkled her carefully painted face and pleaded, 'I
haven't got time, Terry. I'm expecting someone.'

'He won't come for ages. You depend on me.' He pointed at
me. 'Put the kettle on, tell him what he wants to know while I
wait outside. There's a good girl.'

'No.'

Terry tapped Maureen's shoulder.

'Do it. Tell him everything. Maureen.'

He left. She stood in the centre of the room, looking unhappy. Looking uncertain.

'I don't want any tea,' I said. She ignored me and went to
the sideboard for a bottle of port wine and some lemonade. She
didn't offer me any.

'I don't like port,' I said.

'So that's okay,' she said with her back to me. When she'd

mixed the drink to her satisfaction she sat on the sofa and smiled at me.

'Are you comfortable?' I asked.

'Fine.'

'Good.' A long time passed. Eventually I said, 'Aren't we going to talk?'

'No,' she said.

Another long time passed. I could feel the veins in my temples throbbing. They were beating out a tattoo. Sleep, Jenner. My eyelids closed for the briefest of moments before I gained control again.

I said, 'Your friend hasn't come.'

She ignored me.

'Maybe he's just late,' I suggested. Empathy Jenner, that's me. You've got to start somewhere.

'Terry's told him to push off,' she said bitterly. 'That's why he went out there.'

Another silence. Her gas fire hissed where there should be a hearth. There was none. The gas fire was set on the wall, and was entirely unnecessary as the little flat was centrally heated. I felt so tired. I was sweating, I realised. I could barely keep my eyes open as I waited for her to speak. I could barely keep my eyes open but I didn't dare force the pace with her.

'Why did you come here now?' she said. She drained her port and lemon.

'Terry brought me.'

'What's wrong with you?'

Good question. I was near to fainting.

'I feel a bit ill.'

'You look it. Lie down,' she said.

I obeyed. I kicked off my shoes and tucked my hands under my face like we used to at school after lunch, when the nuns told us to take a nap. Some nap. I woke in the small hours. I could feel the leather creases of the chesterfield on my face. Maureen was motionless, sitting opposite me. Her glass was full again. A blanket lay over my shoulders. I shivered. The fire was still lit. She didn't seem cold.

'What's the time?'

'One.'

'Jesus.'

'You've got a fever.'

'Where's Terry?'

'I sent him home hours ago.'

'I'm cold.'

She left the room for a second and came back with an eiderdown. Only women over sixty have an eiderdown. It was dark green with diamond stitching. She fetched me a glass of water too. It stung my throat like whisky and made my gut ache.

'What the hell is that?'

'Water. Shall I make you some tea?'

'No. Thanks.'

'You were talking,' she said. 'While you were asleep.'

Was I?

'You were dreaming.'

'No.' I said weakly. But I was. I closed my eyes and remembered. I had dreamt about the past. No one dreams more about the past than me. I worry about the past. I'm a setter-to-rights of the past. I know little about the future except it is to come, even in my dreams. I'm a philosopher in my dreams. I'm bloody clever in my dreams. If you know about the future the only thing that's certain is that you know nothing. If you know more about the future you're cleverer than I am even in my dreams, which I doubt. I know about people, that's all, and what we can say about people relies on the past. The future was hidden from the people we were just as the past is revealed to the people we are. This paradox torments me. I am constantly tempted to set things right which can't be set right, to try to avoid things which have already happened. Why? Guilt. After all, I'm still here, alive and kicking.

If in the past we had known what was to come we would have tried some avoiding action, don't cross that road, don't walk down that street, don't meet that person, go hungry, don't go into that restaurant. Where would it end? We'd wind up clucking over our own futures like a mother hen. Here comes the paradox, though, running, stumbling, bumping around the corner: each of us, however cunning our evasions, would have failed to change the net result. Why? Because the result is just that. An outcome. Only ever seen over your shoulder. Philosophy, see? I know all about philosophy. Albert Camus, drive my car. I can't. I'm sweating bloody buckets.

I was waiting above a *calanque* outside Marseilles for Amy. We'd gone to visit her mother. Patricia, like the song. If only she'd been light, like the song. She had coarse features that said more Slav than Frenchwoman. Patricia owned a bar above the *calanque* where they sold something that looked very like fried whitebait. I never asked exactly what it was. The mother didn't work in the bar, of course, she simply owned it. Actually she lived in a Paris suburb and had a lot of stocks and shares. She didn't work at all. I think she inherited the bar from her father. He'd been a southern peasant. She'd inherited her manners from him too, from the way she ignored me. It was the only time we ever met, but Patricia hated me on sight. The feeling was mutual. I never knew fat gold chains looked so bad on oiled, burnt, wrinkled, female skin. I lie. Of course I knew. I'd just never been closely connected with someone who looked like that.

We'd gone for lunch. A thousand miles for lunch. The mother roasted a rolled piece of beef in the bar's little private kitchen. Before she put it in the oven she'd cut up some garlic and put it in the joint. Patricia shoved her fingers into the meat, two fingers in a gesture which was pure obstetrics. Her digits emerged pink and bloody. I wasn't sure if I'd ever eat meat again. I'd left Amy and Patricia to discuss the price of whitebait or how hard it was to park a new Mercedes in Marseilles without it getting scratched. I'd gone down to sit on the limestone rocks in the creek, surrounded by brown, almost naked perfect bodies. The sea glistened a dazzling oily light at me. The sky was so bright it was white. I had no sunglasses. I sat on the rock and peered through my fingers. The flesh made pink venetian blinds over my eyes. I sat on my rock, more

conscious than ever of my awkward body. I felt like a casualty.
I was. No self-pity now, Jenner, I warned myself. The sun beat
on my head. The light prised open my fingers. A child smiled
and allowed herself to fall back in the water. Above me I knew
Amy and her mother were licking their bloody chops and
wondering where the hell I was. It mad me feel like a sacrifice
to a couple of jaguars. They knew where I was. They were just
waiting for me to come back with my tail between my legs,
waiting with that certainty and superiority women sometimes
allow you to see. I shivered. My stomach turned over. Was it
the sun or the cepes I'd eaten on the way down? I felt like
getting in the water. Beside me it looked black and cool and
soothing. I could have done with a swim but couldn't take all
the staring. A man with jet black hair and olive arab tones in
his skin swam past me, then climbed out on a rock and shook
himself like an otter. Nearby his stunningly normal family
were preparing a picnic. Wife and two kids, one of each. He
skipped and tip-toed across the rocks to join them. They all
laughed. For a moment a pang of anger and jealousy touched
me. What bloody right had they? I'd never felt more foreign. I
stood and began to climb up the side of the *calanque*. I walked
past the wooden shack that housed the bar. It stank of roasted
meat. Outside the back of the bar a pile of past-it whitebait
rotted. The stench close to it was unbelievable. I climbed a
white dusty road onto the barren cliff. I found my rented car, a
white Renault. I ran the engine so the air-conditioner could
come on. I dozed for an hour, maybe two, like that, curled-up
in a white Renault, switching the engine off now and then to
avoid it overheating. Switching it on again to avoid me
overheating. As I had climbed the side of the *calanque* I'd
decided Amy would have to go. That was three months ago
and I'd done nothing about it. Why? Cowardice? Loneliness?
I'd instead semi-detached myself from her. Our affair hadn't so
much been strangled as been caught on a stifled yawn. I woke
with a start, baking, and reached out for the Renault key to
start the engine and the air-conditioning again. I didn't find it. I
was in Maureen's flat.

'Do you want more water?'

'If only. I can't.'

'Why?'

'My throat hurts too much.'

I must be straight with Amy, I thought. I wish I had been. 'I'm sorry, but you're failing to fill the shoes of someone else and even though you're doing it well in your own way, it's no bloody good.' That's what her mother had smelt on me, the disloyalty of my heart. It's a kind of faithlessness which nothing can mend. I made a mental note to be straight with Amy. Again. If only I had been straight straight away. Don't flatter yourself, matey. Amy couldn't give a toss. Judy could and she's marrying someone else, someone she'll hate soon if she doesn't now. If only I could find some way to intervene. If is the important word. If, if, if. If my brother Joe in nineteen-sixty-eight could have foreseen the gas trench falling in and crushing him even as he dug he never would have dug... it. If. But dig he did, as surely as my father smoked all those rollies and drank all those whiskys that killed him in the end. Now he must have known what that would bring.

I indulged myself. I dreamt a few more regrets. Why not, once you've got started? I don't remember my mother, not really, so I have to speculate her face, draw her up from a few photos. If I could do better, I would. If. If I had known that there would come a day when only one of us was left alive and that the one would be me I would have done anything (I do not exaggerate here, I mean ANYTHING) to avoid it.

If. There I go dreaming those 'ifs' again. But if I'd known our last meal had been our last meal I'd have clutched my family to my then small-child's breast and held them then for all and ever, even my amorphous and ill-defined mother, who in my memory has to do with a photo for a face. Even my brother, who truth to tell didn't like me much. We were, after all, the same stuff, Joe Boy and me.

In my dream I'd remembered it was Joe who told me Mickey DeWitt had Tommy Slaughter killed. In my dream he thought that was funny. Very funny. Why?

I dropped Maureen's glass, not meaning to. It didn't really matter. I'd drunk the water. She took the glass and tucked my arm under the eiderdown again.

I remember where I was when Tommy Slaughter died too. It was nineteen sixty eight. I was in a youth club in Woolwich, St Mary's, with a girl who had a reputation for going bandy but wouldn't for me. She nearly would but nearly's not enough. If I was going to get my hand inside her drawers I should have brought a crow-bar. I remember thinking, 'This must be what sainthood is like. Me and Saint Mary ablaze in a bus shelter. But ablaze with all our clothes on, and our hands visible for all the world to see.'

While Mary lit up Woolwich with me Tommy Slaughter was getting it in Greenwich. Bang bang bang bang. He was no saint. Slaughter was Bermondsey's own one-man missile crisis, a self-appointed psychopathic Khrushchev, a forty-year-old conscience-less bastard. By my day, by the time I remembered him, Slaughter had gone 'up West', buying into night-clubs, taking over rings of whores from Maltese pimps who were without his contacts in the police. By the time I *remember* him (as opposed to remember what I know about him) Slaughter had a network of go-betweens, lesser yobs who would arrange his affairs, collect his money, pay off his bent coppers.

How did I get to Greenwich? It's a long way from Dockhead. Miles. I know. I missed the last train and had to walk most of the way back.

Maureen was sitting opposite me in a blue housecoat now. She'd taken her make-up off and wore fluffy mules on her feet.

'I'll get a cab.'

'You won't. Just sleep. Terry will come for you in the morning.'

'I'll phone my girlfriend.'

'She won't like it.'

'You don't know her.'

'It's four.'

'Four what?'

'In the morning.'

'I should phone her.'

Why? Why did I suddenly feel the need to commune with Amy in the middle of the night? For a moment I had no idea. Then I remembered my note to myself. Be straight with her.

Joe drove me. That's how I got to Woolwich. I remember. I met a girl from Woolwich and asked her for a date and Joe drove me out to her house. She lived in a tiny house on a huge hill. Joe drove me in some car he'd borrowed. It was a flash car. I'd love to say it was a Jag-you-are but I really don't remember, even in a dream. Was it Slaughter's car? No. It couldn't have been. Slaughter loved driving himself. He loved his Jag. There were things Slaughter did for himself. Like drive the Jag. And kill people.

Slaughter was a real killer. His first effort that I remembered was a man with hatchet holes in his head lying in the Sunday morning sunlight in the square before the next-door flats to ours. It was autumn and leaves swirled around his clotted blood, as if they were interested. Revellers from an all night knees-up stayed on their first floor balcony, unsure, also interested. The man with the holes was famous in Bermondsey for having crossed Slaughter some months before, and had seemed until then to be fireproof, or to live a charmed life. When we saw the hatchet headed body in the square we all knew who'd done it. The police came, took the body, knocked on all the doors. No one knew anything. If Slaughter wanted to impose his will, if he wanted to frighten people he had the reputation of doing his dirty-work himself, wiring his victims up to the mains and pausing over the switch to ask did they agree with him. They did. The police only asked politely 'did you see anything?', so everyone said 'no'.

Tommy Slaughter's end came on a Saturday night and Sunday morning too. It was nineteen sixty eight. On the Saturday night he went to a house down the Grange Road, Bermondsey. Slaughter – so the story goes – thought he was going to a meet with a Maltese pimp, some feudal baron come down from Soho to pay homage to King Tom Slaughter. Why Grange Road, Bermondsey? Safety, I expect. It's not much of a road. There was a swimming baths down the other end in those days and when they chucked out streams of slick, wet-headed kids used to flow towards Tower Bridge Road, the nearest pie-and-mash shop. It's gone now. As they ate their clothes itched. Too much chlorine. I know. I'd been one of them in my time.

I'm sure that Slaughter reckoned more than one Maltese gangster would have stuck out amongst this mob of slick haired midgets and bag-on-wheels-toting old ladies. He was right, but being right didn't stop his motor being found on Crooms Hill, Greenwich the next morning, doors open, leather seats soaked in blood, occupants noticeable by their absence. Tommy Slaughter and Freddie Phillips, his driver, disappeared... whoosh, just like that, taken up by UFOs, except they left their blood behind.

So the view was Tommy Slaughter underestimated the Maltese. According to my brother he'd underestimated Mickey DeWitt. Ordinary people didn't care how Slaughter died, just that he'd died. The rumour got around that Slaughter and Freddie Phillips had been popped into a concrete pillar supporting the M40 at Notting Hill. It's a wry thought, the two of them there for all eternity, trapped in concrete with lorries rattling their teeth as they passed over, unable to get as much as a game of dominoes going between them as they sat side by side, waiting for the end of the world. I never believed in it myself. They must have had quality inspections on the concrete of the M40 and more simply Crooms Hill, Greenwich is not on the way from Grange Road, Bermondsey to Ladbroke Grove. Bang bang bang bang. That's how it must have been. Bang bang. Bang bang. For the two of them. Some shot, eh? Unless it never happened.

Joe drove me to Woolwich the same day Slaughter died in Greenwich. I think he may have driven me there in Slaughter's car. No wonder he laughed when people talked about Slaughter's death. He drove Slaughter's car to the appointed place. But Slaughter wasn't in the car. I was.

Years later, dreaming on Mobile Maureen's chesterfield, it occurred to me that Crooms Hill is quite posh, but that no one had seen or heard a thing. No gunshots, no cars pulling up, no men running away, no voices. No moans, groans or dragged heels. That's something else we have in common. All of us. Middle class, working class, law-and-order, Neighbourhood Watch or not. We all suffer fear.

'You talked in your sleep,' Maureen said.

'I dreamt.'

'I know. You were talking about someone.'

'I dreamt about my wife,' I lied. Anyway, she's not my wife any more. Instead I've Amy down the Old Ford Road. Who '*as come to Engerland for zee decadence*', she told me once, straight-faced. She calls herself an artist, but doesn't look like she's running up a big bill at Rowney's. Apparently you do not need to invest much in paint or clay to become an artist now. It can be your life. It can be your leavings. It could be your crap, literally. It could be a video of your crap. It can be whatever can be interpreted by whatever the viewer brings to it.

'Does there have to be a viewer?'

'No.'

'Then it sounds like a description of a sewer to me.'

'You don't understand.'

Amy explains why and what I don't understand to me like she's talking to the world's oldest man. Amy has a thoroughly French liking for (and misunderstanding of) philosophy, and has acquired English friends with nancy accents and mouths like coal-holes who also claim to know what's what in the thinking stakes. Amy's friends do not think much of me, a one-legged, dirty and frequently dishevelled cockney private detective. They think Amy has merely acquired me as a sign that she embraces decadence. Or is it the bourgeois? Amy's friends hold dinner parties where they shout the odds about time and existence and our future and why we're here. It makes them feel clever. Amy carts me along to these dinner parties and I sit there wondering, 'Why am I here?' Now there's an existentialist impasse. Amy's friends shout at me, 'Got it, Jenner? Got it now?' All right, all right. I've got it. Don't shout. I ain't deaf except in the one ear.

I play dumb for Amy's chums. Not only do I know what a paradox is, I can spell it. I've been to dinner parties in West London. Also I've argued myself round in circles, without even needing an audience.

*

Later I woke again. My father had taken Maureen's place opposite me, as if it was the most normal thing in the world. I didn't complain, though he looked pretty young. If he'd still been alive he'd have been ninety-nine. But he sat before me, sixty-something in a white no-collar shirt with his worsted trousers nearly up to his armpits and his black hair slicked back into a widow's peak, and he said, '*I know I'm hard on you. I wish I could take everything that was in me and tie a bow around it and hand it to you. I wish I could get the experience in you by some direct, magical method. But I can't.*' Which was bollocks. It was the way he would have talked to Joe if he'd had the nerve. Actually my father never would have revealed himself like that. And also, while we're having a clear out, it wasn't the way he would have talked to me. Ever. He was never once 'hard' on me. I was his baby. So what was that all about? It just goes to show how much you can trust dreams.

*

I don't know how much later Maureen made tea. She poured into two almost transparently thin china cups while I watched. It still wasn't light outside. I felt a lot better. The eiderdown was soaked with sweat. It made me cold. She was dressed now in a nightie and dressing gown. She sat by my side and handed me the thin china cup. I sipped it. She'd softened. I took my chance.

'Do you know how my brother got involved with Slaughter?'
'No.'
'But you knew Slaughter?'
'Yes.'
I waited. I drank my tea. I sat up and threw off the covers.
'You're better?'

'No. I just can't afford to croak on your sofa. Tell me Maureen, what do you know?'

Maureen stretched her arms in front of her. She flicked the fingertips away from her. Fear, anxiety – it's not tiredness, that stretching.

'So what became of him, this fearsome friend of yours?' I asked.

'You know.'

'Tell me.'

'Someone done him and his driver both. People say they're propping up the motorway out by Ladbroke Grove. The police found their motor down in Greenwich full of bullet holes and blood.'

'You remember it well?'

She looked me in the eye. 'It was a lovely car.'

'You sound as if you'd been in it.'

Maureen sipped her tea.

'Of course I had. Lots of times.'

'I mean that evening.'

'The police took me to see it afterwards because they'd found my prints in it.'

'No others?'

'No.'

'Not my brother's?'

'Not that they told me.'

'Not mine?'

'Why would yours have been in the car?'

'Joe gave me a lift in it.'

'Well not yours or Joe's. Just mine.'

'Why?'

'How the hell do I know why?'

I gave her a few seconds but she didn't speak again.

I asked. 'What do you think happened to Slaughter?'

Maureen sipped her tea again, but this time put it down deliberately and crossed to the window.

'No idea,' she said, looking out into the night. I could see her face reflected in the glass, edges softened by refraction, image on image. I went and joined her. Stood close behind her. Now I could see both our reflections in the glass, darkened by the glass, and so could she.

'You've recovered.'

I hadn't and it was obvious. But Maureen was again obsessed with her own thoughts. She barely looked at me. Eventually she said, 'I expect he told you about the passion wagon.'

'Terry said you were famous for it. He was quite proud of you.'

'Terry Crisp was proud of *me*? It was *his* idea. So was the nutty defence in court.'

'For a laugh?'

Maureen shook her head. 'Of course not. Who does things like that for a laugh, Jenner?'

'Then....'

'Revenge. Terry paid me a couple of grand to get revenge for him.'

'How?'

'There were some coppers at Tower Bridge he wanted to embarrass. The guy who ran the Gangs Squad, for a start. One or two others. Terry knew that if we could make a laughing stock of them, it was the most he could hurt them. It was best revenge available. Then the people who run the police force would sack them.'

'It doesn't work like that. If he's of that sort of rank they'd just promote him and ship him out.'

'I didn't say it worked. It was just what Terry wanted. Anyway, nothing hurts policemen more than being laughed at.'

'Why did Terry want revenge on them?'

'He thought they were responsible for your brother dying.'

'Were they?'

Her face in the window stiffened slightly.

'What did my brother do?'

'He was a navvie.'

'Yes. He dug gas trenches. All muscles. Between the ears too, my father used to say.'

'Poor boy.'

'What did my brother do?' I repeated.

'He did a bit of muscle for Slaughter.'

'Come on Maureen. I mean, what did he do when Slaughter died? What was his part in it?'

'I don't know. Really I don't. I wasn't there at the end.'

'Could he have been present at the end?'

'Yes. Joe could've.'

'But you weren't?'

'I had a drink with them in a house somewhere in Bermondsey.'

'Grange Road?'

'That's it.'

'Who was 'them'? Who was there?'

'Tommy, Freddie Phillips, Micky DeWitt, Ralph Purnell.'

'You?'

'And another couple of girls.'

'Janice?'

'Janice?'

She wasn't convincing.

'My brother's bird,' I said. 'Janice Conkey as was, Lola Purnell as is.'

'Yes. She was there.'

I peered past our reflections into the dark. She turned to face me, very close to me. I could feel her breath and smell her cheap perfume. I'd begun to like her but now I had to suppress the most intense sensation of disgust. It washed over me like a wave, then left.

'Did Terry Crisp tell you how they got nicked?' She asked.

'Yes. The robbery.'

'It was a set up. The police knew that he and Joe were knocking over banks.'

'How do you know?'

'Terry told me. He also told me your brother agreed to act as the man on the inside in Slaughter's gang.'

'He *what*?'

'He was a police informer. Joe gave them the inside track on Tommy Slaughter.'

'Why?'

'Why do I get to tell you? I'm wondering that myself.'

'Why did Joe help them?'

'They had him and Terry for the robberies. Terry was no use, he was rowing his own boat. But your brother was on the fringes of Slaughter's gang. And he really wanted to be in it. Really wanted. Just as the Gangs squad really wanted to be in it, too. So he was their man. The police stood back and let Joe dig...' We looked at each other for a second. 'They let him have his way, as long as he was their man. Joe got them enough evidence to jail Slaughter.'

'How do you know?'

'He told me.'

'But they didn't do it.'

'No.'

'And you still haven't explained why.'

'More tea?'

'No. Thanks anyway.'

She would have preferred me to ask for tea. Instead she had to plough on. Plough into it.

'The Gangs Squad told him the Robbery Squad would put you in the frame for the bank robberies, with Terry and Joe.'

'Me?'

'You.'

'But I was a teenager.'

'I know.'

'And the robberies were done by two men. Not two men and a boy.'

'Two men. Three. What did they care? This is the sixties. If the police tell the witnesses there were three robbers, there were three robbers. If someone insisted there were only two, they'd simply have claimed you'd been one of the two. Anyway, you were a kid. Who knows whether they would have actually done it.'

It was an assertion, not a question. But I asked myself the question. Who knows? Greasy, of course. My grubby guardian angel. He knows whether they'd have actually framed the teenage Jimmy Jenner or not. No wonder he has a guilty conscience.

'Joe was a dreamer. A fantasist,' I said.

'He was in the real world. He became a member of Slaughter's gang and he did what the police asked him to until they had enough to put Slaughter away. And he did it to stop the Robbery Squad framing you. What more could you want from a brother?'

'Is that supposed to make me feel better?'

'I don't care whether you feel better or not. I'm telling you. That's what your brother did.'

No wonder my father was angry when Joe had died. Terry had persuaded the young PC Greasy to tell my old man how helpful his elder son had been to the police. My father had had to think his way down the same grubby path I'd just followed. Greasy wouldn't have told him about the implied threat to me, but the old man would have worked it all out eventually. He was very clever, my old man. Cleverer than me and Joe put together. No subtlety of the situation would have escaped him. he'd just have been hurt that he didn't foresee it.

'I'm tired now. I'm going to bed. You can sleep on the sofa,' Maureen said. 'Terry can fetch you in the morning.'

But I turned to look for my shoes.

Twenty seven

I LEFT MAUREEN'S. Downstairs it was raining again, real full-blooded English rain. Water crept over the welts of my shoes. It only matters in one. I should buy a galosh. I walked towards Cambridge Heath, thinking, half-meaning to go home and sleep. Then I decided to go back and get a cab. I hung around Bethnal Green. A house nearby sported a blue plaque to an ancient boxer. The streets were silent and empty. I trembled in the darkness until I could cop a cab to Dockhead. It's not easy to get one during the night. They start by giving you all that, *'that's over the river, ain't it? I ain't going that way mate'* spiel. I tell them straight, *'I don't care what way you're going. I ain't asking you for a lift, John. I'm hiring you.'* You have to make sure you're sitting in the back of the cab before you say this, otherwise you end up standing in the gutter with a neat line of tyre marks over your toe-caps and you're still no nearer to Dockhead.

I rode shivering across Tower Bridge in the hour before dawn. Below me the tarted-up southern bank glittered across the water, Bermondsey by moonlight. My Dad unloaded barges where there are restaurants now. My feet had trodden those pavements so much when I was a boy I felt as if there should be ruts, Jenner-ruts worn into the surface of the flags. The ruts would be doubles, since I had two legs when I wore them. Passing the darkened windows I wondered about the people behind them. God knows who lives in Bermondsey now. Everyone I knew has left or is dead. Everyone I knew is obliterated. In nineteen-seventy the docks closed and in nineteen-seventy-one Bermondsey closed. I changed my mind and the cursing cabby drove down the Tower Bridge Road, all the way to Grange Road. The Caledonian market was all lit up and dealing like hell, even now before five. Antique dealing is another job for insomniacs. We drove slowly along Grange Road, the cab driver not knowing where he was going, me not knowing from which house Slaughter was abducted all those years ago. Half of it has been rebuilt since. If Bermondsey kids want to swim now they have to hoof-it to Rotherhithe. We went back through the Neckinger and under the long dark railway arch in Abbey Street. The roads have changed but the smoke smuts in the arch remain the same, older than me. I passed my childhood under Victorian smuts, a hundred yards from the first railway station in London, which isn't there any more and wasn't there for long.

By the Drill Hall I stopped the cab and got out. I paid him off and paced the street, looking, looking, looking for a sign of an ancient crime. The old junction with Jamaica Road had been further down. I paced out where the abandoned Protestant church would have been. I looked down at my shoes. So that meant Joe Boy's ditch was here. I stood in the road, staring at a small square of tarmac between my shoes. A gaunt-looking young copper stepped out of the darkness. He could have been a ghost he moved so quietly and he wore a heavy woollen cape, something they don't do much now.

'This is a dual carriageway sir.'

'What?'

'You can't stand here.'

I followed him to the kerb.

'Have you been drinking?'

'No. I couldn't sleep.'

'You could have been killed there. Standing in the street like that.'

'Well I wasn't.'

'What's the problem?' His face was pale. His eyes were dark and hooded under the peak of his helmet. His voice was soft, comforting, almost a whisper.

'That's where my brother died. I couldn't sleep and I came and looked at it.'

'I'm sorry sir. Was it recent?'

'Nineteen sixty eight. When you were in primary school.'

'Before, sir. I was bouncing on my Daddy's knee in nineteen sixty eight.'

Now we both stared at the square of tarmac. His radio squawked softly, MP, MP, MP. He clicked it off.

I said. 'How deep is a gas trench, do you reckon?'

'I don't know. Two, three feet. Maybe four.'

'Not six?'

'No.'

'It's sewers that are six feet isn't it? No one puts gas mains right down there.'

'Yes sir.'

The policeman and I stood at the side of the road for a few minutes longer, watching the patch of tarmac. Nothing happened except a few cars drove slowly over it, their drivers aware of the uniformed man standing at the side of the road. Nothing was meant to happen. The events were in my head or in the past. The copper was polite enough but stood close enough to smell my breath and when I left I saw him writing down a few notes. *'Accosted lunatic in Jamaica Road. Talked about sewers and gas mains. No alcohol taken. Doesn't seem dangerous. Proceeded in a westerly direction. Made point with Sergeant Nobby at oh-six-four-five hours. Refreshments at eight.'*

I walked back down Abbey Street, under the long dark arch of my youth, past the sleeping council estates, past the buried monastery, past the railway arch where Hitler's bombs had buried a hundred and fifty of my putative countrymen and women. They've no memorial, except word of mouth. As dawn came up I drank a cup of antique dealer's tea from a mobile tea-bar in the Cally, sweetened as for a shock victim though I don't like sugar in my tea. I walked round the stalls and bought a bible, sixteen something. Sixteen brown-ink-smudge. Before or after the civil war? An expert could say but I'm no expert. The bible had been printed at a time when such streets as there were here were filled with our ancestors, Christians and Jews, Englishmen, Germans, Frenchmen. When did they all become one? The bible smelled like a cave. Open it and bats would fly out. I paid an awful lot for it and I had no need for the bible but I read it on a bench in Spa Road for an hour, dozing as I skipped and delved alternately, smoothing the

fragile pages with my fingertips, snoozing in the cold and
damp until I was woken by a passing car sounding its horn.

I went into the Spa Road bakery when it opened, would
have stamped my foot against the cold if I could have, was
waiting at nine on the doorstep for the Bermondsey Library to
open. It had shrunk since my day. Who'd done that? You can
shrink a library by taking the books out, but I mean the fabric
of the place. Take a few rows of bricks out? Knock an inch or
two off each marbled step? I was in the diminishing world of
my youth, shrunken as if seen through the other end of
binoculars. My youth was still sharply focused, but reversed.
Tiny. I was looking up from the dark, in London's abyss, standing on the steps of the public library with a group of raggedy
men. The seekers of warmth; unemployed, poor retired, down-
and-outs and one-legged detectives. The library hall lights
flickered into life and so did we. Halt, lame, unwashed and –
from the smell of some – incontinent we sprang to our feet,
pushed through the door, poured into the Newspaper Reading
Room. I gave the burly and bearded library assistant his first
request of the day. South London Press. Second-half of
nineteen-sixty-eight.

'All of them?'

'Each and every.'

'Are you looking for anything in particular?'

'A man.'

I searched on. I found no pictures. Tommy Slaughter may
have existed in newsprint, or in the memories of his victims, or
in the imaginations of one-legged middle-aged Bermondsey-
born obsessives. But no one had taken a photo of him. I
couldn't believe it. I went to the counter and demanded a
broader range of newspapers. They suggested I went out on
the tube to Colindale. Local public libraries apparently restrict
themselves to local papers and to microfilmed copies of *The
Times*, endlessly handy if you're a Lilliputian wanting to read
old Court Circulars, but not much use in tracing the squalid
activities of a lot of villains in south and east London *prior* to
any appearance in the Old Bailey. *The Times* only reports things

that *have* happened. Since Slaughter died before anyone could take him to court and make him famous in the 'Ronnie and Reggie' sense, he did not feature. The fan whirred in a microfilm reader. The man at the machine next to me was asleep with his head on the white Formica surface of the microfilm reading table. Spittle leaked from his mouth onto his beard. I felt in my pocket for some change. I went out to the library foyer and found a phone under one of those ancient pierced aluminium acoustic hoods.

Whitehall, one-two, one-two. Edgar Lustgarten eat your heart out.

'Extension forty-eight twenty-two please.'

'Hello?'

'Judy?'

'Yes?'

'Write this down.' I read the number off the booth. 'Could you ring me back?'

There was a faint sigh, sorely-tried patience leaving a woman's lips. The telephone felt like it was melting in my hand.

'Okay.'

She put the phone down. After she'd rung off I called Terry to ask him if Lochinvar had shown up. He hadn't. I rang Leon but he hadn't seen the cab either. I left directions with Leon. Terry didn't need them. Then I began the trudge down to the Tower Bridge Road and the hope of a cab for hire.

Twenty eight

THIS ISN'T CONJECTURE because I asked her.

On one side of London a one-legged, knackered-out but partisan detective receives a phone call from his long-legged blonde ex-wife. She's in a phone booth outside the Roman Catholic cathedral in Westminster and the phone booth smells like someone died in it. I know. She told me. It's her second call to her correspondent and she doesn't like speaking to him. It makes her nervous.

'You'll get me the sack,' she said.

But she listened.

Later, in a building in the old, eastern centre of the city, a lock clicks and turns. A hammered-glass door opens. It leads into a dusty room crowded with filing cabinets. The floor is covered with ancient paper debris. A blonde woman enters and pockets a key. She told me about this too, but a long time later. She steps across the rubbish on the floor. She opens a filing cabinet. A drawer screams as she opens it. Her finger moves back along the crystal files. Slaughter. The woman takes out the file and begins to read. The file contains reports, witness statements, black and white photographs, even press cuttings. There are dockets to represent items borrowed from the file. The blonde woman doesn't like what she reads. Meticulousness is a two-edged pen.

The blonde woman steps back across the paper debris. She leaves. The deadlock clicks over and the room is quiet again.

*

Meanwhile I was in my cab to Shoreditch. At this rate the cab-drivers of London will adopt me as their patron saint, or at least give a day's holiday in my honour. Jenner Day. I went back to the bank in Shoreditch and got my best photo of the old guy in the windcheater at Sydenham. Then I went to Myddleton Street. Registry of Births Marriages and Deaths. I was so tired my head was banging, as if my brain was loose in my skull. My eyes were sore and the back of my neck ached. Really ached. I went back to Dockhead, this time on a bus from Aldwych. I dozed and dribbled in a seat on my own on the upper deck. I nearly missed my stop, but I didn't. It's as if the sound takes on a different quality when you get there. It's as if the very fabric cries out, *'you're here Jenner. You're home.'* I got off the bus and rang Leon again from yet another phone box, this time opposite St Saviour's Dock. Still no Lochinvar. I crossed the windswept dual carriageway, walked round my private corner into the old main road, opposite the Drill Hall and outside the mission. I was hidden from traffic now. I was in a private island of my own past. I waited and waited outside the mission hall. And thought.

It was all bloody obvious. Why can't I see things which are bloody obvious?

Twenty nine

GOD IS LOVE. To the English words are more powerful than pictures. God is Love was a sign on the mission hall opposite our flats and the words hung over me more powerfully than any mawkish Spanish madonna, more powerfully than any Sebastian (surely the patron saint of holes if ever there was one), more powerfully than any nailed-up Christs. God is Love. Be good. He's hanging over you. The Word. What does it mean? Now it bothers me. When I was a boy it simply existed, hanging in the air, to my mind then just one more ghastly proddywhack epithet flickering among all the others. We were even less tolerant then. Anyway, why did we need a 'mission'? What were we, Zulus?

At three in the afternoon in the gathering half dark, with the sodium lights flickering to life already and a watery winter moon glowing coldly above me, I stood with my head aching and my eyes smarting sore under God is Love. I was holding a plastic bag full of papers. It was more than twenty-five years since I'd moved away, left Dockhead for good and all. For the very last time. Spending a day there was eerie. Going back is like pulling on an old overcoat. It feels bespoke. It's full of long forgotten smells and textures. Like putting your hand in the pocket and finding a bus ticket you remember buying. A two-penny half to Millpond Bridge, in this case.

I used to wait just along the street from God is Love for the bus to school every day and wouldn't have been surprised if my bus pass was in the pocket of that oh-so familiar overcoat. I used to wait there with a girl called Theresa who'd been to primary school with me but now ignored me, on account of puberty. She had farted once in gym and blamed me by the simple resort of pointing and laughing. Theresa was a proto-feminist. What does she do now? Probably heads up a bank dealing room. I stood with my back to a wall and my eyes closed thinking about the girl who farted and laughed.

A woman's shoes sounded in the distance. Click, click, click.
I opened my eyes. Judy approached through pools of flickering
yellow street light. She came around the Abbey Street corner of
the Drill Hall. She wore a blue suit and red shoes. She held a
red umbrella to match over her head. She kissed me.

'It's not raining.'

'It was. Look at you,' she closed and rolled the brolly. 'You
look terrible. And when did you shave last?'

'I don't know.'

'You're tired.'

'I didn't sleep last night.'

'That's obvious. Where did you spend the day? In a ditch?'

'In the library. In the council planning department. At my
bank. Here and there.'

She sighed. 'So, what did you find, 'here and there'?'

I waggled the plastic bag. 'All sorts. Look.'

I sorted through the sundry papers in the bag. I took out one
of the photos of the man in the windcheater.

'I got this in Sydenham.'

'When?'

'When I was there. He was there when DeWitt was killed.' I
said.

'You didn't say you had photos.'

'No.'

'Well Jimmy that's two witnesses. You and the grey-haired
man.'

'Who said he was a witness? I said he was there.'

'So... ?'

'He's the hit man.'

'He killed DeWitt?'

'Yes.'

'You saw it?'

'No. But he did it.'

'He won't need much of a defence lawyer against witnesses
like you.'

'But he did it. A young fellow in a van gave him the gun.'

'Did you see that?'

'I saw him pass a little parcel, then a few minutes later
DeWitt was shot, then Ralph walked past me with the gun in
his hand. He was obviously going to get rid of it.'

'How come you know that Ralph didn't shoot DeWitt?'

'My superior knowledge of human nature. DeWitt was in
more danger of the building collapsing than of Ralph shooting
him. Ralph isn't a shooting person.'

A silence. Something was bothering her. I assumed it was
me. Looking back, I should have known it wasn't, but I wasn't
feeling very sensitive. I grew tired of waiting.

'Did you get what I asked for?'

She took out two photos from her bag. The first showed a
man in his late thirties. He wore what looked like a black
Italian suit and was leaning against a Jaguar. He looked like an
extra from *La Dolce Vita*. In a way he was. The photo might
have been posed by an Italian film-maker. It also showed a slim
and attractive blonde dolly bird of the nineteen-sixties. Janice,
or 'Lola' as she preferred to be known now. Tommy Slaughter,
dark-haired, slim, hard-looking, was behind her wearing a
dark suit and dark glasses, hands in pockets, leaning against
his car. A line of tall, Georgian-style railings ran out of Tommy's
profoundly black side. Behind the railings were a lot of tall
Georgian-style windows and doors. It must be *that* Jag. It
looked too black in the photo but who can say? It could be
orthochrome film. I could just make out the shapes of two men
sitting in the Jaguar. Who? I could see the shapes but not the
faces. Freddie Phillips? Joe Boy? Who knows? Once you start
looking for someone you see them everywhere.

'That's Tommy Slaughter?' I asked.

'Yes. Do you remember him?'

'Sort of. Well, I think I do. Your memory plays tricks sometimes.'

She handed me the second photograph. In it Tommy
Slaughter stood next to the same woman. Janice. They were at
a shop opening in East Lane, as people from Bermondsey call
it. Slaughter was staring out of the picture, as if someone
standing just out of the frame had said something important to

him and he was thinking about it.

'The grey-haired man is Tommy Slaughter,' I said, as I gave her my photo again.

'Well?' I wanted her to agree.

She didn't answer. She knew I was right.

'What does it mean?' She asked.

'Come with me,' I said.

'Where?'

'Not far.'

We walked round to the junction of Abbey Street and the new Jamaica Road. I showed her the bit of tarmac. We had to look from the kerbside rather than go into the carriageway. There was plenty of traffic.

'Under there is where my brother died.'

I opened my plastic bag again and took out a drains and services plan.

'Look... no gas. There are gas pipes on that side of the road, but right in where the pavement is, not in the road itself. And this side... ' I pointed at where we were on the plan, '... there are no gas pipes down this side of the road and no gas pipes in the middle of the road, where, according to this picture in the *South London Press*... ' I took a photocopied photo from the plastic bag, '... Joe boy died. Right in the middle of the road. Here.'

Judy looked at the photo, then at the road. 'It doesn't look like the spot.'

'They've knocked down a church and built a dual carriageway since. What do you expect?'

'How do you know it was here?'

'I know. Believe me *I* know. I was born there.' I pointed at the flats. 'Anyway, you can orient yourself in the photo by those buildings.' I pointed at some other flats and the Felton Club, still extant in their nineteen-sixties positions, then at the same buildings in the photo. 'Triangulation.'

Judy paced along the pavement, looking at the tarmac. She looked at the plan, she looked at the photo from the *South London Press*, she looked at the buildings. 'Wherever it was, it wasn't in the gas trench, Jimmy. The gas trench was tens of yards away.'

'Exactly. And he worked for the Gas Board. What would he be doing in someone else's trench?'

'You couldn't be mistaken?'

'No.'

'So what's the theory?'

'That someone enticed him into the sewer trench and then backed a truck full of earth on him.'

The rain began again. Judy put the brolly up, tilted it slightly to invite me in.

'I'm not too much of a scruff?'

She smiled for reply and passed her arm through mine.

'You'll do.'

We stood arm in arm in the rain, looking at the tarmac.

'Joe couldn't have just been in someone else's trench?'

'What, gone to borrow a cup of sugar?'

'No. But if not then...?'

'If the right person asked him, he'd get down there. Like if Janice his bird came over and said, 'I've dropped my purse down that hole' or 'I've dropped my bangle down that hole'.'

'Any evidence for that?'

'None whatsoever.'

'So why say it?'

'The Borough Surveyor in overall charge of the road-workings was Ralph Purnell. He subsequently married Janice and then she changed her name to Lola Purnell. The young D.C. who did the accident report was Greasy Parker. Here... here's a court report on the inquest. See... *'Detective Constable Parker said...'*.

'Parker's a common name.'

'It was Greasy. You know it and I know it. Greasy Parker, Janice, Ralph and Tommy Slaughter are all somehow implicated in Joe's death. Lola Purnell is Janice Conkey. Joe Boy's old girlfriend. She married Purnell six months after Joe died.' I reached into the plastic bag, feeling like a magician, and pulled out a copy marriage certificate. The certificate was in the name of Janice Conkey, spinster of this parish and Ralph Purnell, bachelor. Judy read it. I pulled out another certificate, this one of birth. Lola Purnell, using that name, had given birth to Lola Junior two months after the marriage.

'How do you know Lola Purnell and Janice Conkey is one and the same woman?'

'I met her, that's how.'

Now Judy had to think. Some misplaced detail intruded, disturbed her sense of order. I knew.

'Slaughter had to retire,' I said. 'The old Gangs Squad down at Tower Bridge had him in their sights, so he had to find a way to disappear. My brother helped Slaughter stage his own death in Crooms Hill, Greenwich. He drove Slaughter's Jag up there and left it smeared with blood. Then he came home, mission accomplished. Only a small group of people knew Slaughter wasn't dead. Ralph and Janice. Mickey DeWitt and Joe. The only one who wasn't part of Slaughter's inner circle was Joe. Six weeks later, Joe had an 'accident'. Now the thread is cut. Slaughter has left Mickey and Ralph well set up while he takes on a new personality. He's home free.' 'How did he know Janice would be loyal?'

'She was pregnant with his daughter.'

Judy didn't speak but her look said, *I don't believe you.*

'How do you know?'

'I'm guessing, of course. But Slaughter seems to have a big interest in the daughter.'

'Janice married Ralph,' Judy said.

'And changed her name all round. I know. It's a cover. A dash towards respectability.'

'Why?'

'I dunno. Women are like that.'

She didn't bite. 'Why wasn't Ralph the father?'

'You've never seen a more unlikely married couple than Ralph and Lola Purnell.'

'Us?' Now she bit.

'Nope. Maybe you and the Scotchman.'

I can wound too.

'Why do you think it started up again?'

'Ralph found a floozie and said he was leaving Lola One. She decides to put the frighteners on him by hiring me as a private detective. She figures, he'll spot me and have an attack of brown underpants and come crawling back into the arms of Mummy, chequebook and all. But instead of running to her, Ralph runs to Mickey DeWitt, and they have a war conference at the Glass Balloonist, to figure out what to do. Ralph is there, and Slaughter and Lola Two and Mickey DeWitt. The latter has clearly already suggested a no-good plan of action, because Slaughter shot him, then and there. And he already had it planned.'

'Mickey?'

'Slaughter. Aren't you listening?'

'How do you know Slaughter had it planned to kill Mickey?'

'Because I watched Peter Kay give him the gun outside the pub before he went in.'

'Peter Kay?'

'Slaughter's go-for. He's a bit younger than me. He wears brown boots.'

'And what plan of action suggested by Mickey DeWitt brought about his early death?'

'I don't know. *You're old, turn yourself in. Don't worry, we'll get you let out for having Alzheimer's*, like the geezer from Courage.'

'Courage?'

'Guinness. Like the geezer from Guinness.'

'He wasn't a multiple murderer.'

'So you believe me?'

'Nearly. Not this bit. Convince me.'

'Well the most likely is this. Mickey had come a long way since the sixties. He was set up. Rotary Club, property developer, big house in Esher or Epsom or somewhere, lovely blonde daughters, all that crap. He doesn't want to have his boat rocked, leave alone capsized. They'd already had a huge fright when Freddie Phillips' body had to be moved...'

'Freddie Phillips.'

'Slaughter's driver. He disappeared with him on Crooms Hill Greenwich.'

'But his body was moved.'

'Recently. He was walled up in a house in Leyton, but that new motorway ran right over the top of it. They'd have knocked down the house and found him, so Mickey and Ralph Purnell had to dig him up and rebury him in Epping Forest. Later, when I turned up, apparently dogging Ralph Purnell, Mickey first plan was to have someone shoot me. When that proved difficult he started to think about who's the weak link. Who does he know that's really *dangerous*? Me? DeWitt himself? Ralph? Or Tommy Slaughter? Slaughter's favourite. After all, if Slaughter's already dead, he can go missing and no one will notice. So I guess Mickey probably made polite noises to Tommy Slaughter, 'oh dear, we'll all stick by you,' and polite enquiries in Soho or the Old Kent Road about finding a hit man who would see off Slaughter. And Slaughter got to hear about it. So instead of a war council on how to see off Jenner the conference in Sydenham turns instead into an execution for DeWitt.'

'Any evidence?'

'Speculation, every single bit of it.'

'Jimmy.'

'It fits.'

'Does it fit Ralph and his girlfriend?'

'Same story. Burning a bridge. Protecting himself from discovery. Tommy Slaughter would do anything rather than have that light shone on him.'

We began to walk slowly together towards Tower Bridge, still arm in arm. We crossed the road by a Catholic church, modern, brutal and ugly. Apparently they say mass in English facing the people, and then can't figure out why no one goes.

'According to them we're not divorced.' I told her.

'According to them we're not married,' Judy said.

'That's not true. It's a sacrament celebrated between us. The priest is a witness. You need to mug up your RS if you're going to get married again.'

'*We* were married in a registry office.'

'But it still existed as something between us.' The words were like rocks in my throat.

'Jimmy... I have to tell you something.'

Oh please no more confessions. Why do I always have the feeling that when she tells me some intimacy it will be the worse for me?

'Go on,' I said, despite myself.

'It's about Tom.'

'Why bring him up?'

But she didn't bite.

'Before he was in the murder squad, he ran my department. Criminal Intelligence. That's where we met.'

'Good for you.'

'We have... our department has responsibility for all the dormant supergrasses. The ones who've been to prison and come out. The ones who've never been inside....'

'And the ones who are missing presumed dead.'

'That's right.'

It hit me like a train.

'Like Slaughter?' I said. My jaw felt numb.

'Yes.'

'Does he have a file?'

'Yes.'

'What's in it?'

'Not much.'

'But he does? And the Gang Squad boys at Tower Bridge in nineteen-sixty-nine must have known he'd staged his own death.'

'Yes.'

'They must have helped him stage it.'

'Looks like it.'

'What about Freddie Phillips?'

'No mention.'

'I expect that was private enterprise on Slaughter's part.'

'Yes.'

'Or Joe's.'

She didn't speak. Nor did I, for a long time.

'Slaughter was a supergrass.' I had to think about that. It made sense. Sort of. 'But Slaughter's never been in court,' I said. 'Supergrasses all stood trial.'

'Only the later ones.'

'.... or gave evidence at trials.'

'It depends how important they were. Some would never be put on public display in the witness box. It all depended on their status.'

'What status would Tommy Slaughter be?'

'What do you think?'

I didn't answer. It was obvious.

'First of the supergrasses,' she said. 'Remember he disappeared in nineteen sixty-eight.'

'His record still exists? The physical file?'

'I've held it in my hand.'

'Did Tom Mack know about him?'

'He could have done. Yes.'

'Greasy told Lola One to employ me as a private detective.'

'Why?'

'Because she'd gone to him and complained that Ralphy was just about to give her the heave-ho. Greasy knew my presence would intimidate Ralph. Think about it Judy.'

She did.

'I'm Joe's brother. Ralph's bound to have seen me at some stage. I'd discount that usually. So what if your subject sees you? As long as they don't do it every morning for a week, so what?'

'But?'

'But that only works if your subject doesn't know who you are. I'm Joe Jenner's brother. It's written all over me.'

'He'd have recognised you.'

'Yes. And when he did it would remind him.'

'Of?'

'Why he and Janice had spent their lives together.'

Judy smiled.

'Why should this be Greasy's idea?'

'First, it was done via Menke, famous intermediary between coppers and villains. I think Lola went to Menke and asked him what she should do.'

'So Menke knew Slaughter is alive too?'

'Not necessarily. He knew Janice or Lola had a problem and she would have told him it was associated with Greasy. Menke talked to Greasy and...'

'And?'

'That's reason number two. How did Lola, or Janice, as I knew her, think up the ploy of using me to intimidate Ralph? It's too psychological for Lola. Hiring someone to lurk around and unwittingly intimidate someone has a copper's mentality. Lola is stupid.'

She thought. I waited. I wanted her to make the connection for herself.

'You don't like it?' I asked eventually.

'I don't see what Greasy has to gain from exposing you like that. He probably knew there was a dirty past to it, Jimmy...

'Definitely. Not probably.'

'He probably knew Slaughter was still alive.'

'Yes.'

'So why would Greasy pursue a high risk strategy like that?'

'I know. Greasy was all for calming things down. That's why he was following me around like Hamlet's dad, making sure I didn't die in the course of being a stooge. It couldn't be Greasy. It needs to be someone with another agenda. Someone who only stood to gain, not lose if my name became mud.'

She looked at me for a long time. She saved me the trouble.

'Tom Mack,' she said.

'Greasy's boss. Your boyfriend. He must have thought he'd been dealt a Royal Flush.'

'He doesn't gamble.'

'No. He doesn't. Why take a chance when you can get someone else to take it for you?'

'And Greasy's role?'

'Benevolence.'

'Greasy couldn't even spell it.'

'He's been a copper for thirty-five years. He needs to do something for conscience's sake, before he retires. He works for Tom Mack. Tom used me, Greasy decided to be my guardian angel. I was his project. His thirty five year indulgence. He knew me and my story inside out. Better than I did.'

She rubbed my hand.

'You're so bitter.'

I couldn't argue.

'What will you do?'

'Me? What will *I* do? You're the policewoman.'

'It won't stand up. All this is guesswork, Jimmy.'

'Of course. But someone's murdering people. You can't just hope it'll go away.'

'So what should *I* do?'

'You'll have to tell Tom Mack. '

'Then he'll know....'

'*He'll* know that *you* know he's a mischievous, hard-ball-playing self-obsessed bastard who will do anything to get his way. He wants to get his way with you but he wants a lot more to move the next step up the greasy pole of promotion. Still, what's new about that? It's a type. We've both met them.'

'And I'd thought you liked him.'

'Don't blame me. It was you who wanted to have his baby.'

Now why did I say that? She looked like I'd punched her.

'I'm running out of offers, and the clock is ticking, Jenner.'

I could have swept her into my arms, or something romantic. Instead, I watched, tongue-tied except for sarcasm as she checked her watch. We were deep in Shad Thames by now. The spice warehouses still had that dank, eastern pungency, though they'd stopped carrying spices thirty years ago. It's in the walls. In the mortar. Between the cobbles. I turned away from her. I breathed deep. I love that smell. My youth savoured of Courage breweries, fresh bread, bonded sherry under railway arches, malt vinegar in the vats on the Tower Bridge Road, spice on the docks in Shad Thames.

'What is it?'

'The smell of spice makes me feel secure.'

She laughed. 'I'll buy you a drink,' she offered. 'There's a bar at the end.'

'Thanks, Jude. I'd like that.' I kissed her. She didn't react. 'Another time.'

'Okay.'

'Soon. Somewhere nice. Like a date.' I could have bitten my tongue off.

'Come off it,' she said.

She was still holding my hand. I felt awkward, like a kid.

'What are you going to do about Tom?'

'What are you going to do about Amy?'

'Sack her.'

Now she kissed me. Her lips were soft and she smelt of freshness. I wanted to climb inside her clothes, just to be there, next to her. I wanted her freshness next to me always. Ear, nose and throat had only been a medical speciality up until now. I wanted to hear her, smell her, touch her throat for ever.

I looked into her eyes as we kissed in the dark, narrow cobbled street under her umbrella. Now the scent of spice had changed forever. It was removed from the box of my childhood. Filed under 'man'. I was lost in her arms forever. Lucky me. But I had business to do before 'forever' began.

Part three

The Last Days of Tommy Slaughter

Thirty

LATER WE WALKED across to the City. The rain had stopped but the water was still on the ground, glistening in the artificial light. The evening had begun already. I can't stand this. It's always dark, it's always wet. If it's not raining now it will do soon. I'm going to move to Australia or South Africa. Anywhere but in this rain.

And Slaughter? Only patience was required from me. Judy would tell Tom Mack what to do. Tom and his perverse conception of justice would catch up with Slaughter, once Judy spelled out what his best, his only plan of action should be. Like most men in his position, scandal and black marks were the things Tom Mack feared most. If he took timely action he would probably be able to blame Slaughter-the-rogue-Supergrass on some long retired and preferably dead copper. I could just see them now, a posse of senior detectives doing the honours, standing around in dark suits wringing their hands at the funeral of some long dead rozzer's reputation.

Only patience was required from me. Slaughter would be arrested. No doubt in a few days unattributable reports would surface in the papers that the body in the forest was Freddie Phillips. I wet my lips. I could still taste him. All of Slaughter's best works were buried, but not all of them was buried.

Meanwhile I needed to set a few things straight. We crossed London Bridge on foot. Judy kept a half a pace away from me, as if she'd thought about it by now and needed a little distance. No, surely not. I looked at her and at my own reflection in a bank on the bridge approach. No. She smiled at me.

'What?'

'Nothing. I'm just looking at you,' I said. Behind the plate glass doorway a doorman in a comic opera dictator's suit sneered at us; what's that beautiful bird doing with a limping scarecrow? I linked my arm with hers for a few paces, kissed her goodbye, then swung away. The man in the dictator's outfit was still watching. Up yours, jobsworth. All deliveries at the back door. Alone again I headed for the tube east. Lola Two clearly knew what was her real dad's stock-in-trade. She was there when he shot DeWitt, she received visits from Peter Kay. When Slaughter had given me the Bob Danvers Walker bong at Freddie Philips's graveside, from where had he followed me? Lola Two's place. She was in it up to her pretty neck. Malcolm Boyce had spotted her straight away as Slaughter's daughter. His meet with her in Oxford Street had been some form of blackmail shakedown. That's a dangerous game, Boycey. I stopped and thought about him for a moment. The translucent go-for. He had some nerve. I'll give him that. I found a phone box by the Monument. I tried to ring Boycey and warn him. No joy. A voice in a sardine can fielded my call.

'This is Clean Air Contracts. Please leave a message after the tone.'

Push off. And 'Clean Air Contracts' really, with a bum like his. Please. I spent weeks sitting in a car with him. I *know*.

I steeled myself to go to Old Ford and sack Amy the 'artist'. It had to be done, if only to be fair to her. Isn't that what we always say when we're going to be a shit to someone? 'It's only fair to you. I only want the best for you.' Be fair. Actually the truth is that a more beautiful and less neurotic woman has cast her cloak at me, Amy. I surrendered immediately, of course. Well, I have a history with her. We're an unlikely couple.

I went down the tube at the Monument. Warm air passed my face as I descended. The air touched my face with stale smelling fingers. The old nicotine taste of a million fags, smothered as their owners went down the stairs, mixed with the tang of newsprint and beery breath. Broken carbons and fast food cartons swirled around my feet. The fingers of warm fetid air touched my face again and clutched at the plastic bag in my hand. There was a distant rattling of train wheels. Subterranean London beckoned, girt in creamy tiles. A rush of

air and the train roared in. The sound always scares me
slightly, even on a nearly empty platform. And the smell would
make a strong man throw up. In the tunnels of brick and soot I
rode on polished rails. I imagined the men who'd built the
tunnels sweating in their dingy, dangerous hole. For a second I
was in the shallow grave again. I thought about Tommy
Slaughter and his photograph. All dark suit, crisp white shirt
and style, Italian photographer style. Even Tommy Slaughter's
way of terrorising was intended to indicate his panache. I took
the photograph of him out of my carrier bag and held it in my
hand, as if the print was security, as if it was the only copy and
I was scared to let go. The tube train sped under the City
streets. I held him in my hand. Where are you Tommy? Except
in my picture? I closed my eyes. I tried to fill my mind with
other images. It didn't work. I looked around the carriage. No
one met my eye. Who could blame them? I picked up an
abandoned Evening Standard. On page three it said, 'Body
found in shallow Forest grave.' If Slaughter reads the paper he
knows I'm not dead, otherwise the paper would read 'bodies'. I
hurled the newspaper aside. No one reacted.

Rocking in our false tweed seats we Londoners passed
under the churches, under the walls of the old City, under the
Aldgate pump and the bell foundry, under the streets of dirt
and the ancient feet that trod the road westwards to the City,
eastwards to Essex. There had always been a road here. No
doubt dead Romans were buried by the side of it, never
expecting to have dead Victorians disturb them so that new
Elizabethans could dash under them. The train rushed through
the brick and soot tunnels. The steel wheels clacked and
complained. We turned the corner at Aldgate East. We
travelled under the cockney countryside towards the cockney
marshes at Bow. Now Jenner takes the road to Essex, but not
too far. I passed under the road in the steel train, bright wheels
spinning, riding on polished steel rails. My neighbours never
looked into each others eyes nor my eyes during our journey,
each of us alone in some profound, untouchable way. I don't
know if I could have contained myself if someone had met my

eye. I was bursting, I wanted to yell, 'I have set things to rights.' Of course I hadn't. But it was in my grasp. I may look like a limping, unshaven, unslept tramp but I have won the woman and arranged defeat for my enemy. Who was the enemy? Tommy Slaughter, of course. Are you sure, Jenner? The fact that arresting Slaughter would crash-land Tom Mack's career was fortunate collateral damage. Joe wouldn't mind fate dealing me a favour as I took his revenge. I closed my eyes and clutched the photograph of septuagenarian Slaughter. The steel wheels of the tube train squealed as the driver applied the brakes, and in my mind I could see the scene as Tom Mack arrested Tommy Slaughter. Now that was a union over which I'd happily officiate.

I left the tube and walked down to the Old Ford Road. I was very tired. It seemed to take forever. Roman Road was the usual mess. Stall-holders chuck most of what they bring to market onto the street; a Freudian slip, an outward sign of inward tackiness. Sell it or sling it, buy it and sling it. The new consumerism, missing out the junk man. I trod over broken glass, almost stumbled on a cardboard box. I put my hand on a stall to steady myself.

'You all right mate?' Asked a tiny man in a huge tweedy flat hat.

'I'm all right.'

I ducked down a side street. I felt better in the inky black shadows. I clasped the plastic bag tighter to my side. I reached Amy's building. My rented cab was outside in the private yard, as if Lochinvar had come but never gone again. It was a token, one which didn't call for much expertise in interpretation. I didn't have to pretend to be a red indian and follow his paw prints until I found Amy. Lochinvar was giving her one. Bastard, with my money in his pocket, fetching her my flowers, driving here in my rented cab. I still had the silver napkin ring in my pocket. I'd make him wear it as a throat warmer.

I hobbled up the fifty-eight steps. On the stone landing outside her door was a small, wooden three-drawer chest. Its surface was distressed by use. The veneer was peeling and its

feet were rough and blackened. Amy had bought it meaning to
paint it and make something irresistible in the line of bedroom
furniture, but for now she'd lost the urge so it waited outside
the front door. Between the small distressed chest's feet stood
Lochinvar's designer pumps. Amy hates sight, leave alone the
smell of trainers. She'd have made him leave them there. On
the peeling veneer top rested Lochinvar's green black and
yellow Alice band. Cheek. I picked up the shoes and went
downstairs again. The door to Serge the sculptor's studio was
unlocked. I went in. The room was echoing and cold. It was
empty apart from tools and materials, as if Serge had decided
to make something but wasn't sure what yet, so he'd just
gathered together tools and materials and pissed off to give
them time to orientate themselves in the world of art. Later, he
would beat them into something. Serge is the last metal bash-
ing sculptor in captivity. All the others have gone conceptual.
His studio should be a museum. On one side of the room stood
a bandsaw. I put the Reebok Classics into a clamp on the
bandsaw table and started up the machine. Passing designer
pumps through a bandsaw is very satisfying. The hum of the
motor, the soft growl as the saw bites into the leather, a faint
burning smell from the compound rubber soles. Mm-mm, I
could do this for a living. Jenner's recommended system for
dealing with pent-up fury. Angry-ish, I had to fake the outrage
slightly. After all, I was just about to dump Amy. But she didn't
know that and neither did Lochinvar. He needed to be kept in
his place.

I returned the Reeboks to *their* place under the small stressed
chest outside Amy's studio door, all four halves, perfectly
placed in twos. I stood back to admire my work. As I did I
noticed Amy's door wasn't closed properly. It was the tiniest
crack ajar. Why did I do what comes next? It's my nature.
Nosey Jenner. I pushed. It gave. I pushed more. It gave more.
Inside was pitch black. I leaned inside the door-jamb. In the
past I'd have said the room had the silence of the grave, except
now I'd experienced it and it isn't so silent. Blood rushes or
worms chomp. Either way it isn't silent. I let go of the door and

stepped inside. Amy's space was so cold. Unnaturally cold. I
reached for the light switch.

'Hello?'

No reply.

I clicked it. The studio had been turned into a giant work of
art, if work of art means interpreting blood smeared over the
walls. A work of art is what you bring to it, according to Amy's
chums. This one should be 'studio still-life with dead negro'.
Lochinvar lay on the floor. His hair had been pulled from his
head. The scalp had come with it. His fingers and toes had
been smashed and his eyes gouged out. His clothes lay ripped
around the floor, as if they'd been torn off him by a giant dog.
He was a pathetic, heart churning site. I stood in his blood,
feeling wretched. What the hell had I done to him? I could
have told Leon ,'no, he's just a stupid kid. You keep him.' I
could have simply refused, point blank. Instead Lochinvar lay
at my feet, a negro out of the school of Damien Hirst, while his
blood was spread around the walls, a more traditional
painting. I screamed anger at Tommy Slaughter and his pal
Peter. I made noises I never knew were in me. I lay on Amy's
dusty sofa and sobbed, wishing the sight away. I gathered
myself. I moved Lochinvar's body into a more comfortable
position, as if I really needed to. As if it would help him. The
dragging exhausted me, and I fell over several times, slipping
in his blood. Where the hell was Amy? I dragged out the
paintings of the previous tenant, peering into the back of the
racks. No Amy. I looked under the bed. No Amy. I screamed
and shouted around the empty loft after her, Amy, Amy, Amy,
but there was still no Amy. Now I was covered in Lochinvar's
blood, just like him. At least I was still alive. I found a towel,
took my clothes off and turned on the light in the shower
cubicle. A figure was curled up in the footwell. I opened the
shower door. Amy sat in the bottom of the shower, fully
clothed. She didn't move. I stood naked over her. I lifted her
head so that she should face me. Her skin was warm and she
was clearly uninjured, but she closed her eyes and wouldn't
look at me. I went over to the phone and called Boycey again. I

got the Clean Air Contract message again. I yelled into the phone.

'Pick it up you pratt! I haven't got time to ponce about!'

I didn't know he was there at all. He picked up.

'Sorry, Jimmy... if I'd known it was you...'

'Shut up, Boycey. Just get round here and fetch your car and passport.'

'Passport?'

'Yes.'

'Where's here?'

'Old Ford.'

I put the phone down. I showered and asked Amy questions while we waited. She didn't say much. Two men, one old, one young. They'd broken in and started beating Lochinvar during the previous night. The young one provided the muscle, the old one did the beating and hurting. They were looking for me and seemed to think Lochinvar knew where to find me. He didn't know so he couldn't have told them. So much the worse for him. I didn't have the heart to ask why Lochinvar was there in the middle of the night. It wasn't my business. It was his bad luck. Amy had been in the crapper when they broke in. It's on the other side of the landing, so she'd stood horrified outside her own front door, watching through the crack and too frightened to move. Once they'd gone she'd come in to try (and fail) to help Vaughan. She'd spent the day in the studio alone with Lochinvar's cadaver. God knows why she hadn't called the police. When she heard me she thought they'd come back, so she hid in the shower. She has a shower but no crapper in her studio. To have both would contravene some building regulation and imply the studio was a flat. Which it was.

I pulled a dust sheet over Lochinvar. I stripped Amy and showered her too, and changed her clothes. I found her passport. I sat her on the dusty sofa and then I phoned Leon and told him to come round. I told him why he should come. I had to. Then I found some clean clothes, old stuff that I'd left behind when I used to stay there a lot.

Boycey was ringing the doorbell. I took Amy down and sat

her in the back of his Ital. Boycey watched.

'What?' I said.

He stood in the yard next to the cab and looked smug. He smiled and gestured with his elbow. 'That's that cab. I told you about that cab.'

'You can't tell one bloody cab from another, Malcolm.'

'But I can remember plate numbers.'

I gave him Amy's passport.

'Take her home.'

'She lives here.'

'Take her to her mother. Here's the address.' I gave him a slip of paper. 'It's outside Paris. She'll show you. When you get there, stay until I call you. Don't come back to England without my say-so.'

'Why?'

'You know why.'

'I don't.'

'Why did you meet Lola Purnell in Oxford Street?'

'You didn't see me. I checked.'

'I never said I saw you. I saw *her*.'

He didn't answer.

I said, 'You saw Lola because her father is alive. Because Tommy Slaughter is alive and kicking.'

He looked away.

'He knows we know. He also knows we saw him going in to shoot Mickey DeWitt.'

He looked doubtful.

'Go up there and have a look if you don't believe me. Tommy Slaughter is alive and looking for us.'

'Us?'

'He's killed four people to get the photo we took. He's tried several times to make me number five.'

'What are you going to do?'

'What do you think I'm going to do?'

He sucked his teeth. 'Don't. Leave it to Old Bill.'

'They've had their chance. They won't do anything.'

'It takes time. They need evidence.'

'Whose? Yours? Mine? Which form do you prefer? Dying declarations or spirit contact through a ouija board?'

'How about Greasy?'

'All the cops who knew Slaughter when he was active are retired. Most of them are dead. Except Greasy. He's the last. He's not going to rock the boat months before he retires. Who the hell is going to get it in the neck? Only Greasy. All he can do is lose.'

'Who else knew Slaughter was alive?'

'In nineteen sixty nine? My brother. Mickey DeWitt. Ralph Purnell. Notice what they have in common? They're all dead.'

'Mrs Purnell's not.'

'But she's unlikely to talk.'

'They could make her.'

'How? What leverage would the police have on her?'

'Well, what about her daughter? She knows what's what.'

'You've talked to the her. What do you think?'

'No chance.' He walked back and forth a few paces. 'It looks bad. You've got a photo of him a hundred yards from where Mickey DeWitt was shot.'

'*We* have.'

He frowned.

I said, 'Malcolm, I can hear this clicking into place in your mind. If he's looking for me he's looking for you. Right?'

'He won't find me.'

'I got you on the *phone*.'

'But still he won't find me. I have my calls forwarded to my mobile. I stay at several addresses.'

'I don't suppose he was looking until you asked his daughter for money.'

'How did you know about that?'

'I guessed. I guessed she said no, too.'

'She threatened me. She was quite nasty, with it. Foul mouthed. She said she'd cut my nuts off. She didn't look like that, did she?'

'Modern women. Who can say? I expect you got on her bad side, Boycey.' I indicated his Ital. 'Drive her to Paris, okay?'

'Okay.'

'Do not hesitate. Do not deviate. Do not make any phone calls or strike any deals. Stay there until you hear from me. Got it?'

'Got it.'

I looked at him.

'What is it, Jimmy?'

'Danger, Malcolm. You are standing right in the track of an express train. You have to move. Get on with it.'

He did. I waved goodbye as they drove down the Old Ford Road. But it was dark and they couldn't really see me. I didn't really mean them to. I went back upstairs to Lochinvar. I found the keys to the hired cab and rooted in the boot for the Smith-and-Wesson and my mobile phone. Then I waited for Leon in the dark, slumped in the back of the cab with the pistol and phone by my side. Of course he wasn't coming back but I never wanted to be caught out by Tommy Slaughter again. I'd be okay as long as I didn't shoot my ear off answering the phone. Relax, Jenner. Relax. If you can't relax stop impersonating a piano wire. But I couldn't.

Leon didn't take long.

Thirty one

H E HAD LEFT with two middle-aged West Indian men.
They were sombre-looking fellows in casual clothes, not
extrovert yardie types. They were silent too, except for Leon,
who had one question.

'Where does he live?'

'Carter Street. I don't remember the number.'

'I'll find him. I'll be an hour.'

Then they closed the shutter. I searched for somewhere to
rest.

*

The outer door of Leon's garage was a roller shutter with
chipped and peeling paint on it. The colour was indeterminate
in the sodium street light. I knew it was mucky blue in day-
light. At night it was merely mucky. Inside the roller shutter,
Leon's Brixton workshop was a large, hangar-like building. It
was dark and echoing. The floor had that sticky, jammy, oil-
and-dust quality of a garage that's been used for generations. I
swivelled on my good foot in the silence, almost all alone.
Lights shone from two Portacabins side by side in the back of
the hangar. The rolling road was by my feet. The hydraulic
ramp stood by my side. An old grey Transit van was on the
ramp, towering above my head. It had pock marks of red lead
all around its waist. I walked over to the Portacabins. One had
hushed black women's' voices inside. I went into the other.

I cat-napped while I waited alone in the Portacabin. I turned
and squirmed on a dirty black leather sofa. Leon's sofa must
have looked an unlikely purchase in nineteen-seventy-five. It
was a Readers' Wife of a leather sofa. It heated up my arse and
squeaked whenever I moved. Down in the workshop silence
reigned over the rolling road and the hydraulic ramp. Squeak-
ing on my black leather sofa I could hear the black women in
my Portacabin's twin, crying softly over the lost life of

Lochinvar. I'd seen Rosie in there, leading the bawling. They cried a wake for a death which hadn't officially happened yet. Lochinvar's body was still in Amy's studio.

Leon wasn't one hour but three. He came back long after midnight with his sombre friends and something dragging between them, something bundled up with gaffer-tape and covered with a coat. Leon rattled down the steel shutters, then one of the sombre men whirled off the coat, like a magician revealing a pigeon.

'Got him,' said Leon.

Peter Kay was the pigeon. His face was covered in gaffer tape. The rest of Peter looked the worse for wear and blood was seeping from the edge of the gaffer tape. I could offer no sympathy, so I didn't speak.

'He says he doesn't know where Tommy Slaughter lives,' said Leon, while his silent friends industriously secured Peter, spread-eagled below the ramp. They crossed the garage and sat on stools, watching us but leaving Leon and me alone with Peter. Leon ripped the tape off Peter's mouth but not his eyes.

'He says Tommy Slaughter is dead,' said Leon over his shoulder to me. 'But I told him, it's not Tommy Slaughter who is dead. It's my nephew. And his mum and his sister is a bit fed up about it.'

'I don't know your nephew...,' screamed Kay.

'And I'm a bit fed up about it too,' Leon interrupted. 'You can see it from my point of view. Being my nephew.'

'I don't know your nephew!'

I moved into the shadows. I didn't speak. Leon said, 'So, just one question for you. Where does Tommy Slaughter live?'

'I don't know.'

Leon pressed the button on the ramp. The Transit slowly descended.

'What's that?'

'Do you know where you are?' Leon asked him.

'No,' answered Kay. Leon stopped the ramp.

'Think.'

'I can't see.'

'Sniff.'

Peter sniffed.

'What do you smell?'

'Petrol. Oil.'

Leon let the ramp descend again.

'Get it now?'

Peter didn't answer.

'Give me Slaughter's address,' Leon asked again.

'I don't have it... I don't know it.'

Leon kept the ramp descending.

'Do you know who I am?' He asked.

'Some spade,' Peter said. 'How the hell do I know?' 'That's not very nice.' Leon kicked him hard in the ribs, then ripped the gaffer tape from the top half of Peter's face.

'Who am I?'

Peter screamed when he saw the ramp descending.

'Who am I?'

'I don't know!'

'I am not some spade, that's who I am!'

'Okay!'

'Where does Tommy Slaughter live?'

'I don't know.'

I stepped forward from the shadows and lay on the floor next to him, so he could hear me over the machinery.

'Tell him Peter.'

He recognised my voice. 'You.'

'Tell him.'

'I can't. I just can't. Slaughter will kill me.'

'*He* will kill you.'

'Then you'll never know.'

'Slaughter may try in the future. My friend promises to do it, now.'

The ramp was almost on him now. Leon slowed it.

'It won't be quick, Peter. And he *will* do it, believe me.' I could see the pressure of its weight start to press on Peter. Just touching, but it was enough.

'All right! All right. I'll tell you.'

'So tell.'

He did. I wrote the address down. Leon knocked on the door of the Portacabin and Lochinvar's family filed out. Two young women, two older. The men who'd gone out with Leon. One of the young women was Lochinvar's sister Rosie. The room was filled with their perfume. Leon pressed the button to raise the ramp. The two sombre men picked Peter up.

'Why did you kill the black guy in Old Ford Road?' I asked.

'I didn't. Slaughter did.'

'Why?'

'How the hell do I know? Because he does that.'

'How many people has he killed?'

'I don't know.'

'How long have you worked for him?'

'I told you....'

'You told me a load of lies.'

'Not much. I'd done a few things for Mickey. He introduced us. Then after a bit Mickey asked me if I'd help him do Tommy.'

'But you thought there was better money in telling Tommy.'

'Yes.'

'How did he find us in the forest?'

'He didn't. That was his daughter. She saw you hold me up outside the house.'

'Is he expecting me now?' I asked.

'No. He's looking for you. But he's not expecting you. No one knows where he lives.'

'Except you and me. And both Lolas.'

'They're related by blood.'

'And you're related by money.'

'He needs me.'

'No. You need to change your line of business, Peter. You're an unlucky type.'

Leon's middle aged companions stood either side of Peter. He looked at the women. He was scared of them.

'Keep him until you hear from us,' I said.

'Take him to Highclere House,' said Leon.

Thirty Two

WE LEFT A few minutes later. Rosie kissed us both and squeezed my hand. She had fingernails which overhung her fingertips by nearly an inch and wore dark glasses in the dark. Only the fingernails hurt. I felt ashamed because I'd let her down. They closed the shutters behind us. As we walked over to Leon's Beemer I asked him, 'What's Highclere House?'

'A block of flats off Railton Road.'

'What's there?'

'A roof.'

We got in the car.

'What happens on the roof?'

'Accidents.' He looked at me. 'What?'

'I can't leave it like that, Leon.'

'What?'

'You know.'

He sighed, got out of the car, walked back across to the garage and tapped on the shutter. I closed my eyes.

*

If God is Love, Slaughter is Fear. The two icons hung over the mean streets of my teens. I never expected to see either again. Before dawn I drove east with Leon in his BMW. He wore a Barbour coat and a pork-pie hat. My clothes were eclectic. We went through the Rotherhithe tunnel and out towards Essex. The car was laden with so many weapons we could have started a small-arms war. We were a two man Balkan conflict. We didn't speak much. We drove silently east, towards the address Peter had given me.

So much of England is east. It goes on for miles. Humberside. Lincolnshire. Norfolk. Essex. Huge empty, flat lands, tilted slightly so that water runs off and into the sea. We drove into Essex. On and on, against the traffic, through industrial estates and thirties boom housing. Through roadwork after roadwork.

Past cone after cone. They won't be happy in Essex until they have it paved over. Coming from London, you don't see much green before you get to Rayleigh. We turned off the main road there and headed north towards the River Crouch. Then the countryside proper started, a flatland where cows mooched around damp grass, lucky to be out for a day in winter, then a little escarpment overlooking the rivers Crouch and Roach. Another climb took us on to a low ridge, on to a Roman military road. We travelled some miles along this road. It had been modernised by the simple expedient of pouring tarmac on the surface. Leon worried that I wasn't following the map. I didn't need to. We used to come here for holidays when I was a child. The Jenners and Essex are as close as that. More precisely, what's left of the Jenners is like that with what's left of Essex.

Eventually we turned off the Roman road and headed towards the sea. The sky that overhung us was grey and drizzly. I could glimpse the sea below it sometimes. It was indistinct. Grey too. Flat calm.

Leon drove down lanes overhung with green. The houses had long since become infrequent. Sometimes we'd go through a village of white clapboard houses. Sometimes we'd pass an isolated farmhouse. But mostly the road we travelled was empty of cars and houses and people.

Finally the road ended, and became a track through the marshes. We drove along the track until we came to a cinder car park. It was remote, with just a few houses far away on the horizon. The fields between were ploughed for cereal planting and most of the hedges had been grubbed out, so that the ploughed fields were maybe a hundred acres each. On the side of the cinder car park was a dyke, and over the top of the dyke I could see boat masts. Leon pointed to the masts.

'What's that, a marina?'

'It's a quarter of a mile away. That's just winter storage. They pull the boats out for the winter.'

'No marina?'

'Not right here. No.'

There were a couple of rough-looking young men working on a car in the car park. Leon stared through the screen at them.

'So what are *they* doing?'

'Fixing their car. You wouldn't want to get stuck here.'

'So what were they doing here when they broke down?'

'Fixing a boat. How do I know? You want to go and ask them?'

'No.'

The car was a crappy old Hillman Hunter and the young men were obsessed with it, leaning under the bonnet and peering at the innards. The engine fired and they slapped each other on the back and climbed in. They drove away looking cheerful. When they'd gone I pointed to a house about a mile away across the fields. It was a big red-brick farmhouse built to impress the visitor with its ample proportions. The house stood for nineteenth-century wealth and confidence as much as shelter. It had tall hedges and I could clearly see a security gate.

'According to Boycey's directions, that's it.'

'So what's the plan?'

'Wait for dark.'

'That's eight hours.'

'I know.'

'Is that it?'

'No. You can make yourself busy. You go over there and make sure he's there.' I pulled the photo of Tommy Slaughter out of my pocket and gave it to him. 'Accept no substitutes. When you're sure it's him, come back.'

'Okay.'

Leon pulled his pork-pie hat over his eyes and turned up the collar of his Barbour. He took a shotgun out of the boot of the car and filled his pockets with cartridges. He spoke no more, but began to march across the nearest field, careful to conceal himself from line of sight from the Victorian house and looking for all the world like a farmer out shooting rabbits. Only his black skin and a bright white pair of Nike trainers gave the game away. I slid behind the steering-wheel, then settled down in my seat to wait.

Sleep crept up on me like a thief. One moment I was watching Leon's small black unlikely figure trying to look inconspicuous with white shoes and a shotgun, creeping under a hedge, the next the shutters were down. I wasn't so much sleeping as unconscious. I was awoken by a knock on the car's passenger door window. I opened my eyes. The Hillman was parked across the bonnet of the BMW, blocking me from the car park exit. The rough-looking young men from the Hillman seemed to have got it running okay now. The motor sounded as sweet as a nut. They stood either side of my car. One was very close to me; a sallow man, olive coloured skin, jet black greasy hair slicked back to his grimy collar. He wore a grey, German style army coat. His lips moved behind the dirty side-window glass. I couldn't hear what he said but I could see his yellow teeth clenching and unclenching as he spoke. It wasn't friendly. I mean it wasn't *'Got the time, mate?'* or *'did you know your seat-belt's hanging out?'*. His companion was no better-looking. Old 'dirty teeth' clenched and unclenched his gnashers a few more times. I switched on the ignition and wound my window down.

'Get out of there,' he said. 'Out.'

It didn't seem very polite, put just like that.

'I can't. You're in the way.'

'Get out of the car.'

I smiled apologetically and said no more. I wound up the window. His companion dragged open my passenger door. I was too slow to push the plunger on the lock and once he had it open there was no good resisting. He was about thirty, big-muscled, getting fat. Might've been a boxer once. He was unshaven and unwashed-looking too, with mousy-coloured, short cut hair. He ducked into the passenger seat of the BMW, head first so that his face was close to mine and he was leaning across the front seats. His face was grey, as if he'd had cartridge-powder for lunch. He wore dirty jeans and a dirtier sweater. He was so tough he didn't need a shirt under or a jacket over the sweater.

'Get out of there.' his pal commanded again through my

closed window. He chewed off the ends of the words as he spoke, as if the business of opening and closing his jaw was painful. Maybe he thought I wasn't entitled to full-scale words and explanations. He reached inside his jacket.

I pushed the button down by my shoulder, smiled politely and brushed dust off the instrument panel of the BMW.

'Just get out,' said the man on my passenger seat. He knelt on the passenger-seat and laid a hand on my left shoulder. This close, he smelled like an unwashed dog. He pulled gently on my coat. I looked through the window at the guy in the grey jacket with his hand stuck inside it. I thought, if I'm going to get shot anywhere it might as well be here. I turned again, smiled into the driver's big fat face, then jammed the first and second fingers of my right hand into his eyes as hard as I could. The big fellow screamed and put his fingers to his eyes. I pulled my hand back and drove the heel of my palm into his nose, projecting now between his fingers. He screamed again. I flinched, expecting a shot. Nothing happened except the big man blubbed and bled. His companion was running around the car. I started the engine and slammed the beemer into his Hillman, wrecking its side panels and pushing it and him across the cinder car park. I took a handful of the big fellow's hair and tried to push him backwards out of the car. He was too heavy. We just wrestled in the front seat like a couple of Saturday-night teenagers rehearsing their heavy petting. The front wing of the BMW had become caught up in the Hillman. It's ancient thin panelwork had folded. The beemer was stuck and its wheels spun on the cinders, burning rubber.

The sallow man reached the rear-passenger door of the BMW. He climbed in behind me. He reached into his jacket again, then pushed something in front of my face. I stopped wrestling for long enough to read '*Metropolitan Police*' and then, under that, '*Warrant Card*' with two pictures; one an engraving of a coat of arms, the other a photograph of himself, only wearing his hair short and clean and sporting a white shirt and a dark tie.

'Detective Sergeant Andrews,' I read out loud. 'Good likeness.

Who's your boyfriend?'

'D.C. Walter.' Then he leaned very close to my ear and said, 'And you, mate, are nicked.' Then he punched me in the side of the head as hard as he could. There was a great deal of vehemence in the 'nicked', just as there was in the punch. Looking at things from his point of view I could see why. His big sidekick was bleeding all over my clean shirt. Andrews punched my head again and yelled this time because something cracked in his hand as he did it. I heard the crack quite distinctly

D.S. Andrews swore fluently and held his fist and rocked backwards and forwards in the back seat of the BMW. His companion, D.C. Walter, moaned a lot and bled into his own hands, never taking them from his face. He's the only man I ever heard of who bleeds noisily. We three sat together for a minute or two, unable to move. In my case, not daring to. Then I heard a voice I recognised outside the car.

'Jimmy?' Greasy Parker leaned in the car. 'What have you been doing to these two?'

I pulled the little black knob up. He came around and opened the door for me, like a cabby. I climbed out, my head still ringing.

'They're mine,' Greasy said.

'Babies?'

'Sometimes I think so, Jimmy.'

Greasy leaned in the car. 'Fuck off,' he said. That's what the chain of command has come down to. The two detectives climbed out of the BMW. 'Go somewhere inconspicuous.'

'He's buggered up our Hillman,' said the sergeant. Greasy merely pointed. They got in the car.

'What are you doing here?' I asked Greasy.

'We're going to move on Tommy Slaughter. He lives in that house.'

'No? Really. I thought he was dead.'

'So how come you're here?'

'I'm thinking of buying a boat. Co-incidence, eh?' 'Yeah. What have you got in the boot?'

'Well Greasy, we don't want to embarrass each other, do we?'

'No.'

'Whose say-so to move on Slaughter?'

'Tom Mack, of course.'

'What are you going to do? Move him?'

'Nick him.' He grinned and held out his hand. I took it and shook it.

'Tell me, why were you at his daughter's house?'

'I was asking her where Slaughter lived.'

'You didn't have access to his file?'

'No.'

'Did she tell you?'

'She said she'd never heard of him. She's a hard girl.'

'Did you know it was her who'd hit me in the forest?'

'I didn't *know*.'

Then I heard the shotgun, which wasn't part of the plan.

'Get round there!' Shouted Greasy. The Hillman roared off.

There were more shots. Greasy looked at me. I shrugged.

'Look.'

Lola Two was running away from the house. She ran to the dyke, climbed over it and disappeared from view. Greasy saw her too. He turned to me.

'What's happening?'

'Slaughter and Peter Kay killed a black kid last night. They tortured him.'

'Why?'

'They were looking for me.' The shotgun fired again. Now a pistol. Bang bang bang.

'Sounds like the third world war,' Greasy said. He didn't seem all that rushed to go off and do something about it.

'It's the dead fellow's uncle. He's upset.'

Greasy nodded sagely.

'So where's Tom Mack?' I asked.

He grinned. 'In the house. He went in to talk to Slaughter, but Slaughter wasn't there, so he's waiting for him.'

'Come on, Greasy. Do something.'

He picked a mobile phone out of his pocket. He tapped out a number.

'Andrews? There's a coon in there with a shotgun...'

'And a pistol,' I added.

'And a pistol. My friend wants him out again alive.'

I distinctly heard the tinny phone voice say, 'What about the governor?'

'Oh... do your best.'

He was definitely laughing. He clicked the phone shut and turned towards the dyke. We climbed it together, Greasy pulling me. At the top he felt my back.

'Is that an illegal firearm, Jimmy?'

'No,' I lied.

Lola Two was in the field on the far side of the dyke. She was still running, running towards the dry stored boats. There were probably fifty boats there, standing on chocks. Some had maintenance ladders leant against the side. Only one had a seventy-year-old gangster standing on the deck. Tasteful as ever, Tommy Slaughter stood on the deck of a nineteen thirties sloop. He wore a blue canvas top and blue jeans. He looked like any other old codger giving his boat a coat of paint. Another shot sounded from the house and behind Slaughter a flock of geese lifted off the glistening salt marshes. He looked towards us. Lola followed his eye and slowed to a stumble. She hadn't seen us before. Lola was breathing heavily and her legs were covered in mud. Greasy and I descended the bank. Tommy descended the ladder. I know that I shall meet my fate.

'Do you have a gun, Greasy?'

'No. Of course not.'

Tommy did. It was rather like mine. We lined up like a couple of ancient Wyatt Earps, our ancient guns by our sides. Tommy aimed at us, then laughed and let his pistol drop. Lola was still three or four hundred yards away, running like hell. Greasy and I were less than thirty yards from Tommy. He laughed and raised the gun again.

'Jimmy Jenner. In my sights at last.'

'But I'm chasing, not running, Tommy.' I pulled the Smith-

and-Wesson. Slaughter laughed and leaned against the chocks
of his boat. In the distance I could hear a loudspeaker at
Slaughter's house.

'Armed man. This is the police.' They were either trying to
talk Leon or Tom Mack out. They hadn't seen us.

Lola cried, 'Dad!'

Slaughter held his gun towards me. Mine was aimed at his
heart.

'You haven't got the bottle Jenner. You're like your brother.
Gutless when it matters.'

Greasy and I kept advancing. Slaughter pulled the trigger.
The bang when it's aimed at you is greater than you'd think,
and more personal than you'd think. I felt shocked. He's firing
at *me*. Slaughter pulled the trigger again. Greasy went down.
He didn't make a sound at first.

'Dad,' she cried again. I stopped and leaned over Greasy
while Tommy and Lola continued to run out towards the silver
sea. Greasy was in shock, wounded in the thigh. There was a
lot of blood. It spilled onto worm casts in the mud under
Greasy's body. I stood straight again. Slaughter began to back
away. He was in the mud. I was in the mud too. Our steps
slowed. The grey stuff stuck to me. I slipped. Slaughter fired
again, hitting Greasy, as he'd meant to. Greasy screamed. His
forearm was covered in blood too.

'Dad,' Lola called to Tommy. She was by my side now and
ready for a fight. I was thoroughly stuck in the mud. I
transferred the gun to my left hand and held her off with my
right. She fought me. Slaughter laughed. I grabbed her and
threw her to her knees. I put my gun to her head. She knelt
beneath me, quivering. I looked calmer, but I didn't feel calmer.
I pulled back the trigger.

'Put it down, Tommy.'

'You haven't got the nerve.'

He was aiming at Greasy. Lola sobbed under my hand.

'Dad,' she said, quietly.

'I'm not her Dad. I never was. Meet your Uncle Jimmy,
Lola.'

It meant nothing to her. It was meant to shake me. Tommy had timed it wrong. I was too tired, I'd seen too much, been in too much danger.

'You're going nowhere Tommy,' I said. Greasy moaned behind me. Tommy laughed and sat down in the mud.

'Of course I'm not. This is it. The day I waited for.'

'Don't..,' I said. He lifted the gun. I thought for a moment he was going to shoot himself. Of course he wouldn't. He wanted me to do his work for him. He aimed behind me at Greasy again. I fired. The woman under my hand howled. Tommy sat looking at me still.

'No guts,' he said. I'd aimed over his shoulder. He pulled the trigger on his pistol a couple more times. It was empty. He threw the gun down in the mud. He looked frail and old now.

'Dad,' she said.

I stood and walked over to him. Tommy lay back in the mud. It crept around his shoulders, like a suitor. I turned to Lola.

'Run,' I called.

'I can't.'

'Run!'

She tried to stand and failed. I fired the gun over her.

'Run!'

A couple of armed detectives appeared on the top of the dyke near the house. They were pointing at us but they were hundreds of yards away. Lola stood and staggered back towards the boats. The mud was marked by her floundering. Greasy lay nearby. He had his head lifted and was looking at me. I smiled, 'sorry.' I turned again. Slaughter lay before me. Beyond him was a mile of mud, crept over by the shallow tides. Beyond that is Belgium, another eighty miles or so. It was low tide in winter. If we walked for a couple of hundred yards we'd be on the sands, the site of the long lost Roman towns. The sands are covered with good old Thames mud, and the tide covers the mud to ten feet or so there.

I threw the gun to one side and went over to Tommy. He lay in the mud, exhausted now. The water lapped around him. The same water that flows past Westminster. The same water that fills the Neckinger. In a few hours it would withdraw and be a part of the North Sea. But that was then. This is now. For now the sea is rising. I grabbed Slaughter's collar and dragged him upright. The mud sucked at our feet. I marched him a few steps towards the sea. His lips were blue and his face was grey. He stopped and said, 'Where are we going?'

'To meet Joe,' I said. I pressed on, dragging him with me. The sea was cold around my feet. It only mattered to one. Behind us the water had nearly covered Greasy. Lola had nearly climbed the dyke again. Tommy and I had almost met our fate. I slipped my arm around his waist and carried him forward. He didn't resist.